*Pr*ぃ....... ....U WENT AWAY:

"Lou Aronica writes with deep sensitivity of the power of love to transform and heal in the face of overwhelming tragedy. A lovely read."
– #1 *New York Times* bestselling author Susan Wiggs

"Nicholas Sparks fans will rejoice to hear there's a new male author on the scene who writes beautifully about love and emotionally charged relationships. Tears of sadness and joy go hand in hand in this immensely satisfying story. Outstanding!"
– *RT Book Reviews*

"A gem. I couldn't put it down. The characters are people I'd like to know."
– Peggy Webb, author of the Southern Cousins Mystery Series

"*When You Went Away* is a very powerful tale full of laughter, tears, and romantic moments that keep you enthralled with the authors voice. I think every reader will fall a little in love with both this outstanding author as well as this amazing character!"
– Coffee Time Romance

"I truly loved this story. It is so well-written that it's hard to keep yourself separate from the fictional characters. I absolutely recommend this book and plan to read every other work written by this author. Triple-A reading!"
– Fresh Fiction

"*When You Went Away* really surprised me with how much I enjoyed reading this book. Gerry and Reese stole a place in my heart."
– Cheryl's Book Nook

When You
Went Away

Lou Aronica

THE
ST●RY
PLANT

Studio Digital CT, LLC
P.O. Box 4331
Stamford, CT 06907

Previously published as Michael Baron

Story Plant paperback ISBN-13: 978-1-61188-230-8
Fiction Studio Books e-book ISBN-13: 978-1-943486-64-9

Visit our website at www.thestoryplant.com

First Story Plant Printing: October 2009

To Molly, who never, ever went away.
I'm so thankful that Tanya
is purely a product of my imagination.

Acknowledgements

Incalculable thanks to my wife and children, who taught me so much of what has found its way onto these pages. Thanks to Danny Baror, who took the prospects for this novel very personally. Thanks to Barbara Aronica-Buck for the beautiful cover and interior design and for doing it all on a crash schedule. Thanks to early readers Debbie Mercer and Keith Ferrell for their thoughts and encouragement. Thanks to Susan Wiggs for her generous and lovely cover comments. Thanks to Joan Schulhafer for knowing exactly what to do with this. Thanks to all of the musical acts that inspired me during the writing of this novel, especially Ben Folds, Phish, Soul Asylum, and Eric Andersen. And thanks to the New York Yankees, especially Lou Gehrig, Thurman Munson, Don Mattingly, and Mariano Rivera.

The Hearts of Men

What is inside a man's heart? I can't possibly presume to speak for every man, but I can tell you that this question has been a fascination of mine since I was a teenager and I started hearing people say that men weren't in touch with their feelings and that they avoided letting their emotions guide them. That certainly wasn't me, and it certainly wasn't many of the people I knew. Yet this narrative has proven to be a durable one. You see and hear it everywhere – in books, on film, in the media, in coffee shops. I truly believe it is a flawed narrative.

When I began my career as a novelist, I knew that there was only one subject upon which I truly wanted to focus: the hearts of men. I wanted to tell stories from a male perspective that exploded stereotypes and were as honest as I could make them. That has led to this series. You'll meet many men here. Some are just starting their lives, while others have lived it to the fullest. Some are lovers, some are fathers, some are sons. A number of these men have found themselves. Several are still searching. But all of them are facing a moment of dramatic change – a point when who they are and where they are going will be altered forever and when the only way they are going to face up to this change is to explore what's in their hearts.

The second novel in this series is *When You Went Away*. It is the story of a man who truly believed he had it all – a wife he adored, a great family, a good job – until much of it was whisked away with dizzying suddenness. Simply getting up in the morning is a Herculean task, but he has an infant son to take care of, so he needs to carry on. And when joy sneaks up on him, he's nearly as confounded by it as he was by tragedy.

I hope you enjoy *When You Went Away* and its excursion into the hearts of men. I would love to hear your thoughts about it. Feel free to reach out to me at laronica@fictionstudio.com.

Prologue

I dreamt of us in springtime. Maureen and I walked hand in hand through Washington Square Park, an acoustic guitarist playing an Indigo Girls song on one side, a guy throwing a Frisbee to his dog on the other. As we walked, Maureen's sleeveless arm rested against mine, giving me one more reason to be thankful for the dawning of this new season. A teenaged girl and boy ran past laughing carelessly, transforming as we watched them into Tanya at age five, and Eric, her best friend at the time. The park became our backyard. I chuckled as they rumbled by and Maureen leaned into me. She kissed me on the cheek and tittered into my ear, causing the fine hairs on my neck to rise.

Then she pushed me on the shoulder, calling out, "You're it!" and running away laughing like the little girl I always wished I could have known. I chased them both (Eric had disappeared), sweeping Tanya up and carrying her, squealing delightedly and wriggling, under my arm while I sought Maureen, who somehow ducked out of sight. While I looked in one direction, she jumped on my back from the other, causing the three of us to tumble to the ground, Tanya leaping free to pounce on both of us. We wrestled together for a few moments, kissing, tickling, until we lay in the grass, a tangle of arms and legs, gazing up at the impossibly blue sky. *I could stay here like this*, I thought. *I could very easily stay right here and never want for anything.*

A musical tinkling came from somewhere in the near distance, and Tanya gathered her feet under her faster than any little kid should be able to. "Ice cream truck," she said with a joy that was singularly hers, sprinting to the front of the house, knowing that the man in the truck had already slowed in anticipation of her approach and that Maureen and I would soon be behind her with the money necessary for an ice pop or a Dove Bar or whatever else she might want.

Maureen kissed me again at that point, softly this time, warmly, enveloping me with her spring smell. "Do you think the ice cream man will put this one on her tab?" she said, understanding how completely I wanted to remain here and kiss her like this indefinitely.

And then Tanya sat next to us again, her feet tucked under her nine-year-old bottom. "Do the two of you *always* have to kiss?" she said, pretending to be repulsed but at the same time bearing just enough of a glint in her eye to let us know that this was at least moderately okay with her.

"Yes, always," I said and I kissed Maureen again to underscore the point.

She frowned at me, but her mother reached out to grab her and she tumbled toward us, kissing Maureen's hair and settling into her embrace. I rested my head against the two of them, not knowing where one ended and the other began and not caring in the least. And in the languor of this late March day, with the afternoon sun making the air feel warmer than it actually was, I fell asleep on a bed infinitely more important to me than my own life.

The first thing I noticed when I came awake was early morning birds chirping, the sound slipping through the slim opening I left in the window the night before. Then the smell of the daffodils that Maureen planted in ridiculous quantities all around the perimeter of the house. It really was spring. I hadn't dreamed that. And for just a second – that instant between dreaming and being awake when almost anything still seems possible—I believed that everything else about my dream was true as well. My wife was next to me. My daughter, five or nine or seventeen, was two doors down the hall, about to protest that it was too early to go to school.

But the moment receded. And again, Maureen was gone forever, gone from this earth with a suddenness I promised I would never understand. And again, Tanya disappeared from my life, not knowing that her mother wouldn't be here for her if she ever chose to return. I felt each loss as if it had just happened, realizing that the one thing I might have in unlimited quantity was sorrow.

In the past few months, there had been so many dreams. So many moments when they were right here where I could touch them and let them know that they were the absolute essence of my life. Where I could lay my forehead against Maureen's and we could allow our eyes to have hours of conversation for us. Where I could stop time before I floundered with Tanya and give her something of me without taking away any of her. Where I could have said to them, "I'll gladly accept the worst possible moments with either of you over any moment without you."

I wanted to hold onto this dream, but I couldn't any more than I could hold on to the dozens of others I had before. All I could hold onto was the increasing depth of understanding of everything I had lost. Like the insistent repetition of the chorus at the end of an epic song, with every new visit from Maureen and Tanya in my dreams, I came to feel what I had with them just a little bit more – and by extension feel what I could no longer ever have again.

Neither the birds nor the daffodils or any of the other harbingers of the season I loved most could elevate me. Spring was nearly here. And the thought that I would live it without Maureen and Tanya was heartbreaking.

I closed my eyes. *Let me dream again. Let me visit with them for just a little longer.* It never happened before and it didn't happen now. Sleep didn't come easily for me these days and it wouldn't possibly come this way. No matter how much I wanted it.

Reese made his first morning sounds. He never cried right away when he got up. For the first couple of minutes of every day, it was as though the world was just so fascinating to him, so absolutely new to his eyes, that his rediscovery of it took precedence over his hunger. Then the crying would come. Crying that always reminded me, perhaps would always remind me, of the sound of his crying the night I came home to find Maureen.

I didn't want him to have to cry today. And so before his empty stomach imposed its will upon him, I went to his room, picked him up, and held him to my chest. After a moment, we walked toward the kitchen. Past the framed painting of a hobbyhorse, posted outside Reese's door, that Maureen found at the last antique store we visited together. Past Tanya's empty room. Down the staircase lined with photographs of my wife and daughter and even a couple of the new baby.

As we got downstairs, Reese started to fuss a little. We were probably a minute from full-blown bawling. I heated the bottle quickly, using the microwave though I knew that wasn't the best thing to do, rubbing his back, and humming to him in the time this took. I tested the temperature on my arm and brought him into the family room. Almost immediately, he sucked contentedly.

While he drank, I lost myself in the image of the antique quilt on the opposite wall. Maureen and I bought it a month before we were married. It was an extravagant expense at the time, but she wanted it *so much*. "It will hang prominently in every home we ever have," she said. And it did. From the drafty walk-up in Coram to the needy starter three-bedroom in St. James to this, our family home for the past twelve years in Port Jefferson. "This quilt is you and me, Gerry. Woven from separate parts and joined together forever."

Reese stopped sucking and I glanced down at him. He looked at me with fascination in his eyes, maybe even a bit of confusion, and his hand reached up toward my face. I bent toward him, kissing his hand and rubbing my cheek against it. It was only then that I realized I was crying. I let Reese's hand stray over my face, drawing the line of tears down toward my chin. He had no idea what I was going through, just as he had no idea how much his touch meant to me.

I pulled the baby closer and adjusted the bottle. He began to suck again, secure in the simplicity and wonder of his world.

A new season was coming. A new day was beginning. I held fast to the only thing that made it possible for me to face either.

BOOK ONE - Gone

ONE - I Can Only Imagine

I thought about moving to Maine. Or maybe Halifax. Somewhere entirely different from suburban Long Island for the entirely different life Reese and I would have – the life I never planned for him and now needed to make as good as possible. It might have been healthier to move, to not be reminded by the washing machine and the planter on the porch and the crooked street sign at the end of the block and the bagel shop on 25A that Maureen would never share any of these things with me again. But we couldn't move. If we moved and Tanya ever came back, she wouldn't know where to find us. And I refused to believe that she wouldn't ever come home again.

Staying meant I needed to get back to work. And getting back to work meant finding a babysitter for Reese. It's entirely possible that one of the first four people I interviewed for the job would have taken good care of my son. But none of them – three college students and a woman in her early fifties – inspired me to ask enough questions to find out. I didn't want to do this. I didn't want to turn Reese over to someone else. And I didn't want it to be necessary to do so. Maureen and I had been so fortunate that she was able to stay home for the first five years of Tanya's life. It was an idyll I know she cherished. She was only going to be able to get three months this time from her boss, but we hadn't even begun to talk about day care before she died. Maybe she hoped it would be difficult to find qualified help and she would have to extend her stay with Reese. Maybe we should have just planned it that way, even though it ultimately wouldn't have mattered.

If we had, this might have been one less care for her in what turned out to be her final months.

Reese just got up from his nap when Lisa came for her appointment. We were still in his room, watching his musical mobile spin, when the doorbell rang.

"Let's get through this," I said, hugging him to my chest as we descended the stairs. I realized I knew virtually nothing about the woman who was coming for this job. The agency called in the morning with relevant details and I barely listened to them, simply writing "Lisa 2:30" on a pad on the kitchen counter. I expected another college student, but she was obviously older, late twenties, maybe even early thirties.

"Is this Reese?" she said broadly before even saying hello, reaching for the baby's hand, and giving it a gentle squeeze. We went into the family room and I sat on the couch with Reese on my lap. She sat across from us, grinning and burbling at him. He seemed to find this at least a little intriguing and he watched her carefully, not willing to smile, but very content to examine her.

Eventually Lisa looked up at me. "The agency told me about your wife. I'm very, very sorry."

"Thanks. It's been a confusing time."

"I can only imagine." She held me with her eyes for a moment and I got the impression that she indeed had imagined this. That after hearing about Reese and me, she tried to envision what it would be like for a man about to turn forty to deal with the sudden death of his wife and the care of a four-month-old. I found her statement surprisingly moving, even though I spoke at length about precisely this to friends and relatives.

Lisa looked back at the baby. Reese continued to watch her. "Your son is gorgeous, you know."

"He is," I said, kissing him on the ear. I took a deep breath and smiled. "Tell me something about yourself."

She sat back in her chair a little and focused her attention on me again. "I have an M.A. in child psychology from Stony Brook." She must have noticed that my eyebrows rose when she said this. "I know; grossly overqualified, right? Only sort of. You see, after I graduated college, I started a nanny agency and was doing pretty well with it. Then the economy tanked and I went out of business. I thought about doing a bunch of things, and then I just decided that I would enroll in the Ph.D. program and get a job as a nanny myself while I studied. I start school in the fall."

I was disappointed to hear this. "So this job would be a short-term thing for you."

"No, not at all. I'm taking night classes and even doing some stuff at home online." She shook her head briskly. "I wouldn't want to bail on a kid after only a few months."

Certainly, she'd prepped her answer, but it was the right one. If at all possible, I wanted to avoid the heartache of Reese's attaching himself to one babysitter and then being forced to adjust to another in a short while.

"And you really feel like you want to take care of a kid when you aren't in school? Wouldn't an office job or something like that be easier on you?"

She shrugged. "It might be easier *physically*, but definitely not mentally. I don't see myself as the office type. To tell you the truth, I think it would bore me out of my mind." Reese emitted a nonsense syllable and Lisa leaned toward him. "You agree with me, right, Reese? Playing games and rolling on the floor all day is fun. Sitting in an office is a snooze." My son regarded her open-mouthed. I thought about telling Lisa that some of us found office work to be at least marginally fulfilling and then decided against it.

"My hours can be pretty unpredictable," I said, though I had already resolved to get home no later than 6:30 every night.

"For now that's not a hassle. Once school starts in September that could be a little bit of an issue, but maybe all of us will be on a good schedule by then. Assuming you want to hire me, of course."

For some reason, I knew already that I did. Something told me that Lisa would help Reese, that she'd be good for him. I told her she had the job. This was the first spontaneous thing I'd done since Maureen died. And I felt validated in my decision when Lisa stayed for another half hour to talk and play with the baby. Reese definitely responded to her, at least to the degree to which he responded to anything. But he did so in a dreamy fashion. Almost as though she mesmerized him.

"So when should I start?" she said, asking the question I avoided answering in my own mind.

I gave it some thought, though I knew in one sense any answer was a good one and in another that no answer would be good enough. "Does next Monday work for you?" It was Wednesday. This would give me five more days alone with my son.

"Works great," she said, standing up to leave. Reese and I walked her to the door and then, since it was warm enough out, to her car. When we got there, Lisa touched Reese on the cheek. He moved to put her finger in his mouth and she laughed, pulling her hand back. Then she extended her hand to shake mine.

"Thanks for the job," she said.

"Thanks for taking it."

She nodded, looked down at the ground, and then back up at me. "I know this is a big deal. I'll take good care of him."

I buried my face in Reese's scant wisps of hair for a moment and then made eye contact with her. "Yeah, I'm sure you will." She smiled and got in her car and we watched her drive away. Once she did, I got Reese's jacket and took him for a walk in his stroller to take advantage of the nice weather.

If we moved to Halifax, we could probably get by for a few years on our savings. But Halifax wasn't an option. Maybe Lisa was the next best alternative.

I felt like a countdown had begun.

* * *

One day in April last year, I pulled into the garage and saw Maureen taking packages out of her car on the other side.

She smiled at me shyly. Maureen didn't do that. When you've been with someone for half as many years as you've been alive, there's little reason to be shy about anything.

She came over to my car as I got out. "Hey," I said, kissing her and taking some of the packages from her arms. She'd been to the mall, which was odd because it was a workday. "What are these?"

"Nothing, just some stuff we've needed." She looked at me meaningfully. "I was in the neighborhood."

The mall was nowhere near her office. "Why's that?"

She smiled. "You might want to sit down. Or at least lean against the car."

This got me concerned. "Is everything okay?"

"Yeah, I think it is. But you might not." She looked away for a second and then back at me. "I was at the doctor's." She wrinkled her nose. "I'm pregnant."

The statement wouldn't have seemed more out of context to me if Maureen had said, "I'm from another galaxy." This was definitely not something we'd planned or even mused over. It was so disorienting that I couldn't think of a single thing to say.

Tanya had been a surprise, too. A real stunner, actually. We'd only been married a few months, right out of college, still reveling in playing house. *Maybe,* I thought as the notion began to settle in, *our lives were made for sudden additions.*

But this was still mind-boggling. It wasn't as if we'd made plans to turn Tanya's room into a dance hall when she went to college or anything like that, but we were aware that her departure was imminent and that we had a lot of life left to live. Starting over with another baby wasn't one of the options I considered. This didn't mean that I wasn't willing to consider it; only that my aspirations leaned more toward learning another language or discovering the country inns of New England.

I looked at Maureen's face. Obviously, she had much more time to contemplate this news than I'd had and there was no doubt that it thrilled her. In spite of how confounding life with a teenaged Tanya had become, Maureen embraced motherhood. I could feel myself warming to the prospects, to revisiting those nights when Maureen nursed our infant daughter while nestled against my shoulder.

I settled back against the car and pulled her into my arms. "That's great," I said.

"Do you really think so?"

"Yeah, I think I do." I squeezed her and let my imagination run. "I really think I do."

She kissed me tenderly, the kind of kiss reserved for landmark moments. "I guess we won't be running off to London on a moment's notice now, huh? But we're kinda good at this."

"Yeah, we are." It didn't seem the appropriate time to mention that she was great at it and that I was, at best, occasionally effective.

Maureen pulled back, rolled her eyes, and then laughed loudly. "My God, Gerry, a baby."

* * *

When Reese and I got back from our walk, I called the office to tell them I would return on Monday. My assistant started to ask me questions, but I put him off. I would answer all of them when I got back. The rest of this time was for Reese and me.

After dinner, we went into the family room. This had quickly become his favorite place in the house. We would do all of his favorite things over the next few days and hopefully introduce him to several new ones. I put him down on his playmat and he lifted his head, gurgling and doing those little push-ups infants do. He found himself in the mirror on his activity center and smiled.

"You can get away with that now, kid," I said. "When you're a little older, though, you might not want to be so obviously impressed with your own image." The advice fell on deaf ears and he continued to admire his reflection. Who could blame him?

I lay him on his back and held a star-shaped plush toy over his head. His eyes tracked back and forth as I moved it around and he lifted his tiny hand toward it. I brushed the soft fabric against his face and he smiled again. He smiled so easily. I bounced the toy in the air above him and he was transfixed for minutes.

"We'll go to the planetarium when you're a few years older. If you like this thing, wait 'til you see an entire room of them while Pink Floyd is playing."

I decided to put on some music. We usually had music on in the house, whether it was Maureen's jazz or the rock that Tanya and I preferred. But the stereo remained in standby position for the past six weeks. I put my iPod in the dock and searched. Pink Floyd probably wasn't the best choice. Happily, there was no "children's music" on the player. The notion that kids needed to have songs about little lambs or monkeys jumping on beds in order to appreciate music always seemed silly to me. With all of the great songs in the world, why should we serve up mediocre ones to our youngest?

I picked out a Dar Williams album. It was gentle, playful, and melodic; it certainly wouldn't frighten Reese in any way. But it was real music. As the first song started, I picked up a soft plastic caterpillar to show Reese and we played with this for a while.

"Come on," I said. "Let's go exploring."

We walked around the first floor of the house and I introduced him to a number of things that shared his world: the stand mixer in the kitchen, the books in the library, the Tiffany lamp in the living room, the television remote in the family room. And of course the photographs of his mother and sister that were everywhere. I told him what each of these things was and held his hand out to touch every one. He regarded all of these patiently and with varying degrees of interest. I knew this was way over his head, but I wanted him to get accustomed to being aware of his surroundings. I had so much to teach him.

After that, I gave him a bath. There were splash nights and there were lump nights; this was the latter. He simply lay on his bath pillow, holding onto the sides. He didn't seem nervous or uncomfortable in any way, just disinterested. I trickled some water over his chest in search of a reaction and didn't get one, so I decided to wash him quickly and move on.

I dried him off and brought him to his changing table for a new diaper and pajamas. I got the diaper on and then looked down at him. He had an expression on his face that I interpreted as wistful, though it could have been any number of things, including indigestion. He really was a beautiful child, something I hadn't noticed often enough in the sweep of these first few months. I promised myself that I would always take the time to watch him, to see him. I was sure that between worry over Tanya and then everything I felt over Maureen I missed all too much already. Now on top of this I would lose a huge portion of every day with him to work. I had to pay as much attention as humanly possible when we were together.

Impulsively, I bowed down to him and blew a raspberry on his stomach. He laughed – a big, full-throated chuckle. It was the first time I heard him laugh and this made me laugh in response. I did it again and he reacted the same way. He had such a boisterous giggle for such a little person. I picked him up and held his face next to mine, rubbing our noses together before I finished dressing him.

"You just earned an extra hour of playtime tonight."

We went back to the family room. I put on a Jayhawks album, one of my favorites, and sang the songs to him. I let him stay up until his yawning made it obvious that he needed a break. I knew this was excessive on my part, but we had plenty of time to settle into a more defined routine. For four more days, I would indulge him. And myself.

In his room, he fell asleep in my arms. I laid him in his crib and then sat in the rocking chair there, watching his body subtly rise and fall. I'm not sure exactly when I fell asleep, but when he woke me in the middle of the night to be fed, I felt surprisingly refreshed. It was the best I had slept in a while.

TWO - Trinkets and Trifles

On Monday, Reese woke up right after I finished my shower, as though he'd set his internal alarm clock to make sure he didn't miss seeing me off. I felt a strange sense of ceremony to this morning as I gave him a bottle and ate a bowl of cereal. Today, we were beginning the real rest of our lives.

The previous seven weeks had been artificial in so many ways – from the number of people who drifted in and out of the house to the fact that we had spent virtually every minute together. Now I would leave him for a huge stretch of time, as I would five days a week for somewhere around the next eighteen years. I felt as though I should do something to mark the occasion – that I should say something, write something down, or even put a meaningful song on the stereo while we had breakfast. I wound up not doing any of these things, but I refused to see this as an ordinary day.

For some reason, it finally registered this morning that if something happened to me Reese would be an orphan. This wasn't the first time I left him to go to work. But it was the first time I would do so as his only parent. Certainly, there was as much of a chance of my getting stricken down while I was in the house or out shopping with him as there was while I did my job, but it felt like I had a better chance of survival in the kitchen than I would at my office. This was not a healthy line of thinking to follow, and I forced myself away from it by going over one more time the list I had prepared for Lisa. Emergency numbers. Names of friendly neighbors. Toys he liked and things he enjoyed doing. Absurdly, directions to my office. Had I covered everything? Was I forgetting something obvious and important while including a lot of nonsense?

When Lisa arrived, she immediately walked over to Reese's baby chair to pick him up. Reese seemed perfectly satisfied to have her holding him and tweeting at him. At this point, he seemed relatively indifferent to whoever was holding him. I knew the day would come soon when he'd start making distinctions, but that day wasn't today. While I considered this a huge moment in our family life, he was unaware of it and entirely unconcerned. I would keep a mental record of this for him, though. He might want to know about it in the future.

I walked over to them with the list. "I have all the information you should need here. My office number, my cell phone number, his feeding schedule – though you know how meaningful that is – his nap schedule – though you know how meaningful *that* is. There's formula in the refrigerator and he's started to eat a little rice cereal in the afternoon."

"We're going to have a great time together," Lisa said, turning to the baby to add in a higher register, "Aren't we, Reese-y?"

I reached out and took him from her arms. I kissed him on the cheek and we made momentary eye contact before something else in the room caught his attention. Maybe this was meant to be a dry run. Maybe I was only supposed to go through the motions of getting ready for work and handing him over to the babysitter today before doing it for real tomorrow. I kissed him again and held him against me for a few seconds.

"What else do you need to know?" I said to Lisa. She shook her head. "I'm pretty sure I can figure everything out." She reached for the baby and I handed him to her, kissing him on the top of the head as I did so.

"The phone's right there. Eat whatever you want. I bought some cold cuts and stuff and there are some leftovers you might like."

"Thanks."

"I'm only fifteen minutes away if you need me."

"We're gonna be great," she said with a thin smile.

I nodded, understanding the code for *get the hell out of here and let me do my job* when I heard it. She was telling me that I was making more of an event out of this than I needed to. She might have been right, but it certainly didn't feel like it. Reluctantly, I put my sports jacket on, gave Reese one more kiss, and headed out of the house. Even when I got in the car, I thought about going back inside – he would be an orphan if anything happened to me – but I pushed through it and ultimately backed out of the driveway only glancing in the rearview mirror four times on my way out of the neighborhood.

* * *

I asked Maureen if we could go out on what became our last Saturday.

"Go out?"

"I think it would be good for us." We hadn't been out together since that October night when we came home to discover Tanya gone. Reese's bout with colic was over and he was finally sleeping at least a little. And it really seemed like we needed it.

"If you want to," she said. She couldn't have been more unenthusiastic. Maureen spent a lot of time at home when Tanya left, and she hardly went out at all after the baby was born. We alternated between occasional highs over the newness of our son – when he wasn't crying – and deeper lows over the whereabouts of our daughter and the endless frustrations of our inability to devise any way to find her. We'd tried the police, private investigators, grilling Tanya's friends, and a variety of online services I never even knew existed before Tanya disappeared. All proved fruitless and increasingly unnerving.

I normally would have accepted Maureen's listlessness, would have joined her in it as an alternative to my desperate sense of helplessness. But I truly believed this wasn't the right thing to do anymore. We needed a tiny escape from the worry and responsibility.

"Elise is still home for winter break," I said. "I'll give her a call about Saturday night. She loves babies."

Maureen lifted her chin slightly and regarded me head on. "Okay," she said, and I could see that she appreciated that I was taking charge of this.

We didn't talk any more about it until Saturday afternoon. Reese was irritable and I walked him through the rooms of the first floor, jiggling him slightly because this seemed to settle him. Maureen walked up to us, playfully mocking my calming efforts by rocking up and down on the balls of her feet. The fact that she was doing anything playful made me happy.

"So where are you taking me tonight, anyway?" she said. "Fancy restaurant? Seedy hotel?"

"How about a fancy restaurant and *then* a seedy hotel?"

Maureen pretended to give this some thought and then kissed me on the cheek. "How about a neighborhood restaurant and we pray that Reese is asleep when we get back?"

I smiled. "Can we pretend he's asleep even if he isn't?"

She kissed me again. "Yeah, maybe."

A few hours later, we drove down our block and Maureen took my hand. "This was a very good idea," she said, holding my hand to her face.

"I've missed this."

She touched her lips to my knuckles and kept them there for a long moment. "Me too. I guess we didn't realize how easy everything had become, huh?"

"I actually think I did realize it. Maybe I just didn't appreciate it enough."

She squeezed my hand. "Let's take the night off, okay?"

I looked over at her. "Okay." We both knew that it was impossible to truly take the night off. Tanya was always on our minds. Reese was an enormous new presence. But even *trying* to take the night off was a huge deal.

We had dinner at an Italian place we'd visited easily a hundred times since moving to Port Jefferson. Our waitress asked why she hadn't seen us in so long and we told her about the new baby. The Chianti we ordered was the first alcohol for either of us since October. Maureen wouldn't normally have had a drink while breastfeeding, but this was all part of taking the night off. When the wine came, I sipped it and then studied the legs of the wine as they slid down the glass. Chianti had been our drink of choice since we went to Tuscany for our fifth anniversary.

"Castello di Uzzano," she said, calling to mind the five days we spent in a castle in Greve and the night we made love in an olive grove in the early fall air.

"We really need to go back there sometime."

"Our twentieth isn't that far away."

We touched glasses softly. "No, it's not." Tuscany would be the perfect place to celebrate our twentieth anniversary, two years hence. The familiar parts of it would remind us what we dreamed about all those years ago, while the unfamiliar would underscore how those dreams had come alive for us or been replaced by others that bore more meaning. I'd start making the plans. Tanya would be in college then; Reese would be old enough that we could leave him with someone else – Maureen's parents, perhaps – for a week or ten days or so.

We lingered over coffee. The owner brought us a slice of ricotta cheesecake to celebrate the birth of our son and we ate it slowly. It had probably been a couple of months since Maureen had a lazy meal. And even though I ate lunch away from the house, away from the demands of an infant, I tended to eat quickly anyway, as though I expected Reese's call for attention from ten miles away. Maureen and I didn't say much, holding hands across the table, Maureen running a fingernail lightly across my index finger. Her touch still excited and compelled me, long ago having become an essential part of my physical makeup.

"If I called Elise and told her that we weren't coming back until morning, what do you think she would do?" I said while signing the credit card receipt.

Maureen smiled and let her gaze wander just long enough to let me know she entertained the improbability. "Let's go home."

Thankfully, Reese was asleep when we arrived. Elise told us that he'd only settled in his crib a half hour before. When Elise left, Maureen pulled me toward her and kissed me in a way she hadn't kissed me in months. "Thanks for the date," she said, holding me.

"It was a great night."

She nuzzled my neck. "It's still a great night."

She kissed me more deeply then and I ran my fingers through her hair while hers played across the small of my back. There had never been a point, even in those empty days after Tanya left, when I didn't want her, but my desire for her now made me feel like I was seventeen. We uncoupled only long enough to make our way gingerly up the stairs, then tumbled together as soon as we reached our room. And we were in my dorm room in college, or in that olive grove in Tuscany, or on a private beach in Montauk or any of a dozen other places where we could feel our passion for one another in a distinctive and liberating way.

All I knew at the time was that this was a welcome and necessary release, as the dinner had been before it. But would I have tamped back my hunger and tried to record every instant if I had known that this was the last time we'd ever make love together?

Or had I anyway?

* * *

Eleanor Miller, Inc. is a catalog and Internet retailer that began in the early '50s as the pet project of a Long Island housewife while her kids were growing up. It evolved into a national company with annual sales of more than a third of a billion dollars. Its corporate office in Centereach, New York, houses about three hundred employees, with another couple of hundred scattered in various locations throughout the Northeast. We are in the "trinkets and trifles" business, though none of us ever use such terms in public. About half of our products are proprietary with the other half sourced from international manufacturers under exclusive American contracts. Everything we sell is relatively inconsequential – whether a personalized baseball card holder or a teak spice rack – and we don't sell a single item that costs more than a hundred dollars. Still, everything is well made (backed by our lifetime guarantee), all is at least a little bit functional, and much of it is rather clever. People love getting our catalogs in the mail – though most of our business comes online now, all of our research indicates that the catalog still drives it. And for the most part the catalogs love them back.

I started in the marketing department ten years ago, eventually becoming the VP of new product development. I hadn't intended to stay with the company this long, but the regular pay raises, the promotions, and the close proximity to our home pacified me. And the place had grown on me. From the outside, it seemed kitschy and old fashioned, and before I started there, I assumed that the staff would be the same. But in fact, all kinds of smart people worked there, and the upper management had an inspiring sincerity. For the most part, I liked what my job evolved into. There were definitely too many board meetings and budget meetings and meetings of every other sort. But I always had a great time coming up with new items, and brainstorming with the team I put together was my favorite part of any workday. That part felt like play. And if I couldn't say that I would do this work even if they didn't pay me, I could at least say that it felt a lot less like work than everything else did.

As I pulled my car into the parking lot, my gut seized up. The staff here was a form of extended family. Many of them had become genuine friends and many more had come to the funeral or sent condolence messages. But entering the building felt alien to me right now. I don't think I realized until that moment just how completely I had cocooned myself over the past two months. Though I had ample contact with the outside during this time, I paid it little mind. My orbit centered on the kitchen, the family room, my bedroom, and the baby's room. I hadn't expected to feel any hesitation about going back to the office, but getting out of my car took some real effort.

It got worse almost immediately. I could see people's expressions changing when they saw me. I heard them thinking, *there's Gerry Rubato. Gotta be tough what he's going through. First that thing with his daughter, and now his wife.* As I headed to my office, a few people stopped to ask me how I was doing. I had no idea how to answer that question. Certainly, no one wanted the real explanation of how I was feeling. And even if they had, I didn't ever want to be the kind of person who delivered speeches like that. I didn't want to weigh people down with my troubles. I simply nodded meaningfully and people tilted their heads in understanding or touched me on the arm. The pity was nearly as excruciating as the notion that it was possible to reduce what I lost to snippets exchanged in the hallway.

When I got to my office, my assistant Ben was sitting at his desk. He'd been with me for eighteen months and I hoped to get him a promotion before he found a job somewhere else. We'd been in touch every couple of days while I was out, so he was the one person who didn't feel the need to "check in on me" when I arrived.

"I kept the day pretty clear," he said, following me into my office.

"Thanks. I don't know, though. A couple of meetings might be a useful diversion."

"I said *pretty* clear. You have a 10:30, a 2:30, and a 4:00."

"Right." Eleanor Miller was an extremely meeting-intensive company. It wasn't unusual for me to spend the entire day in a conference room. Executive management (which I never considered myself to be, even though the organizational chart said I was) believed that people were at their most efficient when they were "firing off of each other." The upshot was that we spent a lot of time at home on nights and weekends catching up with the work we didn't do while we inspired our colleagues.

"In between, is this an open-door day or a closed-door day?"

I really appreciated Ben. He knew how to ask the question without asking it. "I think it's an open-door day, but I reserve the right to change my mind."

"You got it. It's good to have you back."

"Yeah, thanks."

Ben hesitated for a moment and I worried that I was going to have to fend off his sympathies as well.

"Is the babysitter cute?" he said.

I laughed. First one of the morning. "She's pretty cute."

"Think she could maybe bring Reese to visit his dad sometime soon so I could meet her?"

I shook my head. "She's too old for you."

"I seriously doubt that."

I walked past him and patted him on the shoulder. "I'm going to see Marshall."

* * *

Marshall Grove is seven years older than I am and had been my boss for the past six years. He has two kids; the youngest is Tanya's age. Maureen and I went out regularly with him and his wife Denise. Denise sat with me, holding my hand for a long stretch on the first day of the wake, and the two of them came to visit once while I was home. Reese was having a rough afternoon and they didn't stay long, but it meant a great deal to me anyway. Even though I often couldn't remember who was in the house and when during those first few weeks, I appreciated the effort. Since then, Marshall and I had spoken on the phone a couple of times about business matters.

Looking at us together, you might think that our age difference was considerably greater. Marshall was at least fifty pounds overweight, his hair completely gray, and it took a fire alarm to move him out of his chair. Still, the vitality of his mind was unmatched by most people twenty years younger. He'd been a great mentor and colleague over the years and, at this point, I considered him the best friend I had at Eleanor Miller.

When I approached her desk, his assistant tipped her head accordingly and said it was good to see me. She'd only been with the company six months and probably didn't even know Maureen's name. Marshall was on the phone, but she told me to go right into his office.

When he saw me, Marshall's expression opened up and he reached a hand out for me to shake. I sat down on his couch and waited for him to complete his call. I had long aspired to have an office like his – easily twice the size of mine, with mahogany furniture and thick blond carpeting – but when that thought came into my mind this morning, it felt a little off. As though I was thinking about attempting to compete in the Olympics after doing nothing but watching television for the past couple of years.

Marshall got off the phone and reached out his hand again. This was both a gesture of welcome and a signal to come sit in the chair across from his desk so he didn't need to get up.

"That was just Reed preparing me for next week's budget meeting. She thinks Monroe is going to blow a gasket over our missing the budget for the second month in a row."

I shook my head. "I didn't realize we had."

Marshall threw a paw at me. "Business is soft everywhere. Not just in our sector. Retailers are jumping out of windows." He looked down at his desk at some notes he'd made there and said, "We'll be fine." Then he looked up at me and said, "So, you're back?"

"I'm back."

"Denise really misses Maureen, you know. She told me to give you a kiss when I saw you. I told her we don't do shit like that."

"Yeah, thanks."

"You got someone good to take care of the baby?"

"I think so. She's very smart. She'll probably leave in a couple of weeks."

He rolled his eyes. "You're a braver man than me."

"Not like I have a lot of choice."

"No, I suppose not. Babies. Jeez, I wouldn't have a clue. With Rachel getting ready for college, I'm kind of looking forward to our having the house all to ourselves."

I had no idea how to respond to this and simply sat there.

"You ready to get back in the game?"

I shrugged. "Might need to do a few stretches first."

"Well, do 'em. Christmas is right around the corner."

What Marshall meant was that we had about four months to prepare any new products for the Christmas catalog. "Yeah, I figured I'd catch up the next couple of days and schedule a creative meeting with the team Wednesday or Thursday."

"Do it. And listen, I want you to add a couple more people to your team. Don Richmond and Ally Ritten have come to me with some really good ideas lately. I think they might be ready for the big leagues."

Don had been with the company for a while and I liked him. Ally worked in the marketing department. She had been around for less than a year and we hadn't worked together on anything. I'd heard good things about her, though. Not that it mattered, since Marshall wasn't asking my opinion.

"Sure," I said. "We can certainly use the extra bodies."

"Make this Christmas catalog a knockout, Gerry. It will be good for all of us."

"I'll do my best."

"It'll be really good for *you*. Look, I can't pretend that I know what you're going through, but the best medicine is throwing yourself into your work. It's the only way you're going to get over this."

I had a feeling that what Marshall said wasn't even close to true, but he wasn't saying it as a conversation starter. He seemed distracted, like he needed to get on the phone or summon someone else to his office or something.

"I'd better go find out how much of a disaster my office is," I said as I turned to go.

"Yeah, don't let me stop you. Check in later if you want. I'm glad you're back."

* * *

When he saw me, Ben said that four people had come by. Three had stopped simply to say hello. The fourth had an urgent business question to discuss. As the day went on, interaction with my colleagues continued at that ratio. Most of them acknowledged that it might take me a little while to get up to speed, while some approached me as though I had taken an especially long weekend. In a funny way, I appreciated the latter group more. While I felt a step-and-a-half behind in these conversations, they at least approximated what my work life had been like before. And if I was going to do this, if I was going to spend ten hours a day away from my son, I wanted work to feel like what it had always felt like. To be honest, I'm not sure I could have handled another thing in my life changing completely.

I called Lisa a couple of times during the day to learn that Reese was fine, that she could put her hands on everything she needed, and that she wasn't planning to quit before the evening. I spent the rest of the time returning phone calls and trying to make sense of the piles of paperwork. Concentration was a real problem, though. At any moment, I could find myself transported by a recollection of Maureen or a speculation about Tanya. Then I would be lost in thought for some stretch of time. At one point, I closed my office door for a while when I felt myself losing my composure. If anything, the fact that I could find even momentary distraction in a memo or report made the memory ambush that much more debilitating when it came.

By mid-afternoon, I felt very tired. I had never considered my job physically strenuous, but I seemed to be out of shape, like I needed to build back up before I could be effective for a full day. I never left the office before six, but by 4:30 I was useless.

At 5:15, Ben poked his head in the doorway.

"I hadn't heard any sounds in here for a while and I thought you might have fallen asleep."

"I think I've been reading the same line on this report for ten minutes now."

"Isn't that usually a sign that it's time to go home?"

I shook my head. "I've been gone for so long."

"The company will survive. Go kiss your baby. By the way, I've taken the liberty of printing out a head-shot with my home and cell numbers. Just in case you wanted to give it to Lisa."

"You aren't really that pathetic, are you?"

"It is *not* easy meeting women around here."

I stood up and started packing my briefcase. "Really, leave it all," Ben said. "It'll be here tomorrow. Go be a dad."

Ben was right. There was no way I could accomplish everything that I needed to accomplish on my first day back. There would be time for everything if I didn't stress overly much about it.

I grabbed my jacket and left the office behind for the night.

I had officially survived my first day back in the real world.

If you could call this survival.

THREE - Hearts

"It was a little bit strange, to tell you the truth. The entire day was like this. I mean, it was actually a little weird even being in the building."

Reese and I were in the kitchen – me at the stove making myself dinner and him on the counter in his baby seat – as I told him about my day. Occasionally he would make eye contact, but most of the time his head rolled back and forth, perhaps following a reflection or watching a piece of dust traverse the room. As was the case with my walking him around the house and showing him things, I understood that all of this was going over his head. Still, I wanted to get into the habit of doing it. I wanted to get back from work and let my son know what went on in my life. I wanted this to be one of the things we did at home together. Maybe if communication between us was such a natural thing for Reese that he literally learned it while he was learning how to speak, I could avoid the kind of communication breakdown that dimmed my relationship with Tanya.

And at the same time, it gave me the opportunity to review the day aloud, just to hear myself talk about it and maybe learn something from doing so. It had been an unsettling day. That hardly made it unique among days for me now. But this one had been unsettling – disquieting, really – for different reasons. One was the huge amount of work that had piled up, much of it reminding me (though none of my colleagues would, at least not today) how much time had been lost on the Christmas catalog. Another reason was that the continual stream of sympathy I faced, expressed or not, made me uncomfortable and didn't offer even a modicum of

relief. And yet another was that the place suddenly felt foreign to me. It wasn't mine.

I sautéed some shallots in olive oil and then threw in
a few quartered kumquats, tossing them with my kitchen
tongs a few times to make sure that each picked up a little of
the oil. I cooked the vast majority of meals throughout our
marriage because I loved doing it and Maureen loved eating
what I cooked. My cooking had run through various stages
over the years – from studied and formal when Maureen and
I first moved in together and I wanted to impress the hell out
of her, to simple and casual for a brief period when Tanya
started eating with us, to loose and experimental when it
turned out that Tanya had world-class taste buds and would
try just about anything. And I compiled a considerable repertoire of twenty-minute dishes with big flavors that I could
throw together after coming home from work. I hardly ate
at all the first few weeks after Maureen died. But I slowly
started to cook again, though it was harder to do now that
there was no one to cook for.

When the kumquats were soft, I threw a half-dozen
jumbo shrimp into the pan and let them sear on both sides
before deglazing the pan with a bit of white balsamic vinegar
and a dot of butter. I put the whole thing over rice and sat at
the counter across from Reese, bringing his bottle with me.

"I don't know how you could have the same thing for
dinner every night," I said, holding the bottle up to his mouth
with my left hand while I ate with my right. "We'll get you
on pureed carrots soon. You'll be amazed." Clearly, the conversation didn't interest him much, because he swiveled his
head to glance off at something in the direction of the family
room, the nipple slipping from his mouth as he did so.

The shrimp could have used a little cayenne, but I didn't
want to get up and break Reese's concentration. I watched
the expressions on his face while I ate. Whatever he was looking at was fascinating to him: the bottle forgotten, his mouth
pursing in what I could only assume was some attempt at
communication with the object of his interest. In profile, I
could see his eyes widening and then tightening. Suddenly,

he turned back sharply in my direction, startling me a little by the unexpected movement. Whatever he saw on my face must have seemed funny to him because he chuckled. Tickled by this reaction – I loved the sound of his laughter – I tried for several minutes to get him to do it again to no avail.

However, he did keep his attention on me for a while after that. At one point, he reached for my fork and I let him touch it before pulling it back slightly. He reached out for it again, and I pulled it back again. When I did it this second time, he smiled and reached out again. I kept doing it until he moved on to something else, and I probably would have done it for hours if it had continued to entertain him.

Unlike what I experienced at work, these moments of utter normalcy were a balm. For in these, I got a glimpse of life through Reese's eyes – how just about everything was new for him; how something simple could be so intriguing that you longed to do it over and over again; how it was a good thing that the world reinvented itself from moment to moment. And while I knew that there wouldn't be a single second for me that ever felt like that again, I found comfort in the knowledge that life would be this magical to him for several years.

I finished my dinner and tried to feed Reese some more of his bottle. He didn't seem particularly hungry, though.

"I'm obviously gonna have to tell Lisa to cut down on the candy and ice cream during the day," I said.

I put him in his swing while I cleaned the dishes. During this time, he burbled and grasped at something invisible to me and at one point let out a little laugh for no discernable reason. When I finished, I went to remove him and he protested, so I started the swing again and read the sports section of the paper while he blissed out.

Spring training exhibition baseball games were in full swing and I read a Yankee box score with interest, trying to place the names of the rookies and non-roster invitees. This was always my favorite time of year to read about sports. Beat writers filled the paper with stories about promising young talents and various predictions for another winning season for my favorite team. Once the season began, things could go well or badly. They could go as predicted, or take off in surprising directions. But no other time in the baseball year held as much potential.

I glanced over at Reese, who at that moment stared intently at the floor. Would he be a shortstop like his dad? A fleet outfielder instead? Right now, he most closely resembled third base, so it was anyone's guess what the future held. I wondered how I'd feel if he didn't love baseball the way I did or maybe didn't like it at all. Tanya wasn't a sports fan and I'd been okay with that. But would I feel differently because Reese was my son? Would I feel differently because he was all I had? For now, it was only the preseason of our lives together, and we would find the answers to these questions in the fullness of time.

An hour or so later, I gave Reese another bath and then brought him to his room. I gave him another bottle, but this time I broke out the good stuff – one of the dozens of pouches of breast milk Maureen had frozen in anticipation of her return to work. He drank greedily and I tried to imagine what he thought about when he did. Did he have any sense memory of his mother? Was he more satisfied and contented with this bottle because it made him recall the brief time he'd had at her breast? I noticed tonight that my supply was dwindling, and decided to give them to him every other night thereafter just to extend this gift from Maureen a little longer.

I rocked him while he drank and he seemed groggy. Still, after I burped him, I held him on my shoulder a little longer and sang him a song. Tonight it was Suzanne Vega's "The World before Columbus," which she had written for her daughter. It was one of the several I "covered" at bedtime, ranging from obvious choices like Billy Joel's "Goodnight, My Angel" and Jimmy Webb's "Another Lullaby" to songs that were almost certainly not intended for this purpose, like Phish's "Waste," Marc Cohn's "Silver Thunderbird," and Ben Folds' "The Luckiest."

Reese was asleep when I put him in his crib. The pediatrician had warned me against doing this, but on most nights,

I couldn't help it. There was little in the world that matched the serenity of a baby asleep in your arms, and it was hard to believe that anything that soothed me this way, especially now, could be bad for him.

* * *

I sang lullabies like these to Tanya every night until she was eleven. Those goodnight moments were often the warmest and tenderest between us in a given day. I ceded them grudgingly to her adolescent regimen of showering, hair brushing, and reading books about teen issues to herself. After that, if I were lucky, I'd get to kiss her on the forehead before she turned off her light.

When I talked to friends about how this bothered me, they all recommended I relax. This was what preteen-agerdom was all about. Their evil twins replace them somewhere around their twelfth birthdays and then return them unharmed during their college years. I heard it enough times that I started to believe it. Tanya's grades were great, her friends were moderately socialized, and she was still capable of true warmth and kindness. Certainly, there was no indication that this end in our bedtime ritual would lead inexorably to Mick.

Mick. Philosophy major. Malcontent. Darkener of my daughter's soul.

I made a deplorable series of mistakes with Mick. The first was letting him into the house at all when he wouldn't look at me and when he spoke only to the floor even when he was talking to Tanya. Another was not taking more extreme action when I learned that Tanya lied to us about her whereabouts to go on a late date with him. Yet another was listening to others (including Maureen) who told me he was "a phase" and that Tanya would move on from him soon. And the worst was watching – raging, but watching nonetheless – while my daughter lost the twinkle in her eye, became insolent and cynical, distanced herself even from her mother. All of this was directly attributable to the relationship with Mick that hadn't gone away, and hadn't been a phase but rather a transition.

It wasn't until the day after Maureen told me she was pregnant that we were able to share the news with Tanya. It was the first time we could get on her calendar. She sat on the couch watching the rug, while Maureen and I sat on either side of her.

"We have some big news," Maureen said, placing her hand on one of Tanya's. Tanya didn't pull away, but she didn't grasp it either. Maureen hesitated and Tanya turned her head in her mother's direction. "This was totally unplanned, but it's totally wonderful. We're going to have a baby."

I know that Maureen said it this way to be as inclusive as possible – *we* were going to have the baby, all three of us. And maybe the 10-year-old, the 12-year-old, or even the 15-year-old Tanya would have heard it that way. But the Tanya who sat with us was not prone to inclusion. She lowered her chin to her chest and then swiveled her head to scowl at me. It was the darkest expression I ever saw on her face.

She placed both hands on the couch and without looking at either of us said, "I should have guessed you'd come up with something like this." With that, she picked herself up and ran up the stairs.

I seethed, staring at her back long after she disappeared. Then I stood up to go after her.

"Don't," Maureen said.

"That was a totally unfair thing to say to us," I said tightly.

"I know, but just leave her."

"How often does she get to just slap us down?"

"We caught her by surprise."

"You caught *me* by surprise. I think my reaction was just a tiny bit different."

"Your *circumstances* are just a tiny bit different." Maureen slid over on the couch and drew me back down. "I'll go talk to her in a little while. Let this sink in for a few minutes."

I sat back on the couch and looked up at the ceiling. "That was a *totally* unfair thing to say to us," I said again.

"It was. I'll talk to her."

An hour later, Maureen came downstairs to tell me that Tanya was crying in her arms, telling her that she was worried that the new baby was going to replace her. Maureen did everything she could to assure her that this was impossible.

I took it as a very good sign that Tanya was concerned about this. Clearly, it was an indication that the family and her place in it meant more to her than I believed.

This turned out to be another huge mistake.

* * *

I went to my library, booted up the computer, and checked my home e-mail. Mixed amongst a bunch of spam and newsletters were two personal messages, one from my mother, the other from a friend in Colorado.

My mother spent nearly a week with me after the funeral. It helped to have someone around to watch Reese while I took long walks in the biting January air or lay in my bed trying to feel Maureen next to me. But ultimately it turned out badly when she tried to convince me that Tanya needed to know about her mother and that I had to "do something about it," as though there was anything I could do. I said a few things I probably shouldn't have said, and she was on a plane back to my father in Florida the next day. This new message from her was stiffer and more formal than the ones she used to send. She provided basic information about what was going on with the two of them and asked after Reese and me. I knew I should reach out to her, apologize for losing my temper with her, thank her for her help, but I simply didn't have the reserves required to do this. I knew I would eventually rebuild that bridge. I just couldn't do it right now.

The friend from Colorado was a former Eleanor Miller colleague who wrote much more frequently since hearing about Maureen. Though we weren't particularly close, I found I could write him at length and that he was a good virtual listener with some insightful things to say. This wasn't the first time that the e-mail version of a relationship was stronger for me than the real thing. Obviously, some people just interacted better on the written page than they did in person. I didn't think it made the relationship we'd developed artificial in any way, only functionally different. And I looked forward to hearing from him.

I replied to both of them, writing a much longer message to the friend than to my mother. I spent more time than I usually did telling them new stories about Reese and attached a recent digital photo of him to each message.

After that, I browsed halfheartedly through the newsletters. While I did so, a message arrived from Tanya, immediately recognizable by the FROM ME header she'd used the handful of times she'd chosen to contact us. I looked at it with a start, thinking irrationally that I could latch onto it in some way, reach through the Internet, and pull Tanya back into this house. I felt an odd frisson, as though we had somehow just passed in the ether. Tanya had just hit a "send" button somewhere out there, linking our computers temporarily.

But of course, nothing linked us. Like the others, she'd sent this message through a remailer – maybe hours ago – that made it impossible to trace. This brief interaction between a series of machines left us no more connected than we had been by the dozens, hundreds, thousands of miles between us. Though she couldn't have possibly known that I would be sitting at this desk when the message arrived, it felt like she was baiting me, giving me a peek-a-boo glance, and then disappearing back into the mist. It was so frustrating. And yet I opened the message immediately.

> M&D,
>
> How's the little bundle? Bet he's keeping you up 'til all hours. Hope you're taking your vitamins.
>
> I saw that antiques show on television the other day and it made me think of you, Mom. It still seems totally flaky to me, but I laughed when I thought of

you watching it and trying to figure out how much some old lamp was worth before the host announced it. In this one, some woman thought this creaky chair was going to make her a millionaire and she found out it was worth something like $27. Cracked me up.

Mick and I took jobs for a couple of weeks at a roadhouse. Mick bussed and I waited tables. It was a very cool experience. Not that I would want to do it for a living or anything like that, but I kinda liked talking to all the people who were passing through and getting to know the regulars. We got to crash in the spare bedroom of one of the grill cooks and we got to have all our meals at the restaurant, so we haven't had to spend any money at all, which is cool since that means that now we can go for a while without working and not cut into any of the cash we had with us.

Last night I talked to a trucker and he told me where he was going. It sounded good, so we asked him if he would give us a ride. The owner of the roadhouse didn't love that we were bolting on him, but we definitely never told him we'd be sticking around. For a couple of minutes, we thought he was going to stiff us our last week's salary, but then he forked over the money.

So we're off on the road again tomorrow morning. Just wanted to let you
know that I'm alive and well out here.
Really alive and well. Try to be happy
for me.

Hearts,

T

Try to be happy for me. Tanya had no idea what she was
asking. Even though she was unaware of what had happened
in her absence, how could she possibly think that we could be
happy for her when she just disappeared from our lives? How
could she possibly think that stories of her on the road with
her boyfriend – whom I also happened to despise – would
bring a smile to our faces? How could she think that this was
what we'd been searching for after months of desperate flailing for any clue to her whereabouts followed by the realization, though hardly resignation, that a person could truly
pop off the radar if she chose to do so? I'd stopped spending
a portion of every day trying to find her, not because I didn't
want to, but because I couldn't think of anything more to try.
If I could have latched onto whatever redirected electrons
had beamed this latest message to me and followed them to
the original source, I would have done so instantaneously.
Lacking the magic to pull off that trick, though, I could only
stand in place.

No, I wasn't happy for her. I was confounded, frightened,
and horribly saddened. I wanted her back home with me. I
wanted her to help rebuild our lives together. I wanted the
preteen Tanya – the one who could frazzle me but who still
always amazed me – back in my life. I didn't want her riding
off in the cab of a truck to some new untold destination. I
could never be happy for her if she chose to lead that life.

I was angry now. Where only a short while ago I took
great comfort in the sleeping form of my infant son, the digital version of my daughter had left me incensed. I couldn't get

those last words out of my mind: *try to be happy for me*. Was she so completely insensitive to us that she truly believed this was possible? Or had she so completely forgotten who we were that she thought we might actually find some enjoyment in her escapade? In that moment of anger, I told myself that it didn't matter to me if I ever saw her again. Let her stay on the road. Let her become a footnote in my life. Let her dissipate into the landscape with her miserable boyfriend.

And even as these thoughts came into my head, I knew that I couldn't really mean it.

I went into the kitchen to straighten up, even though nothing was particularly messy. I would bake or prepare something for the next night's dinner. I just needed something to do with my hands. I needed to work off some of the negative energy generated by Tanya's message. I cleaned out two shelves in the refrigerator before I realized how ridiculous the exercise was and I left the kitchen to settle on the couch in the family room, still feeling horribly unsettled.

It was a little after 9:30. I had no idea what to do with this part of the night, even when I wasn't upset about something. This was when Maureen and I would do some reading, maybe catch up on some work, maybe cuddle on the couch, or maybe just shut the bedroom door for some quiet time together. This was the point when I missed her the most, and I missed her horribly tonight. Lisa's first day, going back to work, and Tanya's e-mail had been an onslaught for me. My entire adult life, when stress threatened to overwhelm me, Maureen comforted me. How would my mind ever rest now?

I turned on the television and flipped through the channels, not stopping on anything for more than a couple of minutes. I was too agitated to concentrate, too ill at ease to sleep. So I just kept surfing, hoping that something would placate me.

Even though there was very little chance of that.

FOUR - *Unalloyed Moments*

In spite of all of the gifts Maureen and I got when Reese was born, I needed to buy him some new clothes. He had woefully little to wear on a normal day. People tend to give special occasion clothing as baby presents, assuming either that they are the only ones with this idea or that the child is going to be dressing for dinner nightly. What we really needed were some outfits he could spit up on. That Saturday, the two of us headed to the Smith Haven Mall.

In the parking lot, I attempted to figure out the intricacies of the BabyBjörn baby carrier that I used to tote Reese around, spending several minutes trying out various combinations of clasps and latches. These things had been considerably easier to deal with (though presumably not nearly as ergonomically sound) when Tanya was tiny. I grew a little frustrated and Reese squirmed in his car seat, threatening to explode into fits of screaming at any moment. This was not a happy beginning to our shopping foray.

"That one goes up and over," a man said from a few cars down.

I looked out at him and he walked toward me.

"This strap goes up like this – do you mind?" He gestured toward the carrier.

"No, please."

He reached out and moved a strap, clicking it into place. "I'm sure it makes sense in Sweden."

I unbuckled Reese from his car seat. "How'd you ever figure this thing out?"

"I screwed up a lot and then my wife explained it to me. It really is kind of logical once you do it the right way." I put

Reese into the carrier facing forward. "See? That one you were having trouble with is for support. It only looks like a third leg hole."

"Yeah, I was starting to wonder if maybe it was my son who was built wrong. Thanks for the help."

He waved and started walking away. "Pay it forward. There are plenty of others out there just like us."

With Reese secure in his carrier, the rest of the trip was simple. We walked through the entire mall once to identify our options. It was disappointing to discover that places like Banana Republic didn't have baby sections – *there* was a marketing opportunity just waiting to happen – and the clothing in places like Gymboree just seemed too precious for words. The selection in the department stores was stale and of poor quality. And I refused to pay forty dollars at some of the boutiques for a pair of overalls he'd wear for two months. Ultimately, we settled on Baby Gap and The Children's Place. While at the former, Reese made his first conscious buying decision, seizing on a bright orange shirt and holding it as tightly as his four-month-old fists would allow.

I surely bought more than we needed. But I found I was enjoying this. I never really made these kinds of decisions before. Maureen and I shopped together when Tanya was younger, before she insisted on choosing her own clothing exclusively. But I was just along for the ride. Maureen knew what she wanted, she had great taste, and my opinion really wasn't required or particularly well formed. But as much as I would never choose the circumstances, I liked the fact that these decisions were between Reese and me now. If I thought it would look good on him, then I would buy it. If he liked the color, the texture, or just wanted to grab something, we'd buy that as well. Within an hour and a half, we were finished and would have been done more quickly if the teenager handling the register at The Children's Place didn't slow us down. Thinking about this girl made me think about Tanya waiting tables and claiming to enjoy the work. Would she feel the same way if she kept at it for a couple of months? For that matter, did this cashier's job once seem fascinating before boredom and complete lack of concern for the customer set in?

We still had most of the day in front of us so I decided to stay in the mall a bit longer. We went to a music store and I tried to get Reese to put on a pair of headphones to listen to a song from the new Ari Hest album. He pawed them off and looked back at me contemptuously. Instead, we looked through the CDs while I told him about the Beatles and the Stones and Led Zeppelin and REM, deciding we'd address the classics during this first seminar. He chuckled for some reason at the sight of *Get Yer Ya-Yas Out!* and thought *Rubber Soul* literally looked good enough to eat. Tanya and I spent a lot of time in music stores before she became a teenager. I loved walking around with her, trading impressions of bands and introducing her to new ones. Like so many things in the past few years, this became something we stopped doing, even though we continued to like much of the same music. In fact, by the time she left, my mentioning a new band to her – something I guess I wasn't supposed to be alive enough to do – made her terse and dismissive.

Next, Reese and I went to a sports memorabilia store. I showed him a baseball autographed by Mickey Mantle and another signed by Don Mattingly, my favorite Yankee ever. We browsed through rare artifacts and cheesy tokens to New York's various championship teams. I told him about Reggie Jackson's three home runs, the Islanders' four consecutive Stanley Cups, and Phil Simms' nearly perfect Super Bowl. At one point, Reese decided to lick one of the display cases, but otherwise seemed unmoved by the experience. "I promise; you're going to love this place in a couple of years."

On the way out of the mall, I decided to get a cup of coffee and a donut. At Reese's checkup the other day, the doctor told me it was okay to introduce the baby to certain solid foods (hence the rice cereal). She didn't specifically name Krispy Kremes, but since I was buying one for myself, it seemed impolite to eat it without offering him a taste.

I wasn't really a junk food eater and I kept absolutely none of it in the house, but I had a weakness for these donuts.

Something about the way the Krispy Kreme people glazed them elevated them to some higher form of pastry. I took Reese out of the BabyBjörn and sat him on my lap. I put a little of the sugar on my pinky and then brought it up to his lips. He sucked my finger hungrily and, when I removed it, he continued to work his lips for another taste. I took a bite of the donut and then broke off the tiniest piece for him. He looked up at me approvingly as he moved it around in his mouth, and I knew this was something we would share regularly in the future. However, I wasn't about to feed him any more of something so unhealthy right now. I guiltily finished the donut by myself, reading all kinds of recrimination from his gaze, and then gave him a bottle while I sipped my coffee.

"Reese, you're an excellent shopping buddy," I said to him as we drove home. I flicked on the iPod and sang along to the Jack's Mannequin song that played. We were a couple of boys out for a ride in our car and I felt better than I had in a while. It wasn't until we got back to our neighborhood that I fell victim to another sneak attack, realizing how much Maureen would have enjoyed this trip and how, if fate had been kinder, we would have done it as a family.

I remembered the three of us going shopping when Tanya was six months old. The summer was imminent and the baby needed a new wardrobe. I'll never forget Maureen's giddiness over choosing shorts, sunhats, and bathing suits, holding them up to our young daughter's body with exclamations of delight. Maureen was a dedicated student of everything related to child care, but this was a pure Barbie Doll episode for her, dressing up her little girl. I rarely saw her so uninhibitedly happy. Our budget was very tight in those days and this shopping spree was definitely straining it, but I refused to bring up our finances under the circumstances. We could always make more money. Who knew how many of these unalloyed moments anyone got?

What I remember most about that trip, though, was what happened when we got home. Tanya was asleep in the car and I told Maureen that I'd bring her to her crib.

"She's going to wake up when you take her out of the car seat, you know," Maureen said.

"Yeah, she always does. I can get the monitor and we could leave her in here if you want."

"We could," she said, arching her eyebrows.

"Or?"

She reached over and ran her fingernails along my leg. "It's been a long time since we've made out in a car."

"Have we *ever* made out in a car?"

"Northport Harbor . . ." she said running her fingers up my arm.

"Yes, absolutely."

She leaned over and kissed me, then glanced toward the back seat. "You can do this quietly, can't you?"

"I'm making no promises."

"It would be best if you did. She wakes up easily, remember, and the timing could be unfortunate."

The implications registered and, though it took every bit of my will, I stayed completely silent. We even nodded off together in the car, awakening only when Tanya got up from her nap. It had been one of the truly great days.

Now on this afternoon nearly seventeen years later, Reese and I pulled into the garage of a different house. He smiled when I looked back at him, which reminded me of our little shopping adventure and made me smile as well. But right then, my heart belonged to another place and time and I desperately wanted to see only one face.

* * *

While Reese napped, I got a call from Tate Stax. Tate and I had been friends since second grade and stayed in relatively close touch the entire time. He is taller and considerably more athletic than I am, and during our teenage years he concentrated on being a jock while I spent most of my time playing in rock bands. But even then, we hung together in the cafeteria, went out with friends on the weekends, and spent numerous summer days in each other's company, especially after we both learned to drive. After college, our lives diverged somewhat. I moved back to Long Island with Maureen. He got an MBA from Wharton, did the big-fish-in-a-small-pond thing with a textile firm in Kentucky, then served as comptroller for a mid-size corporation in Columbus, Ohio, where he met Gail, who also grew up on Long Island. When it was time to settle down, they moved back east to live with their two kids, Zak and Sara, now seven and five, in the exclusive community of Head of the Harbor. That Tate made somewhere around three times as much money as I did was something both of us were fully aware of, but it had never gotten between us – though I was very willing to let him pick up the dinner check on occasion.

Since he'd been back, Tate and I saw each other at least once a week, either with our wives on the weekend or alone for a mid-week lunch. We even played tennis together every Tuesday night for a while, but I could barely give him a decent match and we agreed that it wasn't as much fun as it should be. After Maureen died, Tate came around a little more often. He seemed miserable and often lapsed into silences, and I was sure it was because he considered my wife to be a dear friend and felt for my situation. I appreciated his empathy and found myself actually trying to cheer him up at these junctures, which served as medicine for me in its own way.

When he asked if he could stop by this afternoon, though, I knew immediately that something was wrong. He didn't even pretend that he was coming over to check in on me.

Reese and I were in the family room when he arrived. He grabbed a beer from the refrigerator, patted the baby on the head, and sat in a chair across from us.

"Gail and I are splitting up," he said as he settled into his seat.

"You're doing *what*?"

"We're splitting."

"Just like that?"

"It isn't *just like that*. It's been going on for a few months now. We even did three weeks of couples therapy."

"Why didn't you say something to me?"

He looked briefly at Reese then back up at me. "Tanya, the baby, Maureen – it wasn't exactly the time to hassle you with my problems. But I'm moving out tomorrow and I figured you'd be pretty pissed if you learned about this from someone else."

This really shook me. Tate and Gail hardly had a dream marriage, but they seemed fine, and the notion that anyone would choose to deal with this kind of heartache was difficult for me to grasp.

"How are Zak and Sara dealing with it?"

Tate shook his head. "Hard to read 'em. To tell you the truth, I'm a little more concerned with how *I'm* dealing with it at the moment."

"Not your decision?"

"To put it mildly."

I kissed Reese on the forehead and put him down on the playmat with some of his toys. Then I got myself a beer and settled back in.

"What happened?" I said.

Tate looked off into the distance. "I gotta tell you, after months of conversation when I didn't think she was serious and then three weeks with this therapist, I still don't have a freaking clue. I don't spend enough time with the kids. I don't spend enough time at home. I work too much. My eyes are the wrong color. Whatever it is, I can tell you that Gail is royally pissed."

"Maybe she's just trying to shake you up."

"Mission accomplished."

"Maybe she just wants you to make some course corrections and things will be fine in a little while."

Tate took a long look at me and then an extended pull on his beer. "I've got an apartment. We've already told the kids. I'm moving out tomorrow. We have lawyers with huge retainers. This isn't about course correction. This is about dividing up the assets."

I was surprised that he brought up money. "You're not really worried about *that*, are you?"

"I made the vast majority of the cash."

"And you continue to make a massive amount of it. Panhandling probably isn't in your future."

Tate finished the beer and stood up. "The whole thing just sucks."

I leaned forward on the couch. "Zak and Sara are going to need you to come up big for them."

Tate shook his head. "Like I said, the whole thing sucks."

I wasn't sure what to say. It wasn't clear to me whether Tate had come here for consolation or simply to deliver news. I felt for him and I was sure that he had only an inkling of what he was going to experience in the coming months. But I didn't know if he wanted me to talk him through it or just let him stew.

"You okay?" I said.

"Compared to what?"

"Is there anything I can do?"

"Trust me; I wish there was."

"Wanna stay for dinner?"

"I wanna drink myself into oblivion." He turned and looked directly at me. "Mind if I do that?"

I shrugged. "It's fine with me as long as you don't keep Reese awake past his bedtime."

Tate smiled and looked down at the baby. Reese was attempting to get to a yellow plastic ring just out of his grasp and I reached down and prodded him toward it. Of course, it went immediately into his mouth.

"Nah, I'm gonna go. Gail wants me back by six to take care of the kids. She's going out."

"Out? As in *on a date*?"

"I didn't ask. She didn't tell."

I sighed. Tate and Gail were both important to me, but I knew they were going to divide me up along with the assets. "Call me tonight after the kids are asleep. We can bitch to each other for a while."

"Sounds like a great time." He walked past me, thumping me on the shoulder twice as he did. "I'll see ya."

I watched Tate leave and looked off in the direction of the door after he was gone. I was having a very difficult time comprehending that he and Gail were doing this. I went through divorces with friends before – there was a scary stretch when three of the couples we'd met though Tanya split in a six-month period – but to me there was something more dramatic about this one. Maybe it had something to do with being there from the beginning. I could still hear the way Tate lost his worldly-wise cool when he told me he'd met Gail, and the way he confessed how much he loved her when he asked me to be the best man at his wedding.

Or maybe it had to do with the fact that, like me but in an entirely different way, Tate was becoming a single father. He was in for all kinds of rough patches, especially if the proceedings got messy. I wished I had some good advice for him or that he could benefit from my experience. But the best I could offer was that we would go through it together.

I settled down on the floor next to Reese. He'd given up on the yellow ring and had set his sights somewhere in the distance, trying in vain to move himself forward. I picked him up and his head instantly swiveled in another direction, the object of his interest immediately supplanted by another.

To him, as unreachable as most of it was, everything was an option. It was enough to make a guy jealous.

FIVE - Great Toys

I hadn't seen Maureen's sister Codie since the funeral. When she called a few days later, I eagerly invited her to take the trip in from the city that Friday to have dinner with us. Codie and Maureen had been very close and she was the only family I had for hundreds of miles. As an only child, I was accustomed to small families and it never particularly concerned me that ours was little and didn't congregate all that often. But when I considered that my family now stood as Reese and me, I felt a little lost. It meant a lot to me that Codie was coming for a visit.

Five years younger than her sister, Codie was the Type A member of the clan. She started at Hubbard and May Advertising directly out of college and within eight years was creative director. Dozens of larger agencies targeted her over the years, but H&M fended off each approach by giving her more money and more responsibility. Her ever-increasing compensation package netted her a sensational apartment on the Upper West Side, which she saw on the days when she wasn't sleeping on the couch in her office. A partnership was a realistic possibility within the next year.

She also bore a distinct resemblance to her mother – which meant she looked an awful lot like my wife. Codie went for darker colors in her eyeliner and lipstick, and she wore her hair more closely cropped, but her mannerisms were stunningly similar to Maureen's and her smile was exactly the same. It was entertaining to watch the two of them mirror each other in conversation – sometimes making the same gesture simultaneously – and looking at her now was both mildly disturbing and a tiny bit comforting.

I half expected her to postpone our dinner or show up a couple of hours late, both of which she'd done in the past because of her job. But surprisingly, she arrived only a few minutes after I got back to the house myself; Lisa was in the middle of briefing me on her weekend plans when Codie got there. And more surprisingly, she immediately got down on the floor to play with Reese and the new plush airplane she'd brought for him.

Codie was a high school senior with a life quite independent from the family when Tanya was born, and she was away at college for most of my daughter's toddler years. They connected strongly after that, though, and Tanya spent numerous weekends in the city with her. But I never saw Codie engaged with a baby before. And whether it was because he was a living, breathing piece of her sister or because she found him inordinately captivating, Codie spent the entire time I prepared dinner in the family room with Reese.

"He's so cute," she said as she put him in the high chair he graduated to earlier in the week.

"You should get one of your own."

"Yeah, that's a good idea. I could tote him around to client meetings. Or maybe he could hang out in his playpen in my office while I pull an all-nighter."

"People *do* make adjustments when they have children."

"People in other professions."

"Right, I forgot. No one in advertising has kids. Do you really think that H&M would demote you if you dialed it back a little? You threaten to go to the *bathroom* and they give you a raise. I think they understand your value."

Codie let Reese grab her finger and she waved it back and forth. He smiled and then put the finger in his mouth.

"Doesn't matter," she said. "Last I heard you needed a father to have one of these."

I tried to remember the name of the guy she was dating when Reese was born. "Jake didn't pan out?"

She threw me a confused expression. "Jake? Nah, that's been over for months."

"It's hard to keep up with you on this stuff."

"I don't know why it's hard to keep up. When I tell you I'm dating someone, just count forward fourteen days. By then you can be certain he'll be out of the picture."

This was one of the things I never really understood about Codie. Plenty of men – especially Manhattan men – could appreciate and identify with her work life. And she certainly had no trouble finding dates. But even in high school, she kept her relationships very brief and I never heard her talk about a partner with any more enthusiasm than she might a new restaurant.

We ate quietly for a few minutes. I gave Reese strained applesauce for the first time and he took to it with the same enthusiasm as most of the food he tried. Clearly, he was going to be a good eater. I looked forward to cooking for him.

"How are Grace and Ed doing," I asked, referring to her parents.

Codie looked up at me sadly. We managed to go an hour without mentioning Maureen's death, though both of us were almost surely thinking of her the entire time. "They're struggling. Dad worse than Mom, interestingly enough. We were in the middle of a conversation about the *stock market* the other day and he just broke down. They call you, don't they?"

"Yeah, a couple of times a week. But I always get the impression that they're doing it to cheer me up. Lots of questions about the baby. I've invited them to visit a dozen times and they keep putting it off. I think they're not sure what to make of this house without Maureen in it."

"I can understand that," she said gravely.

I pointed a fork toward her. "*Don't* understand that. I don't want you to ever feel weird about coming here." I shifted the fork toward Reese. "He needs his aunt. Especially since she brings him great toys when she comes to visit."

Codie smiled and looked over at the baby. "He really is adorable. He would have wrapped Maureen around his little finger."

"Nah, she wasn't that easy. But he would have gotten most of what he wanted anyway."

She took Reese's hand and kissed it. "Is it scary doing this alone?"

"The scary part is that I *have* to do it alone. Actually doing it isn't that tough. I mean, you keep moving, you know? We're getting by all right."

She nodded and assumed a thoughtful expression that was just like her sister's. "I know I'm out of my depth here, but if there's anything I can do to help, just let me know."

"Do this. Come see us. We both could really use that."

"I will, I promise. I should've gotten out here before now, but, I don't know, there's so much I really haven't dealt with yet. Maureen was always there, you know?"

"I know. For both of us. Always. But I think because of that it's really important that we keep the lines open between us, that we remain family."

"You're right. It'll be easier from now on."

I patted her hand and Reese pounded on his high chair tray, obviously peeved that he stopped being the center of attention for a few seconds.

I cleaned the dishes while Codie entertained the baby and then the three of us played on the floor together for a while before his bedtime. I assumed Codie would go home then, but she stuck around while I got Reese into his crib.

When I returned from his room, she was sitting at the dining room table, having poured herself another glass of wine. When she saw me, she held up her glass.

"Want some more?" she said.

"Just a little. I'm on duty."

She poured some for me and then looked up as I sat down. "Listen," she said, "I got a message from Tanya."

"You did? When?"

"A few days ago. Through a remailer just like yours. It was a really long one. I got the impression that she was unloading."

"About what?"

"About everything. About Mick, and about you and Maureen, and about why she wanted to take off the way she did."

In other words, Tanya had been willing to tell Codie all of the things she had been unwilling to tell us. "What did she say?"

"She told me that she didn't want me to tell the two of you any of this."

I could feel myself getting angry. "Is that a reasonable request under the circumstances?"

"I think it might be. Look, if she had told me anything that could help you find her or anything that suggested she was in any kind of trouble, I'd tell you in a second. But she's always trusted me and as stupid as it might be – I mean, it's not like she's going to know whether I talked to you about this or not – I feel like I need to honor that trust now."

"Just tell me one thing: does she hate us?"

"She doesn't hate you. In fact, this might have less to do with you and Maureen than you think. She wasn't *that* specific, but I think this was a lot more about her need to prove herself as a fully evolved human being to Mick than anything else."

I could feel my bile rise. "She couldn't do that here?"

"Mick doesn't believe in families."

"He doesn't believe in families? What the hell is that supposed to mean?"

"He thinks that families foster codependency and perpetuate dysfunctional behavior."

"Maybe first I'll kill his professors."

Codie reached out for my hand and squeezed it. "She wrote that to *me*. Her aunt. A family member. She hasn't been brainwashed. She's just trying things on for size."

"And what if it fits?"

"Do you really think it's going to fit? You and Maureen raised her."

I looked down at my wineglass. "The last couple of years have been tough."

"They haven't been as tough as you think. I've heard her side of some of those arguments. They aren't very different from your side. That means in some twisted way that you were actually communicating."

"*Were* being the operative word."

"I can't tell you how to feel about this, Gerry. And I miss her like crazy myself. We were real buddies, you know? But with everything that's going on in your head right now, don't make yourself crazy over what you did or Maureen did to drive Tanya away."

"She wants me to try to be happy for her. That's what she wrote in her last message. Can you believe it?"

"So? What's the downside?"

I looked up at Codie as if I hadn't heard her correctly. "What?"

"What's the downside of being happy for her?"

"You've had more wine than I thought you did."

"Really, Gerry, what's the downside of looking at this as something other than an international crisis?"

I shook my head in bewilderment. It was hard to believe that Codie couldn't understand why I felt the way I did. "My 17-year-old daughter has run away with a 20-year-old guy and is riding with truckers to who the hell knows where."

"And you can't do a single thing about that."

I smirked. "Did I forget to mention that part?"

"My point is that feeling angry and frustrated isn't particularly useful to you."

I threw up my hands. "So I should celebrate it instead? Maybe I should start having a better time being a widower as well."

Codie grabbed my face with both of her hands, a gesture that took me completely by surprise. This one was definitely not in Maureen's repertoire. "You're not paying attention to me."

"I think I might be."

"Well then you aren't as smart as I always thought you were. Think about it for a second. Tanya's traveling around the countryside with a jerk. She's putting herself in potentially dangerous situations and she hasn't seen enough of the world to know how to deal with those situations."

"Which piece of this isn't my point?"

"This. Tanya is a really good kid. There's actually a remote possibility that the jerk isn't a *complete* jerk. And she knows a whole lot more about the way the world works than you think."

I spoke sharply. "And you know this because of other things she's told you in confidence over the years?"

"I know this because I'm not her parent and I *have* been paying attention. Is it crazy that a straight-A student would forego her last two years of high school to do something like this? Of course it is. But Tanya was bored to death with school and she was bored to death living in Suffolk County and strolling down the quaint streets of Port Jefferson. Then Mick comes along and exposes her to a whole new way – a much more sophisticated way – of looking at the world and she latches on to it. This is nothing more than an elaborate research project. There is no chance that she's going to be riding with truckers the rest of her life."

"Is there a message here?"

"The message is that it wouldn't hurt you to look at it from her perspective. She's asked you to be happy for her. She has no idea that her mother is gone. And she's out there on a voyage of discovery."

"She's seventeen," I said louder than I probably should have.

Codie took a deep breath. "Gerry, you have every legitimate reason to feel the way you do. But it isn't helping you. At all."

"So I should revel in her experience and laugh giddily when she winds up dead in a ditch." I spit out these words and they felt ugly even as they left my mouth.

Codie looked at me as though I'd truly disappointed her. "When the hell did you become such a pessimist?"

"You *know* when I became such a pessimist."

She looked toward the floor. "I didn't realize both of you died that day."

Hearing this from her, watching her say it the way she said it, made me overwhelmingly sad. I put my head down on the table. Codie leaned over and kissed the back of it. "Only part of the world ended, Gerry."

I looked up and I'm sure I had confusion and distress written all over my face. Codie reached for me and I hugged her. As I did, I felt like my body disassembled. Sobs tore into me. I hadn't cried this hard since the day I buried Maureen. It took me several minutes to regain my composure and several more before I felt comfortable speaking. Through it all, Codie held me, stroking my hair and not saying anything. I didn't realize that she too was crying until I pulled back.

"I'm a total wreck," I said softly, my eyes cast downward.

Codie reached a finger under my chin and raised my head. "Not total," she said with a smile I wish I could have framed.

She stayed until nearly ten. When I calmed enough, we sat in the family room, traded stories about work, and skirted around the edges of reminiscence. Things had already gotten emotional enough for one evening. So we laughed about the cranberry sauce incident from three Thanksgivings past. And we debated the advice Maureen gave her about dealing with a difficult friendship. And we talked about the spring vacation that Tanya spent with Codie – how Tanya came home beaming and how Maureen and I enjoyed ourselves nearly as much doing very different things. But we didn't wallow and we spent more time in the present than I expected us to.

This was by far the longest period of time I had ever spent alone with Codie. I saw her regularly and often picked up the phone when she called the house, but the two of us had never just gone out for a drink, or to run an errand together. The circumstances had simply never arisen. Now I couldn't believe that it had taken this long for us to get to this level.

And crying with her had been a welcome release. Unlike everyone else who tried to offer consolation, Codie truly understood how much I lost. It made a difference. I realized then that feeling for someone's pain was overwhelmingly different from experiencing someone's pain. In that way, Codie and I were linked inseparably. We felt Maureen's absence even more than her parents did. More than anyone who was aware she was dead.

It was nice to know that we had crossed some kind of bridge, that our future visits would be more than ceremonial ones, punctuated by polite conversation and increasingly longer silences. Instead, I would anticipate them with great enthusiasm.

When she left, I pulled her close to me. "This was really good," I said. "Let's do it again soon."

"We will," she said, kissing me on the cheek. "Really soon." And then she ran her fingers through her hair just as Maureen used to and said, "Gotta go."

I stood in the doorway until Codie's car disappeared down the road. Then I went to the library and booted up the computer. No new e-mail worth giving any attention. I pulled up Tanya's most recent message and read it again. *Try to be happy for me.* The sentiment still rankled, but I thought about what Codie said emphatically tonight.

What was the downside? Was it the concern that seeing this from her perspective might make it more acceptable to me that she was gone? Was it the fear that my being happy for her even for a second would somehow authorize her to stay away forever?

Codie was right about a lot of what she said. Tanya was smart and much more sophisticated than most of her friends. I nicknamed her "Queenie" when she was still a toddler because of her regal bearing; she had stopped letting me call her that a few years ago. There was little to no chance she was going to adopt this lifestyle permanently. She was on a kind of elaborate research project that was certainly more perilous than most and could conceivably drive her away from me forever, but one that, if she stayed safe and didn't fall in with the wrong people – two huge "ifs" – could teach her remarkable things.

I'll try to be happy for you, Tanya. I'll try to cut through the misery I feel in your absence and a whole other level of misery that you're not even aware of, to see how this could be a special and meaningful and even innocent time for you. I probably won't be able to be happy for you much, *but maybe I'll be able to be happy for you* a little.

I love you, Queenie. I want you to come home. I want us to pull this family together and gain strength from one another. I want you with me to build a living monument to your mother and for us to remember her in our actions for the rest of our lives.

But if you want me to be happy for you while you're doing whatever you're doing wherever you're doing it, I'll try.

I'll probably fail, but I'll try.

SIX - *Some Other Time*

I began to adjust to my return to work. After a few weeks, I was back into the rhythm of the office. While not nearly as diverting as I had found it to be at other challenging times in my life, the job was something I could focus on for increasingly longer stretches. The deadline of the Christmas catalog lent a certain amount of propulsion to every day.

This wasn't to say that I didn't meditate on the pictures of Maureen, Tanya, and Reese every time I sat at my desk, or that I didn't check in on Lisa more often than was probably necessary (or, from her perspective, welcome). But I began to have ideas again and I could look at the piles of paper in front of me as surmountable.

I was addressing one such pile when Ally Ritten knocked on my door. Until she joined my team, I was only peripherally aware of her. I heard she was smart, others worked well with her, and she came up with some trinket or other for catalogs I hadn't worked on as a sideline to her primary marketing job. In the first couple of team meetings I had with her, I was impressed with her energy and with how quickly she could run with an idea. She quickly made more of a contribution than anyone else did on the team, and I was sure this was something she would be very good at full time. I'm sure Marshall had some notion of this, which was why he told me to bring her on, though he hadn't yet suggested anything like a department transfer.

"Hi, am I interrupting?" she said, standing half in and half out of the doorway.

"I'm plodding through some vendor contracts. *Please* interrupt."

She sat down across from my desk. "What do you think of cookie jars?"

"Filled or unfilled?"

"Well, that's sort of where I was going with this. What about offering a set of personalized cookie jars? You know, 'Mom's Favorite Cookies' or 'Jimmy's Favorite Cookies.'" This way everyone could always have their cookies in their own cookie jar without compromise or, you know, cross-contamination."

"Cross-contamination?"

"Oatmeal cookies don't taste as good if you get Oreo on them."

"They don't?"

"I think a certain sector of our audience might believe that to be the case."

I looked at her skeptically.

"Okay, *I'm* part of that sector," she said. She seemed embarrassed by the admission, as though she told me something terribly intimate.

"Oatmeal cookies aren't allowed to touch Oreos?"

She reddened slightly. "It gets chocolate on them. Then they don't taste as much like oatmeal anymore."

"So it would be better if Mom's cookies and Jimmy's were segregated."

She closed her eyes. "This was a stupid idea."

I laughed. "It's not a stupid idea. We sell tens of thousands of personalized TV remote caddies every year. Trust me; there are *no* stupid ideas. Actually, you satisfied my number one rule for pitching a concept – that *you* be part of the market for it. The first best way to test the viability of a product is to know that you would buy it yourself."

She nodded and seemed to regain a little of her composure. Clearly, Ally had been nervous about pitching me one-on-one and I unintentionally made her more nervous by teasing her.

"If this is your number one rule, shouldn't *everyone* on your team know it?" she said with a smile. Obviously, she gathered her feet under her quickly.

I smiled back. "Now everyone does."

"Thanks. I'll play with this a little and let you get back to your contracts." She glanced over at my desk. "Is that the baby?" she said, pointing to a picture frame.

I handed the photograph to her. "The picture's a couple of weeks old, so of course he looks completely different now."

"He's really cute."

"Thanks."

"Reese?"

"Yeah, Reese. It's Greek for, 'He who doesn't sleep very much.'"

She grinned and handed the picture back to me. At the same time, she nodded toward another frame. "Is that him with your wife?"

I took the photograph of the two of them cuddling that Saturday before our last date together. I touched the frame, but I didn't pick it up. "Yeah, it is."

"This has to be tough for you."

I was tiring of hearing people say that, but it wasn't fair to her to let it show. "I'm getting better at dealing with it."

"You know, you're not giving off any signs of freaking out at all. That's admirable."

"Freaking out really isn't one of my available choices. Not with a baby to take care of."

"I guess you're right. You're lucky to have him at a time like this."

I looked up at her, surprised at the insight of the comment. No one else had said anything like that to me. "You're right; I am. It's hard to wallow when he's around. And it's hard to think that the world sucks when you get a glimpse at how amazing it seems to him."

She settled back in her chair. "You're on an adventure."

I chuckled. "Yeah, like one of those guys who gets thrown into a heroic situation against his will."

"A reluctant hero."

"Something like that."

She reached over and touched the original picture I handed her. "Too bad he doesn't sleep."

"Most of the time it's too bad. Sometimes it's just what you need at 2:30 in the morning."

She smiled and shook her head. "Yeah, I can understand that."

"It's just that, a lot of times, I'm up anyway. It's the weirdest thing how stuff will just creep up on me. Even when I'm sleeping. I'll be floating along and then suddenly something will remind me that I'm that widower with the tiny baby and the runaway daughter." I surprised myself by talking to her this way, since I barely knew her. But she seemed more receptive than most people I spoke to and not at all uncomfortable with these subjects. With most people, opening up made me feel like I was either being boring or feeding someone's prurient curiosity. "It happens to me in meetings sometimes. You can watch for it now that I've told you."

"At which point, I'll bring up something completely inane like personalized cookie jars and snap you right back into the moment."

I laughed. "That's very generous of you."

"The cookie jar thing really was stupid, wasn't it?"

"It wasn't stupid. Work it up."

"You think so?"

"Look, it *might* be stupid, but it's worth exploring a little further. What's the downside?" I smiled after employing my catchphrase of the moment.

"I will." She stood up to leave. "Thanks for the time. They told me you were approachable, but I was still a little concerned about just barging in here with an idea."

"Come in any time. Really."

"Thanks for the invitation."

Ally smiled and left the office. I ran my hand over the picture I showed her. Reese did look very different now. *Are you changing right this second while I'm not with you?* I needed to bring some new prints into the office. Maybe even one of those picture frames that cycled digital images so I could constantly have the latest shots of my son sitting on my desk with me. I was relatively certain that Lisa would object to a nanny-cam.

* * *

Just before lunch, Marshall called me down to his office. He'd just hung up the phone when I arrived in his doorway.

"Messerschmidt's an asshole," he said.

"I'll have to take your word for it, since I have no idea who Messerchmidt is."

"He's the new director of fulfillment. And if you ever spend three minutes in a room with him, you won't need to take my word for it. I wish I could dump the bastard."

"Doesn't he report to you?"

"I spent six months *recruiting* him. I can't just dump him."

"One of the many reasons I'm glad I'm not you."

He gestured for me to sit down and leaned forward on his desk. "Enough with Messerchmidt. I'll get him in line. Listen, I have some great news for you. Corporate wants you on this year's retreat."

"This is that thing you go on every year where you eat a lot and drink a lot and sit by a pool in some grossly over-priced resort for three days?"

"And also discuss corporate policy and make decisions about the future of the company."

"In between massage appointments."

He scowled at me. "A great deal of executive level business gets done at these things."

"Yeah, I think one of the decisions you made last year was to cut T&E by 20%. Obviously the retreat is exempt."

"Do you want to talk about your role in this or not?"

"They really want me to come?"

"I made a very persuasive argument for you. Your presence there will send a message."

"These things happen in Bermuda or someplace like that, right?"

"Longboat Key this year – that is if the accommodations are acceptable to you."

I shifted in my chair. Marshall didn't take particularly kindly to things not going according to his plan. "I don't see how I can do this. There's no way I can get anyone to take care of Reese for that length of time."

He took a deep, impatient breath. "Of course you can. You have a babysitter, don't you?"

"I can't imagine that she'd be up for a long weekend."

"What about your parents?"

"They absolutely couldn't handle it."

"What about Maureen's parents?"

"I really don't think I can ask them."

"Shit, I'll have Denise take care of him."

"Marshall, you're not following me. Setting aside that I wouldn't even consider foisting a four-month-old on your wife for three days, I don't think that this would be a good thing for me to do right now. We're just beginning to develop a routine. There's a huge amount going on in his life at this stage. If this was an overnight, I might be able to pull it off, but three days would be nearly impossible."

Marshall's brows creased. In spite of the fact that he was my boss, we maintained a good friendship by avoiding professional confrontations like this one. "What if this was an essential business trip? Would you beg off because you were too busy playing mommy then?"

"I'd have to give it serious thought. And this is not an essential business trip. You can dub me 'a comer' some other time."

His expression darkened again. "I went to bat for you. You were my pick."

"I'm sure you did and I'm sure I was and I really appreciate it. I need you to understand this."

"This would be good for you, Gerry. You need to get away."

I held up a hand. "Really, I don't. I don't think I've ever needed to be home more."

He scribbled on a piece of paper. He wasn't writing anything. This was simply one of the ways in which Marshall showed that he wasn't happy about something.

"You're really telling me to get another guy?"

"I have to. I'm sorry, but this would be a real hardship for me right now."

"These things happen when they happen, Gerry."

"And hopefully this will happen again when I can take better advantage of the situation."

Marshall crossed something off his to-do list and then looked up at me. "You're making progress with the catalog?"

"We're getting there."

"It's gonna blow me away, right?"

"Let's hope so."

"Yes, let's hope so."

* * *

I was gathering up papers to review at home when Ben came into my office and sat down.

"You're taking all that stuff with you?"

"I am *so* far behind. And I would be even further behind if you didn't do such a great job with the prototype status report."

"Glad to be of service. Listen, a bunch of us assistants are going out for a drink and I was wondering if you wanted to come along."

"I thought your club didn't let people like me be members."

"Usually we wouldn't. But we were talking about it and we decided that you were cool enough."

I looked up from my papers and eyed him skeptically. "You guys don't think I'm cool. You think I'm sad and this is a pity invite."

"No really. It wasn't even me who suggested it. I mean I think the person who suggested it has a little thing for you, but that's not the point either."

"Somebody in your group has *a thing* for me?"

"I think a couple of them think that the guy-with-the-baby thing is pretty romantic."

"Gee, maybe I should start cruising bars with Reese strapped to my chest."

"You promised you would lend him to *me* for that purpose. So are you going to come with us?"

"I can't. Lisa made me promise to be back on time tonight and I have a lot to do after Reese goes to bed."

"Next time, then."

"Some other time."

I continued to put papers in my briefcase, but Ben made no effort to get up.

"Have you been out *at all* since Maureen died?"

"Ben, I have an infant at home. Coming to work qualifies as 'out.'"

"Lisa is never available at nights?"

"I have no idea if Lisa is available at nights. I'm supposed to be home."

"Because Reese will grow up to be a serial killer if you go out for a drink?"

I stopped fiddling with my briefcase and looked him squarely in the eyes.

"I've stepped over that invisible line, haven't I?" he said.

I laughed joylessly and sat back down. "You haven't stepped over the line. And I appreciate the drinks invitation. And you can tell whoever has a thing for me that I'm flattered even if my actual situation is far from romantic. But I'm not ready for a night out. I'm just not. Reese needs me and I need him and that pretty much covers my social obligations for the moment."

"You sure?"

"For now I'm sure."

"We're going to Cameron's. The Five Alarm Wings are addictive."

"My loss. Some other time, I promise."

Ben stood up. He pointed to my briefcase. "Want me to stay here and take some of that stuff off your hands instead."

"Thanks. If I could pass anything off, I would."

He nodded and headed toward the door.

"And Ben, I really do appreciate the invite. Thank the other assistants for me."

"We wanted you to come with us, you know."

"I know."

"It wasn't a pity thing."

"Thanks."

"Some other time, right?"

"Some other time. Definitely."

SEVEN - *Plate Discipline*

The next Saturday, I rushed into the house with several bags of groceries, putting them away with less care than usual. I threw together a fast sandwich for myself, warmed a bottle for Reese, then positioned both of us in the family room and clicked on the television.

The first televised Yankee preseason game of the new year was about to start.

I'd been a dedicated Yankee fan for as long as I could remember. As a child, I was obsessed with them, and even as I discovered new inspirations – music and girls, most specifically – I held fast to my commitment to the team. I scheduled dates around important series. I made bands listen to games on the radio while we drove to gigs. I even slipped out of the hotel room during our honeymoon, while Maureen napped, to watch a game that was critical to the pennant race.

The Yankees were my companions through the toughest times in my life and the best. They served a function for me that others might find in a different form of entertainment – the ability to sweep me up into their world, to make the drama they played out on their stage more consuming than whatever was going on in my head. And unlike any other form of entertainment, none of it was pre-scripted. There was no way to know in advance how things would turn out. The best teams sometimes lost, the poorest teams sometimes won, and how it all happened was a continuing mystery. And so, though I delighted in little other than my son these days, I still looked forward to the new baseball season.

Maureen never shared this passion with me, even during the great Yankees seasons of the '90s with Bernie Williams, Paul O'Neill, Mariano Rivera, and Derek Jeter. She found the game to be slow, a criticism no true baseball fan understands. And while she tolerated the occasional postseason game, I had to watch most of the regular season by myself, which meant that I tended to watch fewer games than I really wanted to. But she always ceded me certain events – like the first exhibition game televised back to New York from Florida.

I especially loved watching baseball in March. Even though, since 1993, the Yankees always had championship-potential teams, there was something exciting about considering their chances for another World Series. And then there were the personal stories that always emerged during this time. The aging veteran five years from his best seasons trying to play himself onto the team in a backup role. The tender-armed pitcher trying to prove that last year's stay on the disabled list was only a detour. And the dozens of rookies with numbers like 87 and 92 on their backs who stood virtually no chance of playing in the Bronx, but *could* be the next coming of Don Mattingly. Standing out from this latter group was Bobby Kitterer, already nicknamed "Kid" Kitterer. He was a 21-year-old from Oklahoma – Mantle country – and he tore up the league while playing for the AA Trenton Thunder last year with a combination of power, speed, and defensive brilliance. It was widely assumed that next year he'd force his way onto the major league club, but this spring training was all about his getting his feet wet. I'd read about him since the Yanks made him their number one draft pick a few years back and hoped he'd get to play a little in this game.

Reese drank his bottle in his high chair, but during the bottom of the first inning as the Yankees came to bat, I took him out and sat him next to me on the couch.

"The leadoff hitter is a total pro," I said to him. "He makes the pitcher work and he sets things up for the other hitters. When you get older, we'll talk about plate discipline. You want to bat like this guy. You want to make the pitcher sweat in the first inning."

Predictably, the leadoff hitter saw eight pitches before stroking a single into left field. The Yanks were on their way.

They wound up scoring twice in the inning, but they gave back the early lead and fell behind 3-2 in the top of the second.

"That's one of the worst things a pitcher can do," I said to Reese. "His team just gave him a lead and he gave it right back. You can't do things like that." It was only the preseason, but like the players, I needed to get my critical faculties into regular season form. And I needed to explain the essentials of the game to my son.

It could easily have been my imagination, but it seemed to me that he paid special attention to the television during the game. The TV had yet to hold any more fascination for him than a spoon or a sunbeam. But I could swear he concentrated on what the players were doing on the field. And while he normally squirmed all over the place – especially since he figured out how to roll over – he sat nestled against my side for the longest time.

The Yankees' manager had planned to use the regulars – who had not started a game together this March and wouldn't have now if not for the television cameras – only four or five innings. It would turn out to be one inning too many. In the fifth, the very same leadoff hitter I lauded earlier ran in after a low line drive and blew out his knee. He seemed to be in excruciating pain and, even before the announcers reported on his condition, I knew he was going to be out for a long time.

"This is trouble, Reese. Real trouble."

Trotting out to replace him was Kid Kitterer. He looked confident and ready. But I wonder if he knew that trepidation filled every true Yankee fan's heart due to the event that hastened his arrival.

Eventually the Yankees won the game 8-6. But it was hard to take comfort in this. Something much bigger than the game had happened, something that would unquestionably affect the team throughout the summer. I had a very bad feeling about the season to come.

Reese fell asleep on his playmat. I picked him up to put him in his crib and then just decided to lay on the couch with him on my chest for a while. I felt a little cheated by what happened during the game, as though one of the few pure things in my life had been sullied. I never liked it when anything went wrong with the Yankees, but this was so much worse than that. One of the key pieces of their foundation was gone.

* * *

That night, Tate came over for dinner with his kids for the first time since splitting with Gail. Zak and Sara ran into the family room, saw Reese playing on his mat, and immediately got down on the floor with him. Tate and I sat on the couch.

"How are they doing?" I said, nodding toward his children.

"They've been a little intense today. Zak wanted everything he could get his hands on at Toys 'R' Us and Sara refused to order a single thing from the menu at the pancake house. I think she needs a nap or something."

I looked down at the three of them playing quietly on the floor. "Maybe they want a baby brother."

"Don't even joke about stuff like that."

"Have you talked to Gail?"

He grimaced. "It was hard to avoid it when I picked up the kids. I tried, believe me."

"I meant have you talked about what's going to happen between you."

"I *know* what's going to happen between us. She's going to steal my house and my money and I'm going to babysit Team Hyperactive on the weekends."

I was surprised that he said that as loudly as he did. The kids didn't appear to hear him, but you never knew what they were actually listening to. Reese seemed perfectly comfortable with them – he rolled over twice already and he didn't just do that for anyone – and Zak was old enough to let me know if the baby was in trouble. I asked him if it was okay if we left the three of them alone for a while and then motioned Tate into the kitchen.

"He's a pretty mature little kid," I said, nodding toward the family room.

"Reese? Don't you think you might be stretching it a little?"

"I meant Zak."

Tate chuckled. "Yeah, he's a good guy. I wish he wasn't so *needy* sometimes, you know?"

"I have a feeling he's going to be a lot needier until he figures out how to deal with this situation you're all in."

Tate walked over to the refrigerator and pulled out a beer. "I guess I'm not entirely convinced that it's that much of a *situation* for them. I mean it's not like I ever saw them very often during the week anyway. I was always working late."

"Trust me; it's a situation. I'm sure they're picking a lot of things up from their mother."

"You mean like the touchdown dances she's doing all around the house now that I'm gone?"

"That wasn't exactly what I was thinking of." I studied him drinking his beer. "What the hell happened between the two of you?"

Tate cast his eyes downward. "I don't know. Different agendas, I guess. But all along, I thought we had the *same* agenda, you know? I had no idea what was going on in her head."

"I certainly never saw it coming and I know Maureen didn't either. She would have said something to me. Gail must have done a hell of a job of keeping everything inside."

"Yeah, I guess. There's a valuable trait. You know, I think she really hates me. I mean, I think she's *thrilled* that I'm gone."

"That stinks. I really feel sorry for you."

Tate shrugged. "Yeah, we'll you're the last person I should be complaining to."

"Give me a break," I said, a little miffed. "You think I can't handle it?"

Just then, I heard Reese wail and went into the family room to see what was going on. He was wedged against one of the armchairs and he couldn't figure out how to roll back in the other direction.

"I think he's stuck," Zak said.

"Yeah, we'll have to unstick him." I picked up the baby and held him for a moment until he stopped crying. Then I put him back on his playmat. Reese immediately looked up – his anguish long since forgotten – and rolled over again. If he found rolling this interesting, he was going to have a ball crawling.

Zak and Sara seemed a little concerned that they'd done something wrong. "Reese isn't very good at steering yet. You think you guys could give him a little nudge if he gets stuck again?"

"I can do that," Zak said manfully. Sara simply nodded. I don't think she'd said a thing since she walked into the house, though she seemed content holding a ring over Reese's head and watching him reach for it.

I went back to the kitchen. Tate was munching on a bag of pretzels he found. "Kids, huh?" he said. "Always need your attention."

"No big deal. I just had to move him back to the middle of the rug."

I started pulling things out of the refrigerator. "I'm making chicken *fra diavolo* for dinner. I assume your kids don't eat that. What should I make for them?"

"I don't know; anything is fine. They love ice cream, I know that much. They could probably make a whole meal out of that."

"Maybe after dinner. Pasta with butter?"

"Whatever."

I looked at him crossly.

"Gail took care of this stuff," he said, throwing his hands up.

"And *you* take care of it now when they're with you. Are you planning to eat every meal out?"

"Why not? I do it when I'm alone."

I dropped the subject, assuming this was something that would come to him in time.

The pasta with butter turned out to be fine with the kids and Sara had three helpings. Zak tried a piece of chicken and said he liked it. He declined a second, but I congratulated him on his willingness to expand his horizons. Both kids found the pureed peaches I gave Reese appealing and happily accepted some of their own. They still had room for ice cream afterward, though.

We watched a movie after dinner and they left when it was time for Reese to go to bed.

"When do you have to bring them back to Gail?"

"Two o'clock tomorrow," Tate said, throwing me a sidelong look. "I think I might make it one-thirty."

I kissed the kids on the foreheads and patted Tate on the shoulder. I couldn't tell which of them looked more beleaguered as they made their way to the car.

* * *

I just got Reese into his crib when Codie called.

"It's a Saturday night," I said. "Shouldn't you be out surveying the social scene or breaking someone's heart or something?"

"I have a cold. I always get colds at the beginning of the spring. I think I'm countercyclical. How are you doing?"

"I don't have a cold. I just finished a relatively upsetting dinner with my friend Tate and his kids, though. He's fumbling around with the early stages of a divorce. How was your day?"

We'd been talking like this regularly since her visit. Most of what we talked about was surface level stuff. She'd tell me about a campaign she was working on, then I would tell her how things were going with the catalog and how Reese had made it abundantly clear that he had no interest in pureed string beans. The mention of string beans would remind her of a restaurant she'd eaten in recently where the menu was built around Chinese long beans. Although, while she didn't say it, I assumed that she didn't at any point in the meal stick her tongue out and let the beans drop onto the table as Reese had done. Her talking about Chinese food would make me think of the surprisingly good pan-Asian place that just opened near work and the conversation would continue in this fashion.

Of course, it was impossible to talk to Codie without thinking of Maureen and Tanya. Therefore, it was only a matter of time before I got to something that was eating at me.

"Do you think she's having sex with him?"

"Do you want me to answer that? Do you *need* me to answer that?"

"You know, I was actually primed for a good lie right there."

"Sorry. Do you know what the statistics are regarding 17-year-olds and sexual activity? Do you know what the statistics are regarding *14*-year olds and sexual activity?"

"Are you trying to tell me something?"

"No, I'm not. Other than what you already know."

"He's twenty. That's a huge three years when it comes to this kind of thing."

"You're right; it is. You're just going to have to hope that Tanya is capable of handling it. At least most of it. And I'm sure Maureen taught her some tricks for keeping boys under control."

I smirked. "Maureen didn't do tricks."

Codie hesitated and I wondered if she was trying to decide whether to revise history for me.

"You're right," she said. "Maureen didn't do tricks with you. That's one of the ways I knew the two of you were going to work, even though I was still a kid. You got all of her. But I'm telling you, she knew plenty of tricks. Older sisters share these things with their younger sisters."

"Care to elaborate?"

"Not really."

We both fell silent for a moment.

"There are so many things I miss about her," Codie said. "But you know what I miss the most? This. We used to talk on the phone almost every day. About stupid stuff a lot. I mean, what percentage of your conversations can be profound when you talk *all* the time? But the lines were always open. I think I miss that more than anything."

"I know what you mean."

"It's gotta be exponentially harder for you."

"I don't think exponents apply in this case." I got quiet again. "My lines are open too," I said finally. "I mean, I know I'm no substitute – certainly I don't know Maureen's *tricks* – but we're family and if you want to talk about stupid stuff with me, I'd welcome it."

"You too," she said softly.

"Do you like baseball?"

"No, not at all."

"Neither did Maureen. We won't talk about that."

"We can. I'll just make sure I'm doing my expense report or something while we are."

I laughed. "That's very generous of you."

"Hey, you know, if the lines of communication are going to be open, we can't let anything be off limits."

"Yeah, I'll keep that in mind. So when are you coming out for dinner again? Reese hasn't been spoiled enough lately."

"Why don't you come into the City? It's time for that boy of yours to learn what *real* living is about."

"You'd allow him to roll all over your Persian carpets?"

"My nephew? He can roll anywhere he wants."

We made a date for brunch the following Sunday and we talked for another fifteen minutes about little things. I envisioned her having these same conversations with Maureen, had actually witnessed them from Maureen's perspective on numerous occasions. I never had anyone I could talk with on the phone like that, and it was a curiosity to me.

"Call me tomorrow, okay?" I said when she told me she was going to go.

"Yeah, I will. Give the baby a kiss for me."

I always felt at least somewhat better after talking to Codie. It dawned on me that we never would have developed the relationship we were developing if Maureen was still alive. She'd call, we'd exchange a few sentences, and then I'd hand the phone over to my wife. There was no way in the world I'd trade that for what I had now, but as consolation prizes went, what was developing here was far better than most.

On my way downstairs, I peeked in on Reese. He stirred, stuck his head up, looked through me, and fell back asleep. He was lucky to have an aunt like Codie, someone who would always dote on him and bring him toys and take him shopping to buy whatever he wanted and stop for ice cream and donuts and maybe a side order of french fries on the way home.

She was yet another invaluable present he'd received from his mother.

EIGHT - Oars

There were intermittent stretches when I didn't notice how much I missed Maureen and Tanya. Times when Reese did something especially entertaining – he recently developed a fascination with his hands that I could watch indefinitely – were chief among them. Unfortunately, they were usually followed by an especially vulnerable instant when the reality of my situation rushed back to the forefront of my thoughts and hit me with a force that was as surprising as it was devastating. And with these attacks came the attendant guilt where I scolded myself for feeling good about taking a break from feeling miserable.

Still, it was part of the process, and these easeful stretches grew as the days beyond Maureen and Tanya passed. Work became more and more involving again. And while social relationships with my colleagues had all but ceased (mostly by my own choice – I wasn't in any frame of mind to be an appropriate companion outside of the office), I found the personal interaction during business hours to be stimulating and even occasionally diverting.

Of all of these, the one that was most refreshing, and in fact the most unexpected, was the office friendship I developed with Ally Ritten. After our conversation about personalized cookie jars, she started visiting my office regularly. We'd bat ideas around, make sarcastic comments about each other's perceptions of the marketplace, and discuss projects already in the works.

"We have to introduce new ornaments every Christmas," she said one day in the middle of another impromptu pitch meeting. "It's expected of us. Isn't it some kind of FTC requirement? So why can't they be ornaments of polar bears in swimsuits?"

"Explain this to me again."

"They make people think of winter and summer at the same time."

"This is a test of some sort, isn't it? You're wondering just how ridiculous an idea has to be before I tell you to scrap it. Am I right?"

Her eyes drifted down a bit. "You think it's a ridiculous idea?"

"You think an ornament of a polar bear in a swim suit is a *good* idea?"

"It came to me in a dream last night."

"See, that's another one of my rules that I forgot to mention – never pay attention to ideas that come to you in dreams. Dreams impair judgment."

She doodled aimlessly on her pad for a moment. "I'll bet Reese would like a polar bear in a swimsuit."

"If it was soft plastic and could fit in his mouth, he'd like it. If it tasted like apricots, he'd love it. He's also not our target demo."

"So you're thinking I should blow this idea off, huh?"

"That was essentially what I was thinking, yes."

She smiled at me. "I kinda knew that. Sometimes when something comes to me in a flash, I can't tell whether it's awful or brilliant. Guess this was the former, huh?"

"Hey, it beats the hell out of Lynch's eighteenth variation on the same damn tote bag."

"Gee, thanks for the compliment." She rested her pen on her pad. "So Reese likes apricots?"

"He bows at the altar of apricots. I introduced him to them last week and now nothing else will do. He has subtle ways of indicating his preferences. Like spitting his peas into my face."

She laughed. "I'm sure you look very distinguished with a little mashed pea on your cheek."

"Not really my color. Carrots are much more flattering."

She picked up the pen and doodled again. "Do you know that your face changes when you talk about Reese?"

That felt like an unusually intimate observation, though I couldn't tell from her expression whether she meant it to be. "It does?"

"Yeah, it does. Your eyes open wider and it really changes the way you look."

"Wow. I'm going to be totally self-conscious about this now."

"Don't be. At least don't be uncomfortable about it. You look great when you talk about him. It's really pretty inspiring."

I wasn't sure what to do with this level of attention. "Thanks. Hey, you know, when you get a really off-the-wall idea you get this sort of glow."

She threw her pen at me. "No mocking allowed."

I handed her pen back. "Sorry."

"I'll let you get away with it this one time." She looked down at her notes and then moved to get up to leave.

"I'm glad my face lights up when I talk about Reese," I said.

"Yeah, me too. You should do it more often."

* * *

The phone rang while I was putting the baby to bed and I let the answering machine pick it up. The message was from Codie and all she said was, "Hi, it's me. Call as soon as you can."

"What's with the sense of urgency?" I said when I returned the call a few minutes later. "Land another multi-million dollar account?"

"I've gotten a new message from Tanya. What do you know about the rock group River?"

"Jam band. Huge concert following. That's about it."

"Have you ever heard of the Riverriders?"

"They're the people who hang outside before their shows, right?"

"It's much bigger than that. There are these roving communities of Riverriders who actually follow the band around while they're on tour. They have all of these ceremonies before each show and even on days between concerts. It's very '60s."

"Why are we talking about this?"

"Because River has just started a six-month North American tour and Tanya mentioned in her message that she's hooked up with a band of Riverriders."

I sprung forward from the couch. "Oh my God, that means we know where she is. Let me get online."

"Pittsburgh on Sunday, Rochester on Wednesday."

It was Thursday. "I can leave Saturday morning."

"Want me to go with you?"

"I'd love to have you along, but I really think I need to do this myself. I can't take Reese with me either. I've gotta call Lisa. I have no idea if she can cover me this weekend."

"*I* can cover you this weekend. I'll come out tomorrow night so you can leave as soon as you want on Saturday."

With every conversation, I grew more and more thankful that Codie was alive. "That would be great. I guess this means our brunch date is off, huh?"

"This is just slightly more important."

My head was spinning. "She's gonna be in Pittsburgh on Sunday. I wonder where she is now."

"That doesn't matter anymore. You know where she's *going* to be."

I closed my eyes and Tanya's face filled my vision. "What do I say to her when I see her?"

"You have a lot to say to her, Gerry. Try not to say it all at once."

I fast-forwarded through a dozen conversations. "My God, I've gotta tell her about Maureen."

"Yeah, you do," Codie said with an unmistakable catch in her throat. "I'll be there tomorrow night, okay?"

"Yeah, thanks. And thanks for letting me know about this. I know Tanya probably told you in confidence."

"There is no way I'd keep something like this a secret from you. If she hates me for it, I'll just have to deal with that."

A short while later, I got off the phone with Codie and sat with it next to me for several minutes. I was excited and nervous and fearful all at the same time, and the combined gravity of these emotions kept me locked in place. For months, I wished for this opportunity, the chance to retrieve my daughter, to bring her back into our lives. Now I was finally getting it.

Sunday couldn't come soon enough.

* * *

The house was quiet when Maureen and I came home from dinner with Tate and Gail that night last October. This wasn't a surprise. Tanya would be out with Mick. She always was these days.

Maureen saw the note first. She went into the kitchen and sat down heavily. She was seven months pregnant and sitting down heavily wasn't unusual, so I didn't pay it much mind. Until I saw the expression on her face.

"Tanya's gone," she said, handing me the letter.

M&D,

Mick and I are heading off on our own. Because of him, I can finally see how pointless and empty my ordered life is. I don't need my average friends, I don't need lovely little Port Jefferson, and I certainly don't need a house where a bratty little kid will constantly remind his parents what a disappointment his big sister turned out to be.

We're going someplace where we can be real and not have to deal with anyone else's expectations.

I'll let you know that I'm alive.

T

"This is a joke," I said briskly. "A taunt. She's trying to shake us up."

"It's not a joke. She wouldn't do that."

"It's conceivable to you that she would run away with Mick but not that she would try to rattle our cages?"

Maureen started crying, covering her face with her hands and weeping into them. I tried to comfort her, but my mind was racing. Where could they have gone? What was Tanya trying to do? She wasn't even seventeen yet; was she out of her mind?

I called the police. "My daughter has been kidnapped," I said when someone answered. Maureen looked up from her tears when she heard this, but I continued. Mick might not have physically abducted her, but he had done exactly that emotionally. He turned her into someone so much darker than she was.

Maureen and I spent the twenty minutes it took for the police to arrive on our respective cell phones because we didn't want to tie up the landline. She called Codie because she knew Tanya adored her and confided in her. Then she called her mother and father, presumably just to vent, as they could hardly do anything from North Carolina. I called several of Tanya's friends peppering them with questions about any information they might have about where Tanya and Mick had gone. The best I could get out of any of them was Tanya's friend Elizabeth telling me that they talked about taking a trip to Montauk before the weather got bad.

"It's because of the baby," Maureen said at a point when we'd stopped making calls at the same time.

"It's because of that bum she's dating."

"It's not just that. Do you remember how she cried in her room after we told her? She thought we were replacing her."

"That was a long time ago."

"She never wanted to talk about the baby."

"She never wanted to talk about *anything*. I could-n't even ask her what she wanted for dinner anymore without getting a snarl from her."

Maureen seemed ashen. Given the advanced stage of her pregnancy, I was more than a little concerned about how this was affecting her. "Gerry, what are we going to do if she stays away?"

"She's not going to stay away." I put an arm around her shoulder and guided her over to the couch. "She'll be back in a few days."

The cops came and we told them what little we knew. Maureen showed them the letter and this essentially put the lie to my kidnapping theory. They asked us questions for several minutes, and with each one I became more uneasy about how they would pursue the case. I understood that they had numerous responsibilities, most far more pressing than tracking down a runaway teenager. But it seemed obvious that they wouldn't come close to dealing with this the way I wanted them to.

Maureen was back on the phone as soon as they left.

"I'm going out," I said.

She put her hand over the phone. "Where are you going?"

"I'm gonna try to find her."

"How?"

"I don't know."

I got in the car and drove, clueless about where I was going. I passed by Tanya's school and the park nearby that kids hung around on Saturday nights. There were dozens of teenagers at both, many with open liquor bottles. I was always so proud of Tanya for not being one of them. I drove onto the campus of the college that Mick attended. Again, there was the sound of wild partying with music blaring that I might have liked under different circumstances. And then I just started driving aimlessly, searching left and right, pent on bringing my daughter back and doing physical harm to the man who stole her. I drove for hours this way, nearly getting into two car accidents because my mind was decidedly not on the road.

When I got back home, Maureen was still awake, seated on the couch, the cell phone and the portable phone by her side. She looked up at me hopefully for a fraction of a second before she lowered her eyes.

"Nothing?" she said.

"Not this time."

Maureen started to cry again. I sat down next to her.

"She'll be back," I said, wondering why I was so strongly convinced that this wouldn't really be the case.

I didn't sleep at all that night, frazzled by the amphetamine kick of anxiety and frustration, unaware of how much anxiety, frustration, and the biggest gut-punch of all – futility – lay ahead for me.

* * *

Reese got up during the night three times on Friday, and I got maybe two-and-a-half hours sleep. It didn't matter. The trip I was taking Saturday morning had me so wired that I would have been fine staying up with him all night.

I let Codie sleep until ten, though I was itching to get on the road. There was no particular reason for me to leave this early. In fact, I could have driven to Pittsburgh Sunday morning and still gotten to the arena in plenty of time. But I wanted to give myself a huge margin for delays and other eventualities. I wouldn't let Tanya slip past me again because of a traffic jam.

Reese was on his playmat, and I was rolling a ball back and forth in front of him trying to pique his interest when Codie came into the family room.

"Sorry about all of the noise last night," I said. "I don't know what was bothering him."

"He made a lot of noise last night?"

I stopped rolling the ball. "He *is* going to be safe with you, right?"

"Yeah, of course. I vaguely heard something. I promise I'll keep my ears open tonight. You ready to head off on your mission?"

"I was ready Thursday night. I'm all set. I have a bag packed and a few new playlists on the iPod – including a couple made up of Tanya's favorites, assuming Mick hasn't convinced her to listen only to trance music."

I went into the kitchen and poured some coffee into a travel mug, then picked Reese up from his mat and kissed him. I walked with Reese and Codie toward the front door. When we got there, I kissed the baby one more time and then handed him to Codie. She hugged me tightly.

"I hope this goes well," she said.

"I'm gonna do everything I can to make it go well."

"I know you will. Stay cool, okay?"

"I will." I kissed Reese one more time. "Have fun with the kid."

"Us? We're going to have a great time. He likes lobster and champagne, right?" She hugged me again and I headed out the door.

I felt buoyed during the first few hours of the trip by the feeling that I was finally doing something about bringing Tanya home. I'd been feeling so powerless. Now, there was great music on the car stereo and I had a true sense of purpose. About an hour into the trip, I put on the live River album that I'd downloaded Friday afternoon. This was the third time I listened to it, feeling like in some odd way this would help me to get to know my daughter better. It didn't hurt that I liked the music, very '70s in feel with numerous tempo changes and long instrumental passages punctuated by occasionally clever lyrics. I would have liked this band a lot in high school or college and could imagine myself listening to them with some regularity even now.

I got off I-78 in Bethel and drove around for a few minutes looking for a place to have lunch. I felt like this trip demanded something better than rest stop food and was rewarded when I found a decent little country kitchen with surprisingly good coffee and a dessert selection that forced itself upon me. While I was there, I checked in on Codie and Reese – he was napping after what Codie described as a "very full morning." Then it was back on the road to another highway that would bring me ever closer to my destination.

Whether it was the lack of sleep catching up to me or the huge stretch of road in front of me, I sagged about and hour later. I tried to pump myself up with U2's *Joshua Tree* album, but even this didn't help. And with this slump came the first doubts I had since Codie's phone call Thursday night. Mellon Arena held 17,000 spectators. How would I pick Tanya out of a crowd this large? What would I do if Mick got in the way? What would I do if Tanya wouldn't talk to me? I clicked off the iPod and drove the next forty miles in silence, suffused in apprehension. This could go wrong in so many ways. I even began to wonder if I should turn the car around.

I thought about what Maureen would have done in this situation. If Codie had called her instead, would she have gone off after Tanya immediately? Would she have worried that doing so was a mistake? The more I thought about this from her perspective, the more I realized that her reaction would have been the same as mine: if there were any chance in the world to convince Tanya to come home, she would take it.

This knowledge fortified me, and as I got off I-376 around 6:30 that night and headed toward the hotel, I knew once again that what I was doing was right and necessary.

Still, having an entire day in Pittsburgh before the concert was much more than was good for me. Now that I was here without any delays, it seemed a little foolish to have arrived so soon. I did as much Internet research as I could about the Riverriders and learned that many of them liked to camp out around or near the concert hall before a show. So after a quick dinner, I walked down to Mellon Arena in the hopes of finding Tanya or someone who knew her. But the parking lot was full for the hockey game that was going on.

I drove for a while, but I had no idea what I was looking for. I imagined scenes from *Woodstock* with sitar music and tie-dyed shirts, even though I knew this wasn't at all what Riverriders dressed like. When I found nothing that looked like a cluster of rock and roll fans, I convinced myself that Tanya wasn't even in town yet and was probably still on her way here from the band's last stop in Cleveland.

I went back to the hotel, called Codie, and kept her on the line much longer than I think she wanted. When I hung up, I tried to occupy myself with reading and television, but found that nothing held my attention. I opened the minibar and poured myself a $10 Scotch, but that did little to help. I went to bed, only to find myself watching *Saving Private Ryan* on HBO at 2:30.

I walked over to the arena again in the middle of the next afternoon. There were four parking lots and, as expected, they were all nearly empty at this time. I wanted to be there before the crowd, assuming most Riverriders would do the same and that this was my best shot at finding Tanya. Of course, it also gave me plenty of time to become anxious and to feel conspicuous passing security guards and parking attendants repeatedly while I made my circuit. Finally, I explained what I was doing. I didn't want anyone arresting me for loitering when my daughter was so close. I approached a security guard in his early twenties, assuming that a younger man would have a better idea of what I was talking about. He knew all about the Riverriders and told me that arena staff had briefed the entire security force about them. The promoters had in fact prearranged that they would be gathering in the West Lot. I wasn't sure how the Riverriders would know this, but there seemed to be some kind of communications net amongst them.

This information made it easier for me to watch out for Tanya. Around 5:00, I saw a van enter with oars sticking from its windows in signature Riverrider fashion. I felt a surge of adrenaline along with another of apprehension as I walked toward it. It had North Carolina plates. Five people got out, opened the back, and pulled out chairs, a hibachi, and a cooler. While one person poured charcoal into the hibachi and another took food and beer out of the cooler, the other three played with a Frisbee. They could have been attending a football game.

None of the five was Tanya or Mick. I thought about approaching this group, but realized that it was ridiculous. Riverriders came from all over the country, and while they communed with one another and even hooked up and traveled in packs, the odds against any one of these people knowing Tanya were enormous.

Over the next hour, the parking lot began to fill and more and more Riverriders staked out their territory. I monitored each car and van carefully. There were dozens of them in this gathering now, maybe even more than a hundred. The air was filled with cooking smells, the scent of marijuana, and the sounds of various River albums playing at high volume. There were still no signs of my daughter.

I was no more than a hundred feet from her when she got out of a green van behind Mick. She smiled back at a laughing, curly-haired woman who helped her unload their cargo.

I found it difficult to move. I hadn't seen Tanya in more than five months and she'd undergone some changes. She now had blond streaks in her brown hair, and it was longer than she ever wore it. She had on jeans with huge holes in the thighs and an oversized denim jacket. But the thing that distinguished her most from the Tanya I remembered was how easily she laughed with her fellows. Mick seemed as taciturn as ever, but Tanya seemed relaxed, extraordinarily comfortable with her environment, and content. I hadn't seen her look this good in years.

This threw me. I had expected the grim, distant girl who last glowered at us from across the dinner table. The girl I sparred with over everything from politics to boyfriends to television shows. The girl who needed saving. To see her call a greeting to someone in another van and dance to whichever of the several songs she heard made me wonder, albeit briefly, if my being here would really do her any good. But my need to have her back with me overrode any other notion.

I found my legs and walked slowly through the cluster of people who separated us. Mick, who sat on a bumper, turned and saw me first, putting his head down and moving around to the front of the van. Tanya didn't notice me until I practically stood next to her. When she did, her face dropped and her eyes, instantly filled with tears, darted away from me. She didn't make any move in my direction.

"What are you doing here?" she said haltingly, wiping at her eyes.

I stopped walking toward her, though I was desperate to pull her into my arms. "Can we go somewhere and talk?"

"I'm not going home with you. Let's just get that on the table right now." Her expression darkened, transforming her back to the Tanya I came to know. "Where's Mom? Oh, right, she has a *different* kid now."

I took a deep breath. "I think it would be a really good idea if we went for a little walk together."

The curly-haired woman approached us and asked Tanya if she was all right. Tanya said she'd be "fine in a minute" and the woman walked away. She turned back and looked at me. "It's a hell of a drive from Port Jeff."

"It was worth it to see you. You have no idea how much I've missed you."

"Why's that? Not enough arguments in the house without me."

Stay cool, okay? I heard Codie's voice in my head. I knew that lashing out at Tanya was counterproductive, as was reminding her that since she was a minor I could force her to come home.

"Something has happened, Tanya. Something terrible."

Her expression softened. There was worry there now. The kind of worry that a teenaged girl might experience. "What are you talking about?"

"Let's go somewhere and talk."

She tilted her head forward and held her gaze. "Tell me."

Never in my life had I imagined this moment. Not with Tanya only seventeen. The confluence of different songs impressed itself on my consciousness as I ran my fingers through my hair. I had prepared to break this news to my daughter. But while I thought of what to say, I greatly underestimated how hard it would be to say it to her face.

"It's your mother."

Tanya took two gentle steps backward and leaned against the van. Tears started rolling down her face almost instantly. Out of the corner of my eye, I saw one of the people from the van look in our direction, move toward us, and then stop.

I wanted to reach out to her. I wanted to hold her as I hadn't in so many years and tell her everything I felt and how much I needed her. But as I approached her, she stiffened and I stopped in my tracks.

"What happened?" she said.

"It was a blood clot to the brain. I found her when I came home from work."

"When?"

"In January."

Tanya turned away, rested her head against the van, and sobbed. Even the cacophony of music couldn't mask this sound. I put my arm around her shoulders. She didn't shrug me away, but she also didn't ease into my embrace. As I held her, Mick came around the other side of the van. I looked up at him as he stood next to us.

"What are you doing to her?" he said.

"Get away from us," I said with more contempt than I ever put in my voice before. If Tanya turned to him then, I didn't know what I would do. But if she even knew he was there, she didn't acknowledge it.

Mick tried to stare me down, but he was completely overmatched. "She doesn't need you," he said thinly.

"Go away now."

He averted his eyes and then turned and walked off. I only wish I could have done the same to him a year ago.

Tanya still hadn't turned around. I leaned into her and kissed her on the head. Her hair smelled foreign to me.

"Come on, Queenie," I said. "Let's go home."

She shook her head slightly. "I'm not leaving."

She said it so softly I could barely make it out over the blare. I shut my eyes and reminded myself that she was in shock over the news. "It's time for you to come back."

She turned at that point, her eyes rimmed in scarlet. "There's nothing there for me now."

If she was trying to hurt me, she was doing a sensational job. "Your friends are there for you. Your aunt." This got a roll of her eyes. She obviously felt betrayed by Codie, knowing this was how I found her. "Your brother. Me."

"Mom's gone, Dad." A tear rolled down her face with stunning rapidity. "I can't be there with Mom gone."

I couldn't conceal everything I was feeling. Not with the way things were going. "Tanya, you're seventeen. What makes you think you're old enough to make a decision like this? What makes you think you're ready to live on your own?"

"I've *been* living on my own," she said angrily. "And I was doing great until you came around."

"You've been living a fantasy. How long did you think that would last? How long do you think it'll be before something comes along that you can't handle and these friends of yours fail you?"

She wiped at her eyes again. "Look Dad, if you wanna handcuff me and throw me in the back of your car, go ahead and try. But that's the only way you're getting me back to Port Jefferson."

Maybe I should have slung her over my shoulder at that point. Maybe I should have tried a more conciliatory approach, something that would make her want to come with me. Instead, I said, "I'm not leaving here without you."

"Then you're gonna look awfully stupid standing in this parking lot all by yourself at two o'clock in the morning."

At that point, the curly-haired woman walked up again and said to Tanya, "Are you're okay? Who is this guy?"

Tanya turned to the woman and said. "Yeah, I'm okay, Marlene." She sniffed and darted a glance in my direction. "This man is my father. He was just leaving."

"I'm really not going anywhere, Tanya."

"Then I am." She stalked off toward the arena.

I followed after her. "You can't run away from this."

She stopped and turned so quickly that I nearly ran into her. Once again, the tears flowed down her face with unusual force. "Do you have any idea what happened here tonight? You shock the hell out of me by showing up and telling me that my mother is dead. Now you want me to go back to Long Island with you and pretend to have a normal life? You have got to be kidding."

"You don't want to handle this on your own."

"I *have* to handle this on my own."

"Why? You have people at home who love you."

"Really? What exactly do I have at home? I have you, who gave up on me years ago, a baby brother who probably dominates the whole household, and I have a million memories of a mother who no longer exists. Does that sound like home to you?"

"I never gave up on you," I said weakly.

She put both hands up to her face. When she brought them back down, I thought I saw – just for a second – that she believed me. But then her anger descended again. "Dad, let me make this as clear to you as I possibly can. If you ever want to see me again – whenever the hell that might be – then you'll leave now. If you try to take me home, I'll leave again. And no matter what, you'll never find me."

In that moment, I knew that she meant what she said. And I knew I couldn't do anything to persuade her. I had no idea why Tanya was rejecting me this way, but she was doing so absolutely.

I closed my eyes and held up a hand in her direction. When I looked at her again, her posture was stiffer. "I'm staying at the Ramada. If you change your mind, I'll be there until tomorrow morning."

She wiped at her eyes again and then turned and walked back toward the van. I turned that way as well, but otherwise didn't move. I watched her collapse into Marlene's arms. The woman patted her hair and tried to console her in a way that Tanya wouldn't let me.

I'm not sure how long I stood there. When I couldn't take it any longer, I went back to the hotel, the rhythms and the celebration following me, tormenting me.

* * *

I never believed that Tanya would show up before I left the next morning. I therefore shouldn't have been disappointed that she didn't. And yet I was.

I had never given up on her. I might have been ineffective at showing her how much she impressed me. I might have built up immunity to the sting of the hundreds of times she slighted me over the years. I might have let Maureen deal with her exclusively too much since she became a teenager, making the preponderance of our interaction verbal sparring matches. But I never once gave up on her. I truly believed that our difficulties were finite and that something more fulfilling was waiting on the other side.

But now, in an effort to bring her back into the fold, I brought her the piece of news most guaranteed to keep her away. A home without her mother was no home she wanted.

As I checked out of the hotel, the woman at the registration desk told me there was an envelope for me. She handed me a note written on hotel stationery. The handwriting was unmistakably Tanya's. All it said was:

> I'm as far away as yesterday Or the rays
> of the setting sun

Was this her parting message to me? Why, after what she said the night before, did she feel the need to punctuate our last exchange with this? Did she think I somehow missed the point?

The lines were from a song, but couldn't remember which one. It wasn't until I retrieved my car and began the long drive back home that I remembered they were the words to a River song that was on the live album, the first two lines of the refrain.

Two other lines followed:

> But one thing I've learned along the
> way
> Is that gone is never really gone

BOOK TWO -
While You Were Out in the World

NINE - Smoother and Sweeter

I also spent a lot of time thinking about Tanya's recrimination that I gave up on her. Surely, this was inspired at least in some part by how stunned she was to learn about Maureen. (And, believe me, I imagined her thinking on hundreds of occasions, "Why couldn't it have been you?"). But she wasn't wrong that somewhere along the line the joy in our relationship dimmed and then was nearly eclipsed by tiffs and coexistence.

Trying to remember the last truly great time we had alone together, I needed to go back before her fourteenth birthday. As was usually the case, it had something to do with food. The kitchen was the one place Tanya and I shared openly and unreservedly together. She took an interest in cooking when she was in preschool, and over the years, I taught her numerous recipes and techniques. To mark the end of the school year, I told Tanya that we were going to put everything she learned into practice in the form of an elegant dinner party for a half dozen of her friends. We spent weeks devising and testing original dishes, drove all the way into Manhattan in search of the best ingredients, and took an entire Saturday to prepare the meal. The result was a level of teamwork that surpassed any we shared before, and Tanya was extremely pleased with the results. She impressed her friends and made me terribly proud of her.

"I think she might be a cooking prodigy," I said to Maureen in bed that night.

"Maybe she'll make huge amounts of money as a celebrity chef and buy us a retirement home on the Costa del Sol," Maureen said, teasing me.

"I mean it. She has much more skill than I had at her age. I wonder if there's a weekend program for her at the Culinary Institute. I'm gonna check."

Maureen laughed. "It was a great meal, Gerry." "It *was* a great meal. And she did most of it. I'm telling you, she's a prodigy. We have to foster this."

Maureen simply laughed again.

The next couple of weeks felt different between Tanya and me. We talked more about things like music and pop culture – things that both of us cared about, but which we didn't really share – and she even took more of an interest in my job. It was a heady time. She was always so much closer to Maureen than she was to me and I never begrudged this (not really, anyway). Though I enjoyed having a taste of it.

But I was a victim of lousy timing. Soon after this, Tanya went away to summer camp for six week,s and when she returned, she wasn't quite the same and *we* were definitely not the same. I tried to get her to talk about the new Radiohead album and she sniffed at me, suggesting with her mannerisms that I couldn't possibly have an opinion that mattered. I tried to get her to watch the DVD of *High Fidelity* with me and she blew me off. I told her that I thought it was time for us to put together another dinner party and she seemed bored by the suggestion. I never did find out what happened that summer, but something had caused our relationship to take two giant steps backward. Maureen bore the brunt of some of this also, but the two of them had so much emotional equity with one another that they could navigate this sea change without capsizing.

I, on the other hand, felt cheated. And when Tanya kicked into full teenager mode, I had no patience for it.

This might look a lot like giving up, though I never saw it that way. It was resignation. I knew I couldn't have the relationship with my daughter that I really wanted and so I made myself accept that it was something less. But I never stopped *wanting* the relationship.

And even now, I still wanted it. I had received no communication from her since Pittsburgh (Codie got one e-mail message that started out stiff and ended somewhat teary), though I faithfully booted up the computer every night. I wanted so much to reach out to her, to have some line of contact. I even considered driving to another River concert to see her again, even though I wasn't sure she was still with the Riverriders. But I understood that I would never be able to retrieve her that way.

I sat in my library staring at the computer screen, willing a message from her to appear. Realizing the futility of it, I pushed away from the desk. I needed an outlet for what I felt. I needed some way of expressing myself to her.

It was then that I remembered the leather-bound blank book that sat in my desk drawer. Maureen gave it to me for Christmas the year before last. At the time, I wasn't sure why she did it – I had never shown any interest in keeping a journal – and when I thanked her, my confusion must have been obvious.

"I don't know why I got this for you," she said. "I just thought you might want to write something down some day."

I opened the book and let it stay blank in front of me for several minutes. Then in the middle of the first page, I wrote the words:

While You Were Out in the World

I would create this document for my daughter. Here, I would speak to her without restraint and without concern about her response. I could share my feelings, let my guard down, and not worry if she were listening or if she judged what I said. I had no idea whether she would ever see these pages, but I knew I had to write them honestly and without inhibitions. I began at the beginning.

> I remember how the responsibility of being a parent struck me all at once. Your mother and I drove to the hospital while she was in labor and it finally got through to me. Before that, I intellectu-

alized what being a father meant, but it hadn't really registered.

And I have to admit that I panicked. The very idea that we were your sole means of support, that we were absolutely responsible for your life, was insanely scary to me. I was 22 years old, out of school a little more than a year, just getting into a groove at work, still caught up in the pure buzz of coming home to your mother every night – and doing something this big, this "no backsies," was daunting. I drove that last mile to the hospital wishing for a traffic jam, as though a delay in getting to the delivery room would actually forestall my future.

And of course your birth did change everything. If you've never heard the name Benny Scarmenti before, it's because my best friend from college came over exactly once after you were born, realized that I wasn't willing to drink myself into a stupor with a 3:00 feeding in the offing, and moved on to another party. The same was true with other friends, who we slowly replaced with parents who had young kids. The focus of conversation between your mother and me shifted from the future to the present – to be accurate, it shifted almost entirely to you for the first couple of years. And I remember realizing with a chill one day after my boss ticked me off that I couldn't just up and quit my job anymore.

But what I didn't realize on that drive to the hospital was how smooth the transition would be. Drinking with Benny had lost its appeal a long time before and if we weren't drunk, he wasn't nearly as much fun to be with. The friends we lost along the way weren't meant to be long-term friends in the first place. I liked talking about your first smile, your first step, your first everything. A lot of the people we met through playgroups and preschool turned out to be great. And I never would have simply up and quit my job, no matter how much my boss angered me.

One of the things I realized was that if you were meant to be a parent at all, the changes don't come as a burden, but as an opportunity to evolve in ways that you wanted to evolve anyhow. This was the secret handshake, the thing that only parents had together. You don't tolerate parenthood. You don't survive it. You grow with it.

I don't know that I ever told you how much you changed me. I definitely know that I never thanked you for it. And as much as you did for me, I know you did so much more for your mother. She was fuller after you arrived. More amazed by life. Even sexier. She became

more of what she was supposed to
become. I guess I should thank you for
that as well.

Anyway, it turned out that there was no
traffic jam on the way to the hospital. I
even found a parking space right away.
I suppose there was a message in this.

It felt good writing this way. And I felt closer to Tanya by
doing it. I was absolutely determined to stay in touch with
my daughter. Even if it was an entirely one-way conversation.

* * *

Reese became much more of a person every day. We had
exchanges now. They weren't sustained exchanges to be
sure, but I did things that generated a reaction from him and
vice versa. I got the impression that he would have a great
sense of humor when he got older. He liked to laugh, which I
suppose every infant did. But he also seemed to love making
me laugh. If he did something that got that response, he did
it repeatedly. And a few days later, he tried it another time,
just to see if it still entertained me. I found it fascinating that
he was learning in this way and always rewarded him for his
efforts.

Reese was the one unequivocal joy in my life. I knew I
could glean messages from the losses I suffered, messages
that applied to the relationship I had with my son. And certainly at least some of what I felt about him had to do with
the fact that he was *here*. He hadn't run off. Fate hadn't
taken him away. But there was much more to it than that. Of
course, I loved him. After Tanya was born, I came to accept
that parental love was included in the starter kit. But I also
really liked having Reese around. He was good company.

This really came clear to me on Opening Day. For the last
several years – since I had enough security at my job to do

something like this without repercussions from my supervisors – I took the afternoon of Opening Day off to watch the Yankees on television. I thought about skipping it this time around because this year was not like any other, and then I decided that would be a mistake. And so with a couple of hot dogs on the griddle, sauerkraut warming in a pot, and pureed butternut squash in Reese's bowl, I turned on the television for the pregame show. Reese was in his baby seat (which he'd pretty much outgrown) on the kitchen counter, and he cooed and waved his hands wildly while I finished preparing lunch. In the last week, he'd become more animated, gesturing and making sounds almost nonstop. I assume it was a warning of sorts that he was going to be crawling soon enough and that he would channel all of this gesticulating into skittering across the floor; that in the very near future, I would need to watch every single move he made.

Though I knew that how the Yankees performed in the preseason offered little indication of how they would do once the regular season began, the news from Florida had not been encouraging. Very few of their pitchers got batters out regularly, and no one in the starting lineup hit the ball with authority. The only player who had an exceptional spring was Bobby Kitterer and the team sent him down to the AAA Scranton team for more seasoning, the Yankees choosing to open the year with a journeyman left fielder they got a week ago from the San Diego Padres. It had been a long time since I felt this skittish about their chances.

I moved Reese's high chair in front of the television along with the hot dogs and the squash. Reese loved butternut squash nearly as much as he loved apricots. A pattern was emerging – he had a decided fondness for smoother and sweeter foods. I knew it was still too soon to introduce him to spices, but I wondered how his appreciation of tastes would change when he discovered ancho chilies, garlic, and salt. Would he still look upon peas indifferently when they were sautéed with onions and olive oil? Would he be nearly so disdainful of string beans once he tried them with Szechwan peppercorns, soy, and ginger? Or was this sweet tooth going to last him a lifetime? Was he going to be one of those marshmallows-on-sweet-potatoes people? And could I really continue to love him if he were?

The introduction of the starting lineups on the field interrupted my thoughts about food. I offered Reese a key fact or two about each player, he absorbed this with little comment, and we finished eating and settled in for the game. I tried to sit Reese on my lap, but he squirmed out of it almost immediately. He did, however, seem perfectly happy to sit next to me on the couch. The night before, I bought him a foam rubber ball bearing the Yankee logo, and he gummed it now while the Yanks' ace stood on the mound and tossed the first pitch of the year – a strike.

"Here we go, Reese. It's a new season."

Reese chewed the ball harder, though it was unlikely that it was in anticipation of another World Series title.

It didn't take long for the excitement of the day to dim. Immediately after that first strike, the Devil Rays' leadoff hitter stroked the next pitch to the wall for a double. Four consecutive hits followed and all of those runners scored before there were two outs. Then, to cap off a dreadful first inning of the first game, the Rays' number seven hitter – who batted .209 the previous season – hit a home run to straight-away centerfield. The Yankees had yet to bat and they were already five runs down.

"They would have been better off with *you* on the mound this afternoon," I said to my game buddy.

The Yankees' starter settled in and the team got individual runs in the third and the fifth. Still, going into the top of the sixth inning, the score was 5-2. As the television broadcast went to a commercial break, Reese took the ball and tossed it to the floor. I figured this was just a function of his endless flailing about with his arms and settled him back on the couch to retrieve the ball for him. Less than fifteen seconds later, he threw the ball again, this time making a series of loud noises to accompany the effort.

I picked up the ball and wedged Reese into the corner of the couch before handing it to him. He held it as well as he could in his little hand and then flapped his arms and sent the ball flying again in my general direction (behind himself, actually, but that's not the point). I laughed at this, causing him to laugh. This also announced to him that it was *show-time*. When I gave him the ball again, he looked at me, chuckled, and then flung both arms outward, the ball flying off to the other side of the coffee table.

Four more times Reese threw the ball and I retrieved it for him. He accompanied each throw with grunts and laughter. Then I handed him the ball again and he took it in both hands and gnawed on it with a dedication that made it clear that our game of catch had ended.

I pulled him up on my lap and he sat there, gumming the ball, until the Yankees rallied in the eighth. Ultimately, they wound up falling short, leaving men on second and third in the ninth and losing 5-4. Reese stayed on my lap the final three innings. I was never happy to see the Yankees lose and I really hated when they lost on Opening Day. But the exhibition of pitching prowess that took place on my very own couch softened the blow considerably. In another five years, Reese's Tee-Ball opening day would be as much of a red-letter day as the Yankees' first game.

I was utterly fascinated with ball games when I was a kid. I always played with a ball in the house, and the constant *thunk*-ing of a rubber ball against the wall drove my mother crazy. I had a catch with my dad whenever possible and, by the time I was six, I not only had Little League in the spring and flag football in the fall, but I always organized games with the neighborhood kids – even playing with the twin four-year-olds who lived behind us if there was no one else around. And if I couldn't get a game going, I went out to the backyard by myself, devising ways to play imagined team games that involved throwing a ball to a particular spot or hitting it or kicking it a certain distance.

I wondered what games Reese would make up with his friends and by himself. He unquestionably had a willing partner to play catch with whenever I was home. Would he be ready to roll a beach ball back and forth by the time he was one? Could he run bases or kick a soccer ball when he turned three?

For the first time, I thought I understood why so many men had a thing about raising "their boys." Certainly, I didn't feel this way because of some gender hang-up I had about sports: I remember listening enviously as Tanya talked about her tiny female friends who played Little League and basketball. I would have gladly played catch with her if she'd shown the slightest inclination toward it. But the difference was that even if we had, I wouldn't have stepped back into my own childhood the way I had after this random game of fetch. Of course, I related to various stages of Tanya's development on a personal level, but Reese would encounter the experiences, rituals, and particular passages that a boy went through. I'd only now come to realize how fascinating that was going to be for me.

* * *

Work was something less than what it had been. It didn't offer a place to hide as had been the case when less overwhelming stresses prevailed upon me in the past. And given my emotional paroxysms, the relative evenness of my days in the office barely maintained my attention. I did my job as conscientiously as I could and offered my staff as much of myself as possible, but I was not fully engaged.

The confounding messages I received from Marshall since my return exacerbated this. Where once he had been my unabashed champion and someone I could talk to about anything, business or otherwise, he now seemed determined to make sure I remembered my obligations to the company. The very mention of Reese made him irritable, and I was back at the office less than a month when he stopped even pretending to be interested in how I was feeling about Maureen and Tanya.

The one thing about Eleanor Miller that kept me fascinated was my developing friendship with Ally Ritten. The day after I returned from Pittsburgh, she stopped in to ask a work question. When I looked up at her to respond, she walked to my desk and sat across from me. She could tell from my expression that something was seriously wrong. We talked for a long time about it, and while it didn't really make me feel any better, it was a relief to be able to get this out instead of repressing my feelings the entire workday.

After that, our office friendship hastened. She made a habit of checking in on me a couple of times a day and I even stopped by to see her on occasion. This was the most active social relationship I had at work since Marshall and I first became friendly. And I relied on it. When my personal pressures became too intense, when my anxiety over Tanya threatened to overtake me, when the mundane nature of my job numbed me, or when Reese did something especially cute the night before, I went to Ally.

Toward the end of April, she came to my office to discuss her progress on a new product. As was typical, the conversation segued from business to personal with me telling her about Reese's fascination with a battery-operated puppy Codie brought him when she last visited and which he had discovered anew the night before. We laughed about his attempts at conversation with the toy and then Ally settled back in her chair.

"Do you think you'd like to go get some dinner Saturday night?" she said.

The invitation shouldn't have surprised me. Certainly, our friendship had been moving in an "off campus" direction for a while. But I was a little flustered and not entirely sure what she meant by it.

"Dinner?"

She wrinkled her nose. "Is this not something you do with colleagues? I kinda thought – "

" – No, sorry, of course I do this kind of thing with colleagues," I said, though I wasn't entirely sure what "this kind of thing" was. "Though I haven't exactly been painting the town since Reese was born."

"Would you like to?"

"Paint the town?"

Ally laughed. "Would you like to go to dinner. Painting the town might be a little beyond both of us."

I tried to think about this without appearing to think about it. "I'll have to see about getting a babysitter. Lisa mentioned something about sitting on Friday and Saturday nights if I promised not to stay out too late. I didn't give it much thought when she said it, though."

"If you can, it would be great. And I promise not to keep you out long."

I smiled. "I think her definition of 'too late' and mine are pretty different. I'll ask her and let you know."

"It'd be fun." She stood up and walked toward my office door. "Give me a call later."

When she left, I felt the momentary thrill of doing something new – quickly replaced by a frisson of concern.

Had I just agreed to go out on a date?

TEN - *Cashmere Blend*

Codie came over for dinner again that Friday. I studiously avoided mentioning my dinner with Ally the next night, though I couldn't really explain to myself why I was doing so. It wasn't that hard to avoid the subject, actually. Since I returned from Pittsburgh, if we weren't on the floor playing with Reese, we were talking about Tanya. I think Codie in some way felt responsible for the way things had gone at the River concert. She had broken a confidence (though she had every reason to do so) and sent me out there and it had all turned out badly. I'm sure in her mind it might have been better if she'd never said a word.

And so we spent a great deal of time speculating. If Tanya was still with the Riverriders, she was in Columbus, Ohio and heading off tomorrow for Kansas City. What did she do during those hours in the van? Did she spend them dreaming about her future or brooding about her devastated past? Could she still smile as freely as she did that night before she saw me or had I wiped the smile from her face? Had the well documented (and I had read every document I could get my hands on) merriment of this band of itinerants soothed her soul, or proven too blithesome, too irrelevant now that she understood first-hand how cruel and indiscriminate the world could be?

And what of Mick? Had he comforted her that night after I left? Had he provided her something in his misguided interpretation of various philosophies to ease her mind, to get her through the oppressive first days? Or had he proven woefully inadequate once real-life darkness obscured the fantasy darkness for which he was equipped? I remembered how the two of them didn't seem particularly connected when I watched them that night before approaching Tanya. Were they just giving each other space, or were they drifting apart?

We couldn't answer any of these questions, but still Codie and I explored them extensively. Just as people recounted the details of some public disaster repeatedly, I found a certain solace in the re-creation of that night and the events that led up to it. I'm not sure why that was. Certainly, it wasn't the belief that if I kept reliving it, I could change the past in some way. But I found that recalling those moments offered me something that passed for understanding. And what I came to understand just a little bit more every day – helped in great part by Codie's familiarity with the situation – was that the results were unavoidable. There was no way that I could have brought Tanya back home. Nothing I could have said, no action I could have taken.

During a break in the conversation, we stopped to admire my son. He could sit up by himself now and this offered him an entirely different perspective on the world. He was pointing constantly, as though his new eye level afforded him an angle on things that suddenly made them new and interesting. Codie sat next to him and followed his outstretched fingers, naming various items around the family room.

"Your parents are missing out on this," I said.

She turned away from Reese and looked over with a sadness that immediately clutched at me. "I know. I can't get them to come up here."

"You wouldn't believe how many times I've tried. I invite them to the house every time I talk to them."

She sat next to me against the coffee table. "It's my mom. There's something going on in her head that I can't get to. I know she misses Maureen like crazy – Tanya too, for that matter – and I know coming up here now that they're gone is very hard. But I never thought she'd be the kind of woman who avoided her own grandson."

"They were insatiable when Tanya was born. Maureen and I actually had to pretend to have other plans in order to get a few weekends alone."

"I know. She complained to me about it when I called home from college."

"This isn't healthy. She needs to come up here and spend some time with Reese. She needs to spend some time in this house and see it as something other than the place where her daughter died."

Codie tilted her head back and neither of us said anything for a minute. "Let's double-team her," she said.

"What do you mean?"

"Let's call her on the phone together. Right now. She'll have a much harder time saying no to both of us at once."

I got the two cordless phones and Codie dialed her parents' number.

"Hey, Ma," Codie said when Grace answered.

"Hello, dear."

"I'm at Gerry's. He's on the other line."

"Hi, Grace," I said.

"Oh, hello, Gerry."

"Mom, Gerry and I were wondering what you were doing a couple of weekends from now."

"Why is that?"

"We want you and Dad to come up for a few days. Reese has been asking for you."

"Reese?"

Codie looked at me apprehensively. "Your grandson, Ma."

"I know who Reese is, Codie."

"Grace," I said, "I'd really love to have you stay with us for a little while. The weather is getting nice up here. And you wouldn't believe the tricks the baby can do now. He sits up, he holds a spoon, he blathers unintelligibly, – a couple of weeks from now, he'll probably be juggling."

"I'll have to talk to Ed about this."

"Mom, you don't need to talk to Dad. You know he'll do whatever you want to do."

There was a long pause on the other end. "I'm not sure," Grace said haltingly.

Codie offered me an exaggerated shrug. "Not sure of what, Ma? What's the matter? Do you have a critical meeting of the gardening club or something?"

"Come on, Grace," I said. "It would be great to see you."

Grace's voice sounded heavier when she spoke. "I don't think so, Gerry. I'm just not sure I'm ready for him."

I frowned at Codie. "Well yeah, Reese can be a handful, but you're an old pro. You kept Codie in line, right? And I'll spot you."

I heard a rushed intake of breath on the other line. "Let me think about it. You know, this isn't a good time. We were due at the Folds' ten minutes ago. I'll call you."

Codie pretended to pound herself on the side of the head. "Mom, I'll call you about this in a couple of days."

When we cut the connection, Codie and I looked at each other. I didn't know what to say, and all she could do was shake her head.

"What do you think she meant by that?" I said.

"By what?"

"The part about not being ready for Reese."

She shrugged.

"You don't think she somehow blames him, do you?"

"Blames him? For what?"

As ridiculous as it sounded to me, I said it. "I don't know, for killing her daughter?" The medical examiner had speculated that the blood clot came during childbirth. Grace knew this.

"Oh my God," Codie said, nearly whispering.

* * *

Reese was crying hysterically when I got home the night I discovered Maureen dead. I knew instantly that something was wrong because Maureen wouldn't let him cry like that. I ran up the stairs, retrieved him, and held him to my chest, trying to alleviate his heaving with only moderate success. Livid splotches pocked his face and his cries were raspy. He had been doing this for a while.

"Maureen?" Toting the baby, I left Reese's room to look for her, growing more apprehensive with every step. I found her lying in our bed, unconscious.

I called an ambulance and tried as hard as I could not to panic. I called Gail and asked her to come to take care of Reese in case I had to go to the hospital. The baby was still bawling and I warmed a frozen pouch of breast milk, feeding it to him while I sat next to her on the bed. As he sucked on the bottle, he began to relax, which was considerably more than I could say for myself. I didn't want to think what I was thinking. I didn't want to wonder what I was wondering.

The paramedics swept in a short while later. They spent about ten minutes working on her and then told me they needed to get her to the Emergency Room. While they were taking her down the stairs on a gurney, Gail arrived. She saw Maureen's body and choked back a sob.

"Thanks for coming," I said, handing her the baby. "I need to go."

"What's happening?" she said as the gurney passed her. She looked horrified.

"I don't know," I said, my eyes riveted to the paramedics. "Pray for us."

"Good luck, Gerry."

I hurried to get in my car and stay behind the ambulance. But I knew Maureen was already gone. After all these years, I just knew it. I stood by and watched while they attempted to resuscitate her, already feeling the pain of separation, already feeling more desperate than I felt my entire adult life.

When they turned off their machines and the doctor came up to me to offer his regrets, I barely heard him. Life without Maureen was inconceivable. Literally inconceivable. I stood over her body for more than an hour, not knowing how to leave her. Not knowing how to take a single step forward without her.

They left me alone to cry, to hold her hand, to say things I don't remember. Eventually a doctor asked if I wanted to call someone to take me home. He said that he had a prescription for me. I told him I could-n't take drugs; I had a son to take care of. This sent him away and I knelt next to Maureen's body again.

When I got to my car, I tried for a half hour to pull myself together enough to leave the hospital parking lot. I couldn't do it. Eventually, Tate came to get me.

Reese was screaming again when we got home. Gail tried to calm him down, but he wouldn't be mollified. I took him from her and walked him, jiggling slightly the way I had only two days before when Maureen teased me and things looked brighter than they had in months.

Eventually, the baby stopped crying.

That made one of us.

> You were always easy to take care of
> when you were a little kid. You slept
> through the night by the time you were
> ten weeks old, you ate well, you rarely
> got sick, and you learned how to crawl
> and walk without destroying any of our
> valuable property (of which, admit-
> tedly, there was little at the time). You
> even potty trained easily.
>
> I'm sure a lot of this had to do with hav-
> ing your mother around all the time.
> She was so relaxed and she loved you
> so absolutely that it probably didn't
> make a lot of sense to you to give her
> trouble. And I think when someone
> constantly gets positive reinforcement
> for good behavior (and your mother
> was very big on positive reinforcement)
> one tends to feed on it.
>
> You certainly made things a lot easier
> when I came home from work. Those
> were "push" years for me. I not only

had to establish myself firmly in my career because it was what I wanted, but because we needed the money that promotions provided. There were times when I came home very late or when I worked after dinner. Even when you were three or four, you rarely hassled me about this, content to snuggle with your mother on the couch and watch Sesame Street videos or play Yahtzee or Candy Land until bedtime.

By the time I finally settled in a little (and the household income increased dramatically with your mother's return to the workplace), you were in elementary school and your world had broadened beyond the two of us. You sometimes had your own work to do after dinner and an endless succession of playdates on the weekends. I suppose I owe my first major promotion at Eleanor Miller to you, since it came via the marketplace study I did while waiting at your Sunday afternoon dance classes.

I sometimes wonder what I lost during those first five years of your life. We had plenty of weekend time together and I tried to get home before you went to bed as often as possible during the week, but I have to admit that I regularly thought about something else while I was with you. I might have been playing on the floor with you and your blocks, but I was wondering about something that hap-

pened at the office or some program I
was developing. The fact that you didn't
notice (or, if you did, you didn't seem to
mind) made it so much easier for me to
do this. But I think I only now realize that
it wasn't you who was missing out on
having me (after all, you always had your
mother), but me who was missing out on
having you.

I had the toughest time getting ready for my dinner with
Ally. I imagined that Reese was coming down with something. I imagined that *I* was coming down with something. I
even imagined that Lisa came down with something and was
going to call any moment to say she couldn't babysit. Ally
hadn't actually named what we were doing a date, but it was
hard for me to interpret her invitation any other way. This
led me invariably to wonder what I was thinking by accept-
ing it. I was about as prepared to go out on a date as I was
to swim the English Channel. Maureen was gone less than
four months and I hadn't begun contemplating moving on
in even the remotest way. And I didn't want to hurt Ally's
feelings by giving her the impression that I was capable of
handling more than a casual friendship at this point. I really
liked her, but there was an excellent chance that I would
never be ready for anything more than a casual friendship.
Maureen and I were together from our sophomore year in
college, essentially since I was out of diapers. That was about
as close to mated for life as I could imagine.

Before Ally suggested dinner, I hadn't given a moment's
thought to dating again. I'm sure my subconscious toyed
with the notion that at forty (a landmark birthday that passed
unceremoniously a few weeks earlier), I was too young to be
celibate forever, but that was as far as it had gone. And since
I liked Ally and I wanted to maintain a friendship with her, I
needed to handle this with more skill than I possessed.

I received a sucker punch of a flashback when I left the
house that night. I left Reese with Lisa every weekday, and

we were very good at making the exchange. But the last time I left him with a babysitter for a night out was that last date with Maureen. And as I drove off to meet Ally, all of it came rushing back to me – the kiss Maureen gave my hand, the conversation about how good this was for us, the anticipation of an entire dinner uninterrupted by the needs of the baby or the weight of end-of-a-long-day tiredness, setting aside for a few hours our endless concern about Tanya, the intense passion when we got home, and the way we held each other in bed that night. I could sense Maureen's warmth against me, the curve of her ankles intertwined with mine as we lay together – and I felt the loss of that sensation as completely as I had on that dismal January night when I discovered her body.

I actually needed to pull over to the side of the road. I looked down at my cell phone and considered calling Ally and begging off, certain that this was the first in a series of panic attacks. For several minutes, I couldn't move. Maureen was almost always on my mind, but there were times when she came so startlingly close to being real for me again that I could barely tolerate the experience. To have her be this near and yet forever unreachable was excruciating.

I didn't know what to do. Ally would certainly understand if I canceled at the last minute. I would explain myself on Monday, she'd talk me through it, and I'd wind up not only feeling a little better, but like I'd made the tiniest move toward getting my feet back under me. But when I realized this – that the person I felt most comfortable talking with about what I was going through was the person I was on my way to see – I convinced myself to continue the evening. I turned on the iPod and listened to some music, willing myself to calm down. After a few minutes, I started to relax a little and gain some equilibrium. Cautiously, I put the car back on the road.

By the time I got to the restaurant, I felt as close to normal as I ever felt these days. Whether or not the worst of it had passed, I had no idea. But I did know that I was capable of continuing. I made up my mind that I wouldn't talk to

Ally about what just occurred unless it happened again. She didn't need my weighing her down like this the second I saw her. And as the minutes passed, I became more and more convinced I could handle myself.

We chose a New American place I really wanted to try. The chef came from an inn on the Connecticut River Valley where she developed a reputation for innovation built upon rock-solid fundamentals. I read articles by and about her in cooking magazines, and the only reason I hadn't been there since the restaurant opened was because Maureen developed a decided preference for comfort food in the months before Tanya left.

Ally was already seated when I arrived. She stood up when I got to the table and I wasn't sure whether I should kiss her on the cheek or simply sit down. After an awkward second, I touched her on the arm of her orange sweater.

"Cashmere?" I said, as we sat.

"Cashmere *blend*. Eleanor Miller doesn't pay me enough for the pure thing."

"Yeah, I guess not. Well, it's a great sweater."

"Thanks. You look nice dressed down. I couldn't imagine it in my head."

"You could imagine me with peas on my face, but you couldn't imagine me in khakis?"

"You're very easy to imagine with peas on your face – don't take that the wrong way."

"It might take me a few minutes to figure out the *right* way to take that comment."

A waiter came by with a glass of red wine for her. She thanked him and both of them turned to me. "They have Morgan's 2005 Syrah by the glass here," Ally said.

"That would be great," I said to the waiter.

While we waited for my drink to arrive, we talked about our Saturdays. Mine involved the usual errands that piled up awaiting the weekend. There were also about a dozen minutes at a local park before I decided that the day was too cold for Reese to stay outside. Instead, after an especially messy lunch, we took a long bath together: Reese discovered his squeaky hippopotamus and the bath book with a sound chip that played "Old MacDonald Had a Farm" (one of the few concessions I made to kiddie songs). The two things entertained him for nearly a half hour.

Ally's Saturday started considerably later than mine did – "Somewhere around 10:30. I like to make up for lost sleep on the weekends." She had errands to run as well, but hers included an impromptu decision to see the new Meryl Streep movie.

"Impromptu decisions," I said. "God, I remember those."

"They're not all they're cracked up to be."

"Yeah, I vaguely recall that as well. And hey, our bath *was* spontaneous. Certainly there was nothing premeditated about playing 'Old MacDonald' forty-seven times."

"Forty-seven different animals?"

"No, the same four because those were the sounds I knew how to make. One of the moral dilemmas of being the parent of an infant. You *could* pretend that an aardvark made the same sound as a horse and he wouldn't know the difference. But if you start lying to your kid when he's six months old, can you ever really stop?"

Ally smiled. She had a gorgeous, reassuring smile that made you think that she was both beautiful and someone with whom you wanted to be friends. It dawned on me that I didn't have any beautiful friends. I had friends who were perfectly pleasant looking, but none of either gender who I would describe as beautiful. Maureen and Tanya were beautiful. Was that enough for me? Was I subconsciously adhering to some quota? Or was I even more subconsciously keeping beautiful people out of my life?

My wine came, and with it our menus. Ally looked down at hers and we concentrated on these for a few minutes.

"Wow, monkfish osso bucco," she said.

"Do you know about this chef?"

"Deborah Gold? Yeah, *Newsday* made a big deal about her arrival a few months ago. And I read about her in *Food and Wine* and *Saveur*."

"Oh you get *Saveur* too? I love how they take you all over the world to the source of cooking. I didn't realize you like to cook."

"I like *reading* about food. And of course I love eating it – is there anyone who doesn't? But I'm a really awful cook." She got a sheepish expression on her face. "It's genetic. Family Services nearly sent me to a foster home because of my mother's pot roast."

"You just need a better teacher. There's nothing genetic about it."

"Do you cook?"

"Almost every night. Even tonight. I braised some chicken thighs and porcini mushrooms for Lisa."

Ally shook her head. "You braised chicken for your babysitter? Don't most parents just order a pizza?"

"I thought I'd offer her a little bonus for coming on a Saturday. Besides, it's just something that simmers on the stove for a couple of hours. It's not like I needed to *slave* over it."

"Feel free to bring me lunch any time you want." She looked down at her menu. "What are you ordering?"

I decided on the barley risotto with spring peas and the seared tuna with *sauce Diane*. Ally ordered the lobster and endive spring roll and found the monkfish osso bucco too fascinating to pass up. The chef prepared the food caringly and presented it with flair and a sense of humor. She clearly understood what went without saying in the best restaurants – that it wasn't enough to appeal to the taste buds, that a dining experience should be delightful on a number of levels.

Of course, the quality of the food would have made no difference whatsoever if things had been uncomfortable or tense between Ally and me. Aside from the obvious concerns about what Ally was expecting from this evening and how I was going to handle any of it, I was equally worried about running out of things to say. Or even that we might find each other unpleasant outside of the office. But that didn't happen.

"By the way," she said, swallowing a bite of spring roll. "I found someone who shares my opinion about Abba."

"You're kidding. How many people did you have to ask?"

"Not as many as you think. Confirmed my suspicions that you're a music snob."

"Only by the broadest possible definition. What is it that you like about them?"

"They're buoyant."

"So's a hot-air balloon."

"Yep, definitely a music snob."

"They also had their biggest hits when you were in elementary school. Don't you think it's time to move on?"

"Are you telling me you don't listen to Led Zeppelin? You can hold onto the past and embrace the future at the same time, you know."

"Abba, jeez."

We kept the conversation pretty much at this level – current events, pop culture, food, work, and, of course, Reese. I checked my cell phone a couple of times just to make sure I hadn't missed a call, but otherwise I was surprised by how in the moment I was. Especially given what a wreck I was fifteen minutes before I got to the restaurant.

It was refreshing and even a little bit exciting to have this kind of night. Other than a business meal a few weeks after Reese was born and then that one night with Maureen, I hadn't been out to dinner in nearly six months. And it felt inordinately good to let things go for a little while.

"This was fun," Ally said as we stood in front of her car later in the evening.

"It was. Thanks for suggesting it."

She smiled. "Maybe we can do it again sometime."

"I'd like that."

For the first time since the night started, I felt a bit strange. I didn't know how to say goodbye to her. The silence that ensued over the next twenty seconds or so was longer than any we endured over dinner. Finally, she pecked me chastely on the lips and, in nearly the same motion, turned and opened her car door.

"I'll see you on Monday," she said.

I stood next to her car until she drove off. It was only when I was alone that I felt the impact of the kiss. It was nothing but the briefest contact and it was entirely possible that she did this kind of thing with friends all the time. But it affected me nevertheless. The only person I kissed on the lips in recent memory – even this casually – was Maureen. And the fact that I found this notable and even a little bit thrilling brought me crashing back to earth.

I'd allowed myself a diverting evening with a charming woman. I found this woman fascinating and I wanted to get to know her better. And when she kissed me at the end of the night, it moved me both physically and emotionally.

How was any of this possible only four months after the death of the woman I dedicated my entire adult life to?

If something this casual could sweep me up, what did this say about my commitment to Maureen? How could I not be so overwhelmed by sadness that an entertaining night like this was impossible for the conceivable future?

By the time I got home, I was convinced that I'd betrayed Maureen and was due some serious self-flagellation. What the hell was I doing going out on a date? This was so utterly inappropriate and so completely wrong.

I didn't realize until I walked into the house that it was after eleven. Lisa was watching television in the family room.

"Everything okay with Reese?" I said.

"He's sleeping like a baby," she said, chuckling at her little joke. She put on her shoes and walked toward the door. "I figured you'd be back an hour ago. You're *almost* going to make me late meeting my friends."

I even screwed up with the babysitter. "Sorry," I said.

"Not a problem. Did you have a good time tonight?"

"Yeah, thanks. It was nice."

Yes, it *was* nice. What was wrong with me?

ELEVEN - Cool

I haven't written to you yet about your mother's dying. That probably speaks volumes about how I'm dealing with it. I don't know why it wasn't the very first thing I wrote about in this journal. It probably had something to do with the look in your eyes when I told you about it. It also had a lot to do with how I felt to have to tell you.

Nothing special happened the morning before your mother died. There were no poignant moments, no expressions that passed between us that said, "Just in case I'm not here when you get home tonight, here's something to carry with you the rest of your life." Reese had another lousy night's sleep and we were both ragged. He'd been up for an hour already by the time I got into the shower. When I got out, both he and your mother were fast asleep again, his little body resting on her chest. I didn't want to wake either of them, so when I finished getting ready for work, I kissed them both softly and crept out of the bedroom.

Even with the lack of sleep, I was still feeling a little boost from the date we'd had that Saturday. Your mother looked fabulous that night. It wasn't just that she was wearing grown-up clothes for the first time in a couple of months. She was radiating. I'm sure some of it was from the simple fact that we were getting away. But I think it was primarily because we were getting away together. We always had that between us. Even when we were mesmerized by your coming into our lives and fascinated with exploring the mysteries of parenthood and the prospects of building a family together, we always made sure to keep some time between us, to keep our love affair fresh. This is advice I'm sure she would have given you when you had a baby of your own.

So I drove off to work feeling good about the future. I was still terribly worried about where you were, but something told me you were coming home soon, that our family would be whole again, and that we would move forward together. The cloud cover had lifted.

So much for instinct.

I've wondered from time to time if I should have awakened your mother that morning to say good-bye to her. If I had known it was going to be the last time, I wouldn't have let it pass with only a faint kiss on the forehead. Or maybe I would have. She was so tired. It would have been selfish of me to get her up – and probably Reese as well – just so I could feel better.

I have very little memory of what happened when I came home that night. The doctor told me that she was irretrievable by then. I truly don't remember what she looked like or felt like. My memory is limited to Reese's screaming. I guess I called Gail (she and Tate have split up, by the way, but that's another story) because she was there to take care of the baby when I went to the hospital. When I left your mother that night, I kissed her forehead one more time. In my mind, the kiss felt the same as the one I gave her that morning, but I know that couldn't have been the case.

Since then, I've had these little periods when everything seems okay. I had another one last night, which I guess is why I'm writing you about this now. It's not that I don't understand that life has to continue, and it's not that I thought that there would never be a point when I could laugh easily or simply have a good time again. But these feelings don't last and they still seem unnatural to me. Not when I have them – at that point, they seem amazingly natural — but afterward. If you and I were going through this together, I'm sure we would talk about that a lot. I'd like to believe we would help each other out, that we would get together on this.

I know I'll always love your mother and that I'll never stop wanting to be with her as much as I did that Saturday night. I just wish I knew how to deal with the rest of it.

I'm sure you're having some of these same feelings right now. I hope you have someone to talk to, even if it's Mick. I hope you find a way to seek some joy out of the rest of your life, and that you aren't letting this destroy you. Trust me; I know how difficult that is. But it's so essential.

We are, after all, her legacy.

I still felt strange about my dinner with Ally when I got to work on Monday. All day Sunday, it served as another thing that crept up on me and threw me off balance. I walked Reese in his stroller, serene in the warmth of a spring day as pleasant as the day before had been nasty, when the memory of Ally's gossamer kiss sneaked into my thoughts, driving me first toward my overreaction to the gesture and then toward the pain of losing Maureen. This was at least one thing more than I could handle at this point.

I stopped by Ally's office on my way to mine. She smiled up at me from her desk and, for the briefest instant, I felt foolish about what I had been thinking.

"Hey," she said. "Did you have a good Sunday?"

"Yeah, it was great. Reese and I walked about four miles."

"His legs must be very tired." She smiled. "Saturday night was fun."

"It was. A lot of fun." I sat down in the chair across from her desk. "But I think we can't do it again. At least not now."

Ally's expression shifted. "Wow. Why?"

"This is going to sound stupid to you, but I don't think I'm ready for this kind of thing."

"What kind of thing?"

"Going out on a Saturday night. Hiring a babysitter. Stimulating dinner conversation." I hesitated and looked away from her. "Kissing goodnight."

"Are you saying I shouldn't have registered us at Tiffany's yesterday?"

"This does sound stupid to you, doesn't it?"

She leaned forward and touched me on the hand briefly. "It doesn't. I get it." She frowned just slightly. "It was a great dinner, though. I don't know a lot of people I can talk to about both Javier Bardem *and* Maldon Sea Salt."

I leaned back in my chair. "Can we wind it back a little? Maybe just keep it in the office? Maybe lunch at the place around the corner every now and then?"

"Yeah, of course. I definitely don't want you to be uncomfortable. I've never experienced what you're going through. You're gonna have to play it out on your schedule."

I was so happy the conversation was going this way. "Thanks. I *did* have a great time Saturday night."

"That's what all the guys say."

I cringed at the hint of an edge in her voice. "Are you angry with me?"

"I'll get over it. I was going to recommend this great Latin place for our next dinner, but I'll just go there with someone else." She smiled again, though I wasn't entirely sure what she meant by that.

I realized I felt more conflicted about this than I expected to be. When I decided to have this conversation with her, I was convinced that it was the only option. But I felt like I was losing something here, which was ridiculous because nothing happened between us.

"Don't go to the Latin place just yet, okay?" I said.

She held me with a meaningful glance. "I'll give you a little while."

* * *

I still hadn't heard a word from Tanya since our encounter in Pittsburgh. That Friday night, though, I received an article about a new Roy Orbison retrospective forwarded from an anonymous e-mail address. Orbison was one of the many musical figures about which Tanya and I disagreed. I thought he was a vocal genius, Tanya thought he sang like a strangled cat. The article was laudatory, almost reverential. Did this mean that Tanya was acknowledging the validity of my opinion? Or maybe she was saying instead, "I guess there are other people out there who are as dumb about this as you are."

Again, I found myself searching for second, third, and fourth levels of meaning in this scant bit of communication from my daughter. Was she sending this along to remind me how different we were? Was she sending it because it made her think of me and she knew I would want to read it? Was she simply doing it to show me that she was still alive? Orbison sang a great deal about grief and sadness. Had she passed this along to let me know that she was grieving? He died much too young. Was she trying to draw some connection between him – and the way he lived on in the memory of his fans – and her mother? The article quoted from his songs, "In Dreams" and "Only the Lonely." Was there something in one of these lines that she meant for me to interpret?

I was still perched in front of the computer looking for answers when Tate called.

"I almost feel ridiculous for asking this," he said, "but I need a favor."

"Yeah, sure."

"Can you take Zak and Sara for a couple of hours tomorrow afternoon? I'm meeting this woman for lunch."

"Couldn't you meet her for dinner on a night when you don't have the kids?"

"It's complicated and she wanted lunch. Do you think you can handle this, or is it too much with the baby?"

"No, it's fine. Drop them off whenever."

Tate showed up a little before noon the next day, brought the kids inside, kissed them on the tops of their heads, and said, "I'll see ya later." I was a little miffed; not at his asking me to do a favor for him, but because he hadn't prioritized his kids during what had to be a tough transition. Clearly, some woman caught his fancy. I knew that Tate was faithful to Gail throughout their marriage and maybe his sudden freedom appealed to him so much that he forgot his responsibilities.

Reese, Zak, Sara, and I ate lunch together and then walked down to the neighborhood playground. Sara spent an inordinate amount of time on a swing, but Zak stayed close by, seemingly much more fascinated with Reese than he was with anything else in the park. He held the baby in his lap while they sat in a play car and then played peek-a-boo with him for as long as Reese continued to smile over it. They shared a teething biscuit and Zak stood over Reese inquisitively while I changed his dirty diaper.

"Is that a pain in the neck?" he asked.

"Is what a pain in the neck?"

"Doing stuff for him?"

"No, of course not. I mean, I can think of lots of things more fun than this." I pointed to the loose bowel movement. "But I love doing stuff for Reese."

"You do?"

"Of course. He's my kid. Your mom and dad love doing stuff for you."

"Yeah, I know that."

He ran off to join his sister and then the two of them went on the seesaw with Reese and me. Reese thought it was hilarious when our side of the seesaw landed on the ground with a thump. He was in an especially good mood this afternoon and seemed to find everything funny. I wondered if he was putting on a show for the other kids. It seemed important to him that everyone have a good time.

On the way out of the park, I bought Zak and Sara ice pops from an ice cream truck.

"Can Reese have one too?" Zak said.

"He's not really supposed to," I said, though I'd given him tastes of everything from Krispy Kremes to *dulce de leche*. "Babies shouldn't eat ice pops."

"I'm not a baby," Sara said abruptly. "I don't like being a baby."

None of us chose to comment on this, though Zak cringed a little.

We got back to the house and I put Reese down for his nap while the two other kids watched television. Tate said to expect him by 2:30, but it was a quarter to three and he still hadn't returned.

While we waited, I taught Zak and Sara how to play Uno. Sara seemed to take great joy in making Zak skip turns or draw extra cards. It was then that I realized what seemed unusual about seeing the two of them together today. From the time Sara could walk, they were extremely competitive with one another and involved in regular, near constant spats. But until this game of cards, they hadn't provoked one another in the least today.

Tate finally got back around four. He walked in, patted the kids, and then said to me, "Were they okay?"

"They were great," I said, glancing over at both of them. "They kicked my butt at Uno, but other than that, they were perfect house guests."

"Wanna play Uno with us, Dad?" Sara said. "Gerry says I'm a *card shark*."

"That's 'sharp,' Baby," Tate said. "And I think it's time for us to go and give Gerry his house back."

I walked them to the door. "How was your lunch?" I said to Tate.

"More delicious than you can imagine."

"Is this something I want to hear?"

"I don't want to make you jealous. Hey, I really appreciate that you did this thing with the kids."

"They were great. Bring 'em by anytime."

"Yeah, right. I owe you one."

Sara kissed me on the cheek and Zak gave me a long hug.

"Thanks for being such a great playmate for Reese today,"
I said to him.

He smiled. "He's a cool kid."

"You are too."

* * *

That Tuesday, Reese had his half-year birthday. We celebrated by throwing caution to the wind and sharing some
chocolate pudding I made. Reese was fascinated with the
taste and, unlike most of the food he ate these days, barely
a drop went onto his face or our clothes. I imagined that at
some point I would have to address the considerable affection that my son had for sweets, but tonight was not that
time.

Before I put him to bed, I also gave him the last pouch
of breast milk Maureen had expressed for him four months
earlier. She had been so diligent about building up a big store
of these. This last pouch had been sitting alone in the freezer
for ten days awaiting this event.

I wondered what Reese would think about this moment if
he knew what was going on. Would he feel like he was losing
his connection to his mother? Would he drink it with extra
care, trying to remember the taste forever? Fortunately, he
didn't need to consider any of this. To him, this bottle was
the same as all the others and I guess in a very real way that
was a good thing.

I thought about how I would memorialize Maureen for
Reese. Of course, there would be pictures, including the
handful I had of the two of them together. But I wanted the
image he had of his mother to be richer, more three-dimen-
sional. I decided to make a habit of sharing pieces of her when
he got older – places we went together, songs she listened to,

food she liked to eat, movies that made her cry, news events that outraged her. There was no way of constructing an accurate image of Maureen in his mind, but I would do my best to give him a feel for her, to help him draw impressions of her that he might have drawn himself if they were together.

Reese drank the bottle hungrily – obviously, the carrots, peaches, and chocolate pudding hadn't been enough – and belched loudly when he finished. I started so sing him a song and then decided to let him stay up a little longer. We watched a Yankee game (which, for once, they were winning easily) and I promised him we'd go to Yankee Stadium when he was one-and-a-half.

* * *

As the product development closing date came for the Christmas catalog, work intensified. This meant taking more of it home with me and sometimes spending hours in my library after Reese went to bed. It also meant that I needed to phone my colleagues at night on occasion. Doing this with Ally one night led to a productive ten minutes on the job at hand and then another half hour about other things. A few nights later, she called me apropos of nothing and we talked for a long time. A few nights after that, I completed the little bit of work I needed to do and then clicked on the Yankee game. I had been in executive staff meetings the entire day and hadn't seen Ally at all. She came to my office sometime after lunch, but I didn't even get the message until after six. While I was watching the game, I decided to give her a call.

"Sorry I missed you today," I said when she answered. "I was stuck with the suits in the conference room."

"Aren't you technically a 'suit' yourself?"

"Bite your tongue."

"I apologize. Anyway, I didn't have any real reason to come see you. I was just stopping by to say hi."

"I would have enjoyed that so much more than the clever banter I had with the finance people. I really think those guys have a different genetic structure than we do."

"I'm guessing they think that people who develop cuddly animal bathmats are pretty weird too."

"You might have a point."

It was a little more than a month after Opening Day. The Yankees were off to a very slow start, winning just 11 of their first 26 games. Also, the injury bug continued to strike, placing two more players on the disabled list, and relegating another couple to day-to-day status. Now, in the top of the fourth, they were down 4-1, again suffering from early pitching problems. At that moment, while I half-watched the game, their second baseman let an easy ground ball slip through his legs and another run scored. I heard Ally exclaim, "Dammit," while I thought the exact same thing.

"Are you okay?" I said.

"Yeah, sorry. I really am listening to you. It's just that this guy on the Yanks just made a stupid error."

"You're watching the Yankee game?"

"I'm *always* watching the Yankee game. I've been a huge fan since I was a little kid."

"How has this not come up in conversation?"

"You're not a Mets fan, are you?" she said with some apprehension in her voice.

"No, Yankees, of course. Always have been. I'm watching the game right now. He positioned himself totally wrong for that grounder."

"He's been doing it all season. They have a real problem at second."

"Item number four, I think, on a huge list of problems."

"I'm worried about them."

"It's early."

"Yeah, but I'm worried."

This was a revelation. For most of my adult life, I didn't have anyone to talk with like this. Maureen and Tanya were ambivalent about baseball and, because we were from Long Island, most of my other friends paid more attention to the Mets. The New York metro area overflowed with Yankee fans, but I had virtually none in my personal acquaintance.

But now I had Ally.

The Yankees ultimately got out of the inning without making any additional errors or giving up any more runs. The broadcast went to commercial.

"Have you seen the new *Food and Wine* and that great tour through Chilean vineyards?" Ally said.

"I don't get *Food and Wine*."

"You don't? I love it. I'll get you a subscription for your birthday. When is your birthday?"

"It was last month."

"You had a birthday last month and you didn't tell me?"

"It was skip-able."

"Birthdays are *never* skip-able. I'm going online right now to order you a subscription. When it arrives, we'll pretend it's your birthday."

"I don't know very much about Chilean wine, either."

"You need me way more than you realize. They're still coming into their own, but some vineyards are producing great stuff. Casa Lapostolle makes one of the best wines in the world." I heard the phone rustling around on her end. "I'm at my computer."

"You're not worried about missing a couple of Yankee strikeouts?"

"Nah, there'll be plenty more where those come from."

"Probably *next* inning."

"So what did you make the kid for dinner tonight? Have you started him on Mexican food yet? I hear babies love *salsa verde*."

"I gave him some guacamole the other night and he seemed to like the way it looked in his hair. I stuck with an old standby tonight: pureed peaches."

"Beech-Nut or Gerber?"

"You're kidding, right? I make my own."

"That sounds like way more work than necessary. Are you afraid the commercial brands will poison him or something?"

"It's not exactly tough to blanch some peaches and throw them in a food processor."

"Sounds tough to me."

"We need to get you over here for some cooking lessons." I said this casually, even though I clutched a little as the words came out of my mouth.

"Ready when you are. As long as you don't mind the risk of collateral damage."

"Game's back on, by the way."

"I'll be done with this in a couple of minutes. I need your address."

"You're really getting me a subscription to *Food and Wine*?"

"You said you didn't have one. I need your address."

I told her and then told her that the Yankees had quickly put a runner on first.

"How'd the team meeting go today?" I said.

"Not the same without you. And some of the kids really act up when the teacher isn't there. But I think we did okay. Morris came up with a fabulous idea, but I'll let him tell you tomorrow. That is, if you're *visible* tomorrow."

"Can't say for sure. I'm telling you, three-quarters of the time I'm with these finance guys, I feel totally unnecessary."

"Come back to us. We promise to make you feel needed."

"Thanks. First and second with nobody out. You really shouldn't miss this."

"I'm doing the credit card thing now. I'll be back in the living room in a second."

We didn't talk while Ally gave the website her credit card information and I watched the next Yankee batter ground into a double play, which left a runner at third with two outs. I moaned and then explained what happened.

"I'm telling you, I'm worried," she said.

"They'll work through this. They have to."

The inning ended a batter later with a pop-up to short. We talked each other through another half inning before deciding to call it a night.

"Mine is in September, by the way," she said.

"Your what?"

"My birthday. I thought I'd tell you now in case you wanted to get me something that required special ordering."

"Thanks for the heads-up."

After I put down the phone, I watched a bit more of the game before I did my nightly check of my home e-mail account. Nothing new from Tanya. I wrote for a while in her journal and returned to the television just in time to see the final out of another Yankee loss.

Would it have been even more fun to talk to Ally about this if the team were playing better?

TWELVE - A Little Impaired

It didn't dawn on me that I had no contingency plan if Lisa got sick until it happened. I had just showered and Reese lay in my bed having his first bottle when she called to say that she had a 102-degree fever.

Irony demanded that this happen on a day when there was a huge amount to do in the office. I needed to deliver the next month's budget numbers by the end of the week, several critical deadlines on the Christmas catalog were imminent, and I was in the middle of completing the specifications for the first new product proposal I came up with since I returned. I really didn't have the luxury of a day off. But since I didn't have a contingency plan, I also didn't have any choice.

As I called Ben to tell him I would be out, I realized that, if I was going to get as much work done from home as possible, I needed a bunch of paperwork from the office.

"Listen, I'm going to swoop in for a couple of seconds in an hour or so. I need you to pull together all the new product data and all of my budget work-sheets and have them in one place for me by then."

"Are you sure? I can bring them to your house if you want."

"No, then my office will be *completely* unmanned. If you're coming here, it had better be to babysit."

"I think both of us know that would be a mistake."

"My point exactly. I'll be there by ten."

It should have been easy to get Reese out of the house. After all, doing this was no different from running errands on

the weekend, something we usually did smoothly and effi-
ciently. But it took an absurdly long time.

First, he squirmed and rolled over constantly while I tried
to dress him. He was definitely no longer the sack of flour of
a couple of months earlier. Now he was in so much motion
that getting him into clothes was a little like playing that
Whac -A-Mole arcade game – one second you think his arm
is going into his sleeve and suddenly it's down where his leg
is supposed to be. Then, once I finally shoehorned him into
his outfit, he spit up on the front of it, managing to catch the
sleeve of my shirt at the same time. This required changing
both of us, though admittedly getting a shirt on myself was a
breeze. Then, as we got into the car, he pooped in his diaper.
I seriously considered letting him sit in it for the round trip,
but didn't think the smell would send the proper message
to any colleagues I encountered. *Of course,* the bowel movement was very loose and *of course,* it leaked through to his
pant leg, requiring a *third* change for both of us.

And then, as we left the neighborhood, I remembered
that I had no more diapers in the bag I kept in the car. Part of
me wanted to play the hunch that he wouldn't have another
dirty diaper in the next hour. But the part that envisioned
Reese leaking onto Marshall's arm proved more persuasive. I
turned the car around.

I didn't get to the office until closer to 10:30, at which
point I barreled into the building as if I were late for a meeting with the Board of Directors. I eschewed the BabyBjörn
thing and carried Reese in my arms, smiling at the people I
passed, but deflecting any effort made by anyone to stop to
see the baby.

I also studiously avoided passing Marshall's office, which
meant taking the long way around to mine. I knew he was
going to be unhappy with my being out and I was sure that
the absolute most inflammatory thing would be to show up
anywhere near him carrying my son.

"Everything ready?" I said to Ben as I approached his
desk.

"Hi, yeah. It's all in your office."

"Thanks."

He followed me in. "So this is Reese, huh? He looks different from his pictures."

"He looks different from two hours ago. That's the way it works at this age."

"Jeez, so you go away for a few days and it's like there's a stranger in the house, huh?"

"I wouldn't know."

The phone rang and Ben went to his desk to take it. I pulled together the papers he gathered for me and then remembered a computer file that I needed. Still holding Reese and the papers in my arms, I reached down to boot up my computer.

"Need a hand?"

I looked up to see Ally standing in the doorway.

"Word is out that there's a guy with a baby traipsing through the building. I used my keen deductive powers to determine that it was you."

I stood up and realized that Reese had been trying to get my computer mouse in his mouth. "Actually, I really could use a hand."

Ally walked over and took Reese from me, gently separating him from the mouse at the same time. I expected him to scream about this, but he was fine. She walked him toward my couch while I started the machine.

"He's gorgeous," she said.

I looked over to see him standing on her lap and playing with her hair. Ally shook her head briskly, which sent strands of hair into his face and made Reese chuckle. As it seemed most adults were prone to do, she immediately did it again, getting a louder response.

"Thanks."

"He has your eyes and your chin. Fortunately, he didn't get your nose."

"There's something wrong with my nose?"

Ally rubbed her nose against Reese's, causing him to laugh again, and said, "It looks better on a grownup than it would on a baby. Do you like to fly, Reese?" Ally raised him over her head and swept him back and forth in front of her. His eyes stayed locked on hers and he smiled the entire time.

I turned to send the file I needed to my home e-mail account, and then decided to make a copy on disk just in case something was wrong with my e-mail. When I finished, I shut down the machine and sat with the two of them.

"He really is incredibly cute," she said.

"You might not have felt that way an hour ago."

"Of course I would have. How could he be anything *but* cute?" Reese settled on Ally's lap and attempted to eat one of the buttons of her blouse. She was right, of course. He was usually cute. She playfully batted Reese away from her button and he pawed her hand in return. They did this a couple of times before Reese's attention fixed on something else.

"Do you spend a lot of time around kids?"

"I have a niece that I just love. She's four now. Other than that, no."

"I have no idea what he's going to be like when he's four."

Reese suddenly dove forward and Ally moved quickly to keep him from falling. Most people who didn't have kids would have nervously handed him over at that point. But Ally turned Reese on his lap so he faced her and then leaned down to him and said, "Don't jump." Then she looked up at me and said, "What's going on? Why'd you bring him here?"

"Lisa is on the DL. It's just me, the boy, and 37 hours of work that I need to do today. He has your necklace."

Ally reached up to touch the hand that held her gold chain, but didn't pry it loose. "Kids like shiny things, right?" she said to me. "Anything I can help you with?"

"Yeah. If you want to do the noon-to-eight shift I'll pay you a lot of money."

"I would in a second," she said, nuzzling Reese again, which may or may not have been her way of getting him to let go of her necklace. "I've got two production meetings today, though. Any *office* thing I can help you with?"

"No, I need to do this all on my own. Thanks for the offer, though."

"Ready to fly again?" she said to Reese before lifting him over her head. He laughed. "He has a great sense of humor."

"Actually, he's flirting. You're seeing his B+ moves right now."

"They're working. Hey Reese, why don't the two of us split this joint?"

I laughed. Reese was having more and more trouble with strangers, but while he was with Ally, he didn't even notice I was in the room. Impulsively, I said, "Hey, how about coming with us on a picnic Saturday afternoon?"

Ally looked over at me while Reese was still in midair. "Really? That would be fun."

"Yeah, it would. The weather is supposed to be nice this weekend and obviously you and my son have a little *thing* going."

She kissed him on the cheek and then sat him on her lap again. "I'd love it. Is he our chaperone?"

I rolled my eyes. While she was graceful about my request to confine our friendship to the office, she didn't let me forget it. "I wasn't necessarily thinking of it that way."

"Well, it works for me. When and where?"

"Stay tuned for more." I stood up. "I hate prying the two of you apart, but I have a ton of work to do and I'm going to be a little impaired at home. I'd better get going."

"Yeah, of course." She leaned forward to kiss the baby on the top of the head and then handed him to me. "Nice meeting you, Reese."

"You guys can hang out all afternoon on Saturday."

"I look forward to it."

* * *

There was one time when events conspired to require me to work from home when Tanya was little. Maureen was in bed with the flu and we had no regular babysitter to call on. I needed to complete a report and, with the nervousness born of a still-emerging career, stressed over the thought that Tanya, two-and-a-half at the time, wouldn't let me do it.

But she turned out to be great about occupying herself and playing nursemaid to her mother. I made enough progress by early afternoon that I took her to an indoor playground for the rest of the day.

It turned out that Reese wasn't nearly that cooperative. I gathered his favorite toys and brought them with us into the library, settling him down on his playmat. Staying in one place was not something that Reese did at all anymore. And there turned out to be a surprising number of items in the library under which he could become stuck. In fact, it almost seemed as though he was doing this intentionally in a sort of infant form of hide-and-seek.

When it became clear that working in the library with him was futile – I had barely reviewed my notes – I tried the family room. This was Reese's home turf, unquestionably his favorite room in the house. He could spend hours in here at a time, rolling over and exploring things, sitting with his play phone or his rings. In the past, he'd even complained a few times when I tried to move him. But that would not be the case today. More and more often recently, Reese propped himself on his arms, rocking forward as though attempting to crawl, but not actually moving anywhere. He seemed to enjoy this and often smiled broadly or even laughed when he got up on his hands and knees. Today, however, he found this exercise consistently frustrating and he spent a great deal of time grunting and whimpering. He would be okay if I sat him up and he wouldn't even attempt to crawl while I was there. But as soon as I returned to the couch and my blank yellow legal pad, he'd get back into position and resume his fussing.

I actually accomplished a tiny bit during his nap. But it was only a tiny bit because the nap – which could run as long as three hours on certain days – lasted all of forty-five minutes. After that, I tried his swing, but he'd essentially outgrown that device, and then the television. Which didn't interest him because there was no baseball game on.

I'm not the kind of person who requires absolute silence in order to concentrate. But I do require time. I don't think well when regularly interrupted. The upshot was that by 2:00

that afternoon, I had accomplished almost nothing. And the pressure I already felt over these deadlines (accompanied by the guilt over skipping another day at the office) mounted. This was when Reese decided to have his meltdown. He simply started crying uncontrollably. None of his toys distracted him and it wasn't okay if I just sat on the floor with him anymore. The only thing that soothed him was my holding him and walking around the house. I did this for a while and then settled him back on his playmat. The screaming began again nearly as soon as I returned to the couch.

And my frustration got the best of me. I didn't expect him to babysit himself while I worked, but I did expect him to do a little more hanging out than he was doing. I could only imagine Marshall's response if I walked in the next day without the budget figures because my son wouldn't let me do them. I picked Reese up from the playmat, plopped him into his crib, and then, for the first time ever, I yelled at him. He seemed stunned by this. Of course, he did-n't know what I was saying, but one of his stuffed animals could have understood the intent of my words. He stared at me, frightened for a moment, and then his face collapsed on itself and he bawled. I threw up my arms and left the room.

I didn't stay away very long. I flung myself back on the couch and tried to work, but I couldn't even begin to do so over the sound of his screaming. And though I knew that what he really needed was more rest and that there was a very good chance that he'd cry himself to sleep in a few minutes, I simply could-n't do it. I went back to his room, took him out of his crib, and walked him around until he calmed. He still heaved when I held him in front of me and said, "You *are* going to let me work tonight, right? Let's go out and play for a while."

I packed him up and put him in his stroller. We went for a long walk around the neighborhood. The weather was spectacular, with signs of an early summer everywhere. Reese had a great time on this trip, pointing and gurgling incessantly. And while he did so, I actually got to think clearly about the budget for a few minutes.

Which I was able to put to use when he finally went into his crib for the night. He slept soundly and I made good progress. I could have circumvented a lot of anxiety (for both of us) if I had simply planned to work at night all along, but I didn't have the presence of mind to think that way. All I knew was that I couldn't let my situation affect my job performance yet again. It was stupid. Certainly, I'd built up enough professional credit at Eleanor Miller that I could afford a little slump, even if Marshall made me feel like a slacker through the entire thing. And ultimately, one missed deadline wasn't nearly as terrible as getting into a mode where I treated Reese impatiently.

It wasn't the first time I was thankful that Reese wouldn't have any conscious memories of this period in our lives. The contradiction there, of course, was that I knew that everything we did together, even the smallest things – perhaps especially the smallest things – helped form him in some way. And the fact that he wouldn't actually remember the things that formed him made it vital that I do my best not to traumatize him.

It was at times like these that I fully understood the awesome responsibility of parenting. It was paralyzing.

Fortunately, I didn't have these moments of clarity terribly often.

I think it's safe to say that I grossly underestimated the value of a two-parent family. I'm not saying that I undervalued your mother, but I don't think I fully appreciated how well we'd divided up the workload in the house or how comforting it was to know that there was always backup when I needed it. I hope she felt the same way.

Your brother can be a challenge sometimes. You weren't as needy as he is.

He's a great kid and sometimes he's a real riot, but he wants to make sure that your eyes are always on him. I can only imagine that this will become even more necessary in the coming months, though at some point I'm sure I'll be able to look at a magazine again without fear for his temperament or physical health. I really wish your mom were here to take some shifts with me.

It's important that you identify what the best things are in your life. The things that do more than just get you through the day. The things that make you want the next day to come. And once you identify those things, it's critical that you nurture them and keep them strong. I think the thing that I cherished most about your mother – beyond the loving and the counseling and the laughter – was the strength of our partnership. We performed as a team even before you were born and so much more so after that. And I do believe we very consciously served and maintained that partnership by talking and planning and giving each other breaks when necessary. I don't recall ever having to ask your mother for a hand. She simply seemed to know how and when to pitch in. We were Lennon and McCartney, Magic and Kareem (that's a basketball reference, by the way).

I can't possibly know what the best things are in your life. It isn't important that I know, though I would love to. What is essential is that you know what they are and that you do everything you can to keep them being the best. Because if your best things go away and you don't have any others to take their place, life can be pretty scary. I'm sure I don't have to tell you that I'm speaking from experience.

Here's the thing: you were one of my best things too. From the first moment I held you, I knew that you were irreplaceable. And as you grew and it became obvious not only how smart you were, but how well you could handle yourself even as a little kid, you became more precious to me. There was never a point in my life after you were born when I didn't define myself by you and your mother. Even when we entered the Dark Period of your teenaged years. Even when your mother became pregnant with Reese. Even now.

I know you're special not only because you're my kid, but also because you genuinely are. You're wise, you're considerate, and you made me proud in dozens of different ways. And even though I know I was a distant second in your heart (or maybe lower when your aunt or your grandparents were around, or maybe even lower than that after you started developing close friendships), you have always been one of my best and most cherished things.

Guess I wasn't always such a pro at maintenance, huh?

THIRTEEN - *Life Support*

"What are you making?"

Codie called right after I began preparing dinner. Reese sat in his high chair with some toys, alternately pounding them and chewing them.

"A cornmeal-crusted chicken breast which I'm topping with a little pineapple-habanero salsa."

"Set the table for two. I'll be there in an hour and a half."

"I'll be waiting."

"I'd love to, believe me. The client I'm working on tonight is creativity-averse. I don't know why he doesn't have someone in his accounting department do the campaign for him."

"So come on out. Reese can put the pitch together while we're eating."

"No, Reese is too sophisticated for this guy. And I actually do have dinner plans tonight."

"Date?

"More like an exploratory interview for a date."

"Sounds very romantic."

"Everything in its place. So what's my favorite nephew doing?"

I put a little bit of olive oil into a hot pan and glanced over at the high chair. "At the moment, trying to put an entire stuffed rabbit into his mouth."

Codie laughed. "Pretty oral these days, huh?"

"Exclusively oral these days. I also forgot how much pre-teething kids drool. I feel like I should dress him in scuba gear."

"There's an appealing image."

I put the chicken in the pan and turned to the counter to get the salsa ready. "So are we still on for the Sunday after next?"

"Absolutely. I'll be there in the late morning. Unless you guys want to come into town for brunch again."

"I think we might want to wait seven or eight years before we give that another try." When I'd finally managed to get into the city with Reese, the three of us went to a restaurant and things didn't work out precisely as planned. The place was far too sophisticated and Reese had no patience for it – something he felt it necessary to voice at tremendous volume. Codie and I wound up taking turns walking with him on the street outside. "Late morning out here would be great."

I put on a pair of plastic gloves. I wasn't usually that wimpy when dealing with hot chilies, but I did-n't want Reese teething on one of my fingers and scorching himself on habanero juice. As I pulled out my chef's knife, I heard a dull thump and then a scream from the high chair. I have no idea what he did to himself, but his face was scarlet and he was wailing.

"What happened?" Codie said.

"Nothing that doesn't happen five times a day. There's no blood." Propping the phone between my ear and my shoulder, I pulled Reese out of his chair. He choked back a couple of sobs and buried his head in my chest.

"Do you need to go?"

"No, he'll be fine in a second. My guess is that he banged his head against his tray. He hasn't figured out yet that this is a bad idea." Reese had already stopped crying, but still had his head down. The chicken needed turning, so I slid him over to one shoulder, the phone on the other, and reached for my tongs.

"Can I say hi to him or is he too upset for that."

Reese lifted his head up and watched me manipulate the tongs, his pain and indignation forgotten. "No, he's totally okay." I put the phone up to his ear. "Aunt Codie wants to talk to you."

I heard Codie's contralto salutations through the earpiece. Reese seemed fascinated by this and leaned his head into the phone. He smiled and burbled. A minute later, I took the phone back.

"He *talked* to me," Codie said.

"You really need to get one of these for yourself."

"I can't believe he talked to me. Do you think he recognized my voice?"

"Of course he recognized your voice. Didn't you hear him say, 'What did you buy me, Aunt Codie?'"

"Don't be a smart-ass. That was very exciting to me."

"Geez, I hope you're tougher on older men."

"My nephew is not a *man*."

"I don't think I have the energy to get into the psychology of that comment. Besides my chicken is nearly cooked and I haven't made the salsa yet."

"I'll let you go. I have to sleepwalk through the rest of this presentation and get out of here in an hour. This guy I'm going out with is a fashion photographer. I might actually need to wear makeup."

"Ridiculous. If he can't tell that you're naturally gorgeous, he can't be much of a photographer."

"Gee, thanks. Can I talk to Reese one more time?" I gave him the phone again, but he didn't react at all to Codie's cooing. Before hanging up, though, I told her he smiled the entire time she spoke to him. She just loved hearing that.

* * *

That night, I checked my e-mail, as I always did after I put Reese to bed. As usual, there wasn't a message from Tanya. But I received a Google alert regarding a new article about River. While I had no idea whether Tanya was still following the band around, it was essential to me that I stay up to date with their press.

This piece focused on a recent concert in Indianapolis and on a ritual bassist Kent Swanson performed a couple of times every tour, going out to the parking lot to party with the Riverriders. I imagined Tanya among this group and wondered what her reaction had been to it. Cool in the face of celebrity, I'm sure, but more than a little tickled inside.

For the first time in a while, I thought about my own days as a rock musician. Though I never got anywhere near breaking through, there was a time in my teens when this was the only important thing to me. Back then, I would have retched to think of working in an office to make a living. The one and only time I ever went on the road was during the summer after my freshman year in college with a rock band that was good enough to book a series of dates along the eastern seaboard. The four of us spent six weeks lugging our equipment from club to club, sleeping in the van, and eating and drinking far too much. It had been exhausting and exhilarating. And it left me with more than a little appetite for the lifestyle – an appetite I lost very quickly when I met Maureen that October and realized how much more fulfilling a romance with her was than burritos and beer at 2:00 a.m. with three guys who had gone too long between showers.

I never told Tanya about that trip – or, as I preferred to dub it back then, my "tour" – though I planned to do so around the time when things between us became tense. In fact, she knew very little about my fascination with being a rock musician. There was the piano in the living room and the songs that I wrote for her on her birthday, but she certainly had no idea that I once dreamed of being in the place where River was now, with followers traveling from arena to arena to watch me play.

Would things have been different between us if she grew up knowing how much this kind of thing once meant to me? Maybe if she saw her father less as the kind of guy who made meaningless things for a living and more as someone who created and dreamed, we would have actually bonded more during her tumultuous years. Or maybe not. Since she wasn't even happy when I told her that I liked some of the new bands she listened to, maybe she would rebelled more. Regardless, holding anything back at this point seemed pointless – especially since I was revealing myself to a leather-bound journal.

Did your mom ever tell you that your dad used to be a rocker? Yep, long hair and everything. I took piano lessons when I was seven and eight and hated it. Back in the olden days, piano teachers didn't believe in training their students through rock and roll, and I thought exercises like "Balloons" or "Hide and Seek," or dumbed-down Mozart and Beethoven was just stupid. But when I was 13, some friends decided to start a band and I wound up being their keyboard player. I started writing songs a year later and by the time I graduated high school, I the idea of being a rock star had become an obsession. I hooked up with a great group of players and we got a bit of a local reputation. Even went out on tour the summer between my freshman and sophomore years at college. I have some of the shows on tape that you can listen to if you promise not to laugh about how dated most of it sounds now.

When I started playing in these bands, I did it for one reason and one reason only: to get girls. Any rock musician who tells you they got into it for any other reason (including fame and fortune) is lying to you. I wrote some of the most dreadfully ridiculous songs because of the impact I thought they would have on the girls listening to them. Treacly ballads to show how deep my soul went. Pounding rockers to illustrate that I could be a "bad boy" (stop laughing!). I was certain these songs would launch me to international superstardom and that women would throw themselves at me wherever I went.

It didn't quite work out that way. First of all, these prefab songs were just plain bad. Second, even though I got to play on stage (though many times the "stage" was a friend's patio during a party) hundreds of times over those rock and roll years, I never attracted many women. Your mother told me that this was because I projected too much sincerity up there and that the women attracted to rock musicians were not looking for "real" guys. And of course, I never became a celebrity. In fact, within a year of meeting your mother, I didn't play in bands at all anymore.

But the happy accident in all of this was the lifelong love affair I began with music. I always liked listening to rock and roll. But once I started playing it – even if my reasons for doing so were less than pure – I extracted all kinds of new meaning from the form. The songs I wrote for myself (as opposed to the ones I wrote for the bands) allowed me to express all kinds of things I couldn't have said easily otherwise. And the sound of the music, whether

it was a power chord played on a dis-
tortion-drenched guitar or a light piano
arpeggio, held trance-like qualities for
me. I came home from school and got
lost in playing. Sometimes hours went
by without my noticing they'd passed.
And none of this was because I chased
a dream of romance or riches. It was
because I'd developed a deep and permanent bond with the music.

Do you remember the songs I wrote
you for your birthday? I did it every
year until you were 14. It was part of
the whole celebration ritual – big dinner, followed by lots of presents, followed by your mother's toast in which
she bestowed her wishes upon you for
the coming year (and yes, she did this
even when you were a toddler) and
finally my birthday song for you. I think
one of the top five moments in my life
came when you were six and I over-
heard you singing one of those songs
in your room.

I don't think I ever explained to you
why I didn't play you a birthday song
at 15 or 16. The main reason I never
explained it to you – and the primary
reason why there wasn't a song – was
that you didn't ask. You see, you never
heard the entirety of your 14th birthday song. The family dinner ran late
(your grandmother told this excruciat-
ingly long story about how the Seniors

Community Center elected her president) and you had some friends picking you up to take you to the movies. I was into the second verse when Lizzie showed up at the door. You came over to tell me and I said that I only had one more verse to go. Your response was, "Dad, I have to leave NOW," and you took off.

I'm sure you didn't mean for me to be as insulted as I felt. But it was obvious that this little tradition had lost its charm for you – underscored by the fact that you didn't even seem to notice that there wasn't a song the next year. I realized then that, while I expressed my love for you by sharing something that I loved, it had gotten to the point where I cared much more about it than you did. And since it was your birthday, that didn't make a lot of sense.

Your mom and I had one of our bigger arguments about my not writing any more songs for you. She told me that she didn't think it was helping our relationship for me to adopt a defeatist attitude. I told her that I wasn't being defeatist, but rather realistic about where we were in our lives at that point. She felt that the difference was semantic.

This wasn't the only conversation that went this way. By this point, you were completely unpredictable and your mom and I felt differently about how to deal with this. She felt that you needed constant reminders that we were there for you. I felt that you needed some space. We debated philosophies a lot and sometimes these debates became heated, perhaps more so than any other conversations we had in our lives together. I think these were the only times we literally stalked away from each other.

And here's the dirty little secret: I wrote songs for you for both of those birthdays, as well as your 17th. I kept them from you because I wanted you to ask for them. And I kept them from your mom because I didn't want her talking you into asking for them. You see, I couldn't stop writing them because I couldn't let go of that moment when I heard you singing my song when you were six years old. And I couldn't let go of the hope that you might wish for these songs again some day and that my instantly delivering them to you would be a watershed moment in our lives.

Yes, I think it was safe to say that the simplicity had fled our relationship quite some time before you ran away.

* * *

I hadn't played the piano since Maureen died.

This was never my primary band instrument. For one thing, one couldn't lug a piano from practice to practice. For another, the piano wasn't very rock and roll. Little Richard and Jerry Lee Lewis could pull it off. Billy Joel and Elton John could. But most of us didn't have the level of cool required to make such an elegant piece of equipment work that way. Instead, I used an electronic keyboard, which I still had in the basement, and I taught myself the rudiments of electric rhythm guitar. There was even a point when I fashioned a strap for the keyboard so I could strut around the stage with it, though fortunately that period didn't last long.

But the piano had always been my main instrument for writing. And when Maureen came into my life, my writing evolved. My lyrics became richer, which was no surprise considering I was in the first serious relationship of my life. But the music I composed became more nuanced and grace-ful as well. I used chord structures I never attempted before. The songs were more melodic and I found the beauty in modulations I never even considered in the past.

I wrote my prettiest songs ever and never played one of them in public (other than Tanya's birthday parties). Song-writing evolved into a very personal avocation for me. It was something I would share with Maureen and later with my daughter. It was something that I did for my family and myself simply because I loved doing it and because it was important for me to express myself this way. Not all of the songs were about my wife and child. Some of them were about how I felt or about an observation I made, and some of them were about utterly inconsequential things. But all of these songs felt different from the ones I had created before. These weren't wannabe hits aimed at making me a rock star. These were songs written with the intention of compiling some kind of personal record.

I didn't quit playing in bands because of Maureen. In fact, she encouraged my playing and told me regularly that she thought I looked sexy (though it was a *sincere* kind of sexy) on stage. But once we were together, playing in bands just seemed so secondary compared to spending time with her. There was no reason to take hours and hours away from our lives to pursue this dream because my dream had evolved. It centered on Maureen now. On the life we were undeniably building and the future that was inextricably a shared one. And where I once vowed to follow my goal of success in the world of music until the bitter end, I found that the end was very sweet instead.

After writing in Tanya's journal, I finally went to the piano. For the first time in months, I wanted to play. My fingers instinctively moved to the two chords I always played when I first sat at the instrument, a Gmaj7 and a C9. I then played (softly, to avoid waking Reese up, though his room was a floor away) one of the first songs I ever wrote for Maureen. This had been a breakthrough moment for me musically, because not only did I use my first augmented chord but also because I rhymed "friend" with "relent," the first time I employed something less than a strict rhyme in my lyrics. I considered this a huge sign of maturity at the time.

After playing this tune, I felt a little blocked. Songs came into my head, but either I couldn't remember the chord changes or I was unsure of a verse. It was time to pull out my old songbooks. And once I did that, I was gone for hours. I went all the way back to my very first one – a loose-leaf binder filled with lined paper on which I wrote lyrics with chords marked over them. My handwriting was a mess back then; I had trouble deciphering some of the innocuous phrases. And the melodies had a humbling sameness, but I still found this excursion entertaining. It was easy to laugh at myself on reflection, even though I knew I took this work very seriously at the time. I played a verse or two from some protest songs I wrote (one on the environment and one on the atrocities in Africa), an homage to a friend who moved away when I was a sophomore in high school, and a cliché-riddled tune I wrote after my first kiss.

A second notebook contained the songs I wrote with my first serious band, a group called Tone. A few of them held up amazingly well. I imagined myself performing these songs, envisioning the fluid solos played by the lead guitarist and the appreciation of the people who listened to them. I hadn't played many of these songs in nearly two decades and my memory had morphed them. I had somehow convinced myself that I hadn't written a single worthwhile tune until I met Maureen, but playing these now suggested something entirely different. There was hardly enough here to make me a household name, but there was more competence – and even a little more inspiration – than I remembered.

Still, when I got to the third notebook, the songs I wrote after Maureen and I got together, there was a dramatic difference. And every one that I played now took me back to another place in our lives. Sometimes these memories were the direct motivation for the songs – the first time we made love, our first trip together, her agreeing to marry me – and sometimes what I recalled instead were the times when I played them for her. Her sitting on my lap while I played with one hand and whispered the song into her ear. Her lounging on the floor next to the piano while we were alone in my parents' house and then pulling me down next to her when the song was finished. Her rocking an infant Tanya back and forth in her arms while I sang to both of them. Her paint-spattered face smiling down at me while I played with equally spattered hands the day after we moved into this house.

As though this music was some kind of psychic life-support system, Maureen seemed revived as long as I kept playing. She wasn't gone; she was here next to me, and intertwined with me. I could follow her out of the living room and into the bedroom, the kitchen, a nearby shopping mall, or the streets of Rome. I could hear her voice, touch her fingers, feel her breath. I knew if I just kept at it, I could keep her here with me indefinitely.

And I slowly came to understand that, just like a medical life-support system, it was all completely artificial. I could keep the pumps going, sing a few more songs to conjure up another receded memory, but eventually I would have to stop and when I did, Maureen would be gone again.

I rested my hands on the keyboard and my head against the piano and the sadness enveloped me completely. I brought Maureen back tonight. By touching on memories I hadn't recalled in years, she became very real. And that made losing her realer as well. This was worse than any sneak attack. I had consciously brought her to me and then saw her evaporate.

A surprising thing happened then. With the tears rolling down my cheeks and my head still against the piano, I fell asleep. And when I awoke some time later, it was with very vivid memories of what had transpired, but with an utterly different feeling about them. I felt enhanced, maybe even bolstered. I knew I could give myself this present again whenever I really needed it. Just about everything I really cherished was in these songbooks and they were always waiting for me. Maybe the magic I generated by bringing Maureen back to me tonight wouldn't always be as strong, maybe in fact it would get progressively weaker, but I knew for a fact that I could touch her in some way by doing this. That was more than I had before. More than I had in what seemed like a very long time.

I got up from the piano and checked on Reese. He lay on his back and stirred when I entered the room, opening his eyes for a moment before rolling over and settling into sleep. I touched his head lightly and then went off to bed.

I'd traveled a couple of dozen years and untold distances tonight. It was time to get some rest.

FOURTEEN - *Like Fire Had Been to the Cave Men*

That Saturday we had our picnic with Ally. It rained the night before and even though the sun was shining brightly in the morning, I thought about calling it off. If the ground were wet, we would have a tough time finding a place for our blanket. Ultimately, Ally talked me into sticking with our plans and we met her at the park under a cloudless sky.

"Did you have to tip the maitre d' to get this spot?" I said to her. Though the park was crowded, she'd carved out a place for us under a tree and right near a stream.

"I called a few people."

"I'm impressed."

She took Reese from my arms to allow me to put down his gear. I wasn't sure what was going to entertain him today, so I brought an inordinate number of toys along with enough diapers and changes of clothes to allow us to stay here for the summer.

This was the first time Ally and I were together out of the office since our "date," and I was a little nervous about it. My invitation to her had been rather impulsive. She knew how I felt about taking our relationship any further and certainly this was something that friends did, but I wondered if she thought I had changed my mind. I still had no idea what my relationship with Ally was supposed to be. We were friends, ones who shared a passion for interesting food and an underachieving baseball team among other things. And she was my go-to person with stories about Reese, complaints about the office, or any little detail that caught my attention in some way.

But while I had no intention of acting on it, it was absurd to think that my interest in her stopped there. Every morning, as I drove to the office, I looked forward to seeing her and I thought about what the first things might be that we would say. This clearly had little to do with our being buddies. This was more than a little unsettling to me, and while I found a way to manage it while we were at work, our having this picnic together roiled things up all over again. How could I possibly reconcile this with the way I felt sitting at the piano a few nights earlier?

"Was I supposed to bring a tent?" Ally said, referring to the vast amount of luggage I had with me.

"You can never be too prepared."

"I think there might be a point at which you can be."

"You haven't seen Reese eat yet. I'll bet you we go through every piece of clothing I have here."

"I think your daddy just insulted you," she said, holding Reese's face up to hers. He giggled and then tried to eat her nose. Ally laughed and then laid him softly onto the blanket. Reese immediately rolled over and propped himself up on his arms.

"Are we eating or playing on the swings first?" she said.

"I vote for eating. Reese got up at a quarter to six this morning, so breakfast was at 6:30. I haven't had anything since."

"Good thing you're hungry. I stopped at Mattarici's and got all kinds of antipasto."

Ally insisted on bringing the food. She laid out a collection of plastic containers filled with smoked mozzarella stuffed with sun-dried tomatoes, marinated roasted peppers, sautéed broccoli rabe, grilled vegetables, and cannellini and tuna salad, along with a wedge of parmesan and a loaf of Tuscan bread. I of course had a variety of mashed things for Reese, though he gummed a piece of crust through most of the meal.

The food and the increasing sunshine took the edge off for me. Ally was as relaxed and easy as she was during our numerous office conversations and we sat quietly, enjoying our meal and taking in the day. Reese seemed relaxed as well, satisfied to stay on the blanket, even though the wonders of grass, trees, and rippling water were only a few good rolls away.

"Mattarici's must be twenty-five minutes from your house," I said as we finished off most of the food. "You didn't need to go all the way there."

"Are you kidding? If I had gone to Subway, you never would have spoken to me again. It's time for the swings now, isn't it?"

We cleaned up and brought Reese over to the playground. Ally pushed him on a baby swing for what must have been a half hour, his reactions ranging from delight to a trance-like fixation on some spot in the distance. At one point, I moved to pull him out and he protested loudly. I stepped back and let Ally continue pushing.

Afterward, we got his stroller out of the car and went for a long walk, stopping for a few minutes to watch some Little Leaguers play a game and then allowing Reese to admire a squirrel for a while. On the way back to the blanket, he fell asleep with his head at a ridiculous angle, which had to be terribly uncomfortable. I never understood how kids were able to do that or how they weren't rubbing their necks for hours afterward. I took him out of the stroller and laid him down.

"How long will he sleep?" Ally said.

"Anywhere between ten minutes and three hours."

"Good to see you can pin it down so precisely."

"We've learned to live with each other's inconsistencies."

She looked over at him and touched him on the leg. "He's really adorable, you know."

"Yeah, I know."

"He smiles so easily. That says something."

"That he's woefully naïve about the dangers that surround him?"

She smirked. "I was thinking that it said that you've made him feel happy and secure." She leaned back on the blanket and raised her face to the sun. "I like watching you dad."

"I don't feel like I've done that much dad-ing today. After all, you were the one playing with him on the swing and pushing his stroller."

"I'm an easy mark because this is a novelty. You probably could have gotten me to change his diaper too if you asked."

"We'd have to know each other a whole lot better before I subjected you to that. There's something about him and sweet potatoes. Medical research could gain valuable information from one of those diapers."

She laughed and patted me on the hand. "Well I think you dad very well."

"Thanks."

We sat together and watched others entertaining themselves in the park. Two kids who couldn't have been more than five tried to play catch with a rubber ball, though neither seemed to have the requisite eye-hand coordination to do it well. A family barbecued sausages while eating huge slabs of watermelon. A mother and her children played tag. An older couple walked slowly arm in arm. A pair of teenagers necked on a bench.

The sun asserted itself in the increasingly insistent way it did in June. I felt cocooned, happily insulated from anything other than the world inside our blanket. Reese's nap was a brief one, probably not more than twenty minutes or so. When he awoke, he propped himself up on his hands and knees and grinned broadly at us. Ally was right. He did smile very easily. When he made eye contact with me, his entire body shook, landing him back on his stomach. But he got up immediately and then, completely unexpectedly, moved toward us.

"Oh, I didn't realize he was crawling," Ally said.

"He wasn't," I said, moving closer to Reese, leaving a shorter distance for him to traverse. "This is the first time."

Reese had been rocking on his hands and knees for more than a week now, but before this, he hadn't been able to propel himself forward. He flopped on his face a moment later, but was up and moving again right after that. I had little doubt that he'd be circumnavigating the family room before the weekend was up.

"This is *very* exciting," Ally said, joining me on her hands and knees next to Reese.

"Tell me about it."

I was at work the day Tanya crawled for the first time and I didn't get to see her do it myself for nearly a week. This was much, much better.

"I feel very privileged to be here for this," Ally said.

Eventually Reese crawled over to me and I pulled him into my arms. "Yeah, me too." While I held him, Reese's head swiveled to take in the world around him, as though he understood that it just got considerably smaller.

* * *

The crawling thing lent an air of celebration to the rest of the afternoon. It's funny that we find something so inevitable so delightful. Of course, Reese would crawl some day. He'd even made it clear to me that the day was imminent. But still, when it happened, it was momentous. And the best thing about it was that *he* didn't know it was inevitable. For Reese, crawling had to be a remarkable new discovery, like fire had been to the cave men or the double helix had been to Watson and Crick. I'm sure the possibilities this new skill afforded dazzled him, and my guess was that he went to bed dreaming of this new mode of transportation that night.

Suffused with excitement over my son's crossing this threshold, I did yet another impulsive thing, inviting Ally to come back to the house for dinner. The three of us were having such a good time together that it seemed pointless to end it in the late afternoon.

I prepared the food while Reese and Ally played on the floor in the family room. Now that it was time to cook, I worried about what to make for her. I had stopped by the fish store on the way home and bought some scallops, but how to prepare them was still very much in question. I didn't want to send the wrong message by making something too terribly formal, and I certainly didn't want to push myself beyond the limits of my talents and fall flat on my face in front of her.

Ultimately I decided we'd start with some orecchiette with artichoke hearts and that I would sear the scallops and serve them with a simple lime butter. There was some asparagus in the refrigerator and I roasted this and made some red rice with almonds to go on the side. I hoped that this evenly balanced my desire to make this dinner casual with my desire to show off a bit.

"You see, this is total alchemy to me," Ally said as we ate. "I kind of wish I watched you make this, but I got a little distracted." She looked over at Reese, in his high chair painting with his barley cereal and bananas. "I know it happens all the time and I've read thousands of articles on the subject, but I just don't see how a person takes these ingredients and makes something that tastes like this."

"There's really very little mystery to it."

"Not to me there isn't."

I was very glad that Ally appreciated the food. I knew I had done at least three things wrong with the food, but she either didn't notice or was too polite to say and I was thankful regardless. I loved cooking for people and had made meals for hundreds of dinner parties over the years. But in doing so, a certain level of complacency had set in. It wasn't that I did-n't care whether people liked what I prepared or not, but rather that I assumed I cooked with at least enough competency to avoid offending anyone. To some degree, that was enough for me. But I really wanted Ally to like this meal. I wanted her to notice how the lime enhanced the sweetness of the scallops, which caused me to use more zest than I should have. I made the asparagus too salty because I wanted her to see how the Arbequina olive oil played against the *fleur de sel*. And I shouldn't have served rice as a side dish after making pasta as an appetizer. But this was a kind of rice I had just gotten online from a small grower and I wanted to impress her with my ability to seek out rare ingredients.

Ally seemed nonplussed by Reese's regular interruptions during our meal. We could barely exchange sentences between his dropping his spoon on the floor, making a variety of noises at the top of his lungs, and otherwise calling attention to himself. This had become part of the backdrop of mealtime at home for me, but tonight I was much more conscious of it; Ally and I usually talked together undisturbed. But she didn't seem fazed by the patchwork way in which we communicated tonight. In fact, she seemed charmed by it.

There was little question that she was taken with Reese. She fooled around with him throughout dinner and even when she was talking to me, she would grab his feet (which he thought was hilarious) or make funny faces at him. This was a bit of a trip to the candy store for her.

But what was more interesting to me was that Reese seemed completely comfortable with her. He was in full-blown separation anxiety mode at this point in his life and he had no patience for anyone who wasn't Lisa or me. Even Codie had a problem with him recently when I left the room. But I could have taken a trip to Aruba and Reese would have been fine with it as long as Ally was around. When she took him from my arms to let me unload my stuff at the park, he went to her without a complaint and they were inseparable after that.

This pleased me. Until this moment, sitting at the dining room table with a son who smiled easily and could now get from here to there on his own and a woman who gave me lots of space while at the same time engaging me, I didn't realize how much I missed feeling good. How much I needed more than a temporary reprieve from sorrow. This was a startling revelation.

I was glad Reese liked having Ally around, because by this point I was hoping she'd come to visit often.

* * *

Ally was sitting on the couch in the living room reading a magazine when I returned from putting Reese to bed. She'd tucked her feet beneath her legs and she leaned against the armrest. This was the least animated I'd ever seen her, and if anything she was more beautiful in repose. I watched her for a moment until she felt my presence and looked up.

"Is he down for the night?" she said.

"You might as well be asking me the meaning of life. Reese's sleep patterns are entirely unknowable."

She swung her legs around and I sat on the couch.

"I had a great time today," she said.

"So did I." I nodded toward the hallway. "Reese too. He told me he was going to ask you to go steady with him."

"Wow, I was hoping he'd feel that way. Do you think you could let him know that I like him too and if he asked me nicely, maybe . . . ?" She let her voice trail off in pitch-perfect middle school girl fashion.

"You two are on your own now. Want some coffee or something?"

"No, I'm fine. Dinner was great. I'd ask for the recipes, but then I'd feel obligated to try to cook them and all those artichokes would have died in vain."

"Maybe we can cook something together sometime. It'll take the mystery out of it for you."

She smiled. "I'd like that. Though I don't mind the mystery."

I sat back on the couch and looked off into the medium distance, not really focusing on anything.

"If I told you that I wanted us to be more than friends," she said, "would that totally freak you out."

"It might."

"I think I still have to say it."

I turned to her. "I'm not at all sure that I can handle this."

Her eyes dropped and she nodded.

"The thing is," I said, "I really want to be able to."

She looked up at me and what I saw in her eyes was something I had no idea I wanted that badly until exactly that moment. It said that she understood, at least in some way, what this meant to me and that she cherished it. It said that she wasn't playing with me and that this was a big deal for her as well. It said that I was safe with her. I'm not sure what she saw in my expression.

She leaned forward to kiss me and as our lips touched, I not only responded, but savored the act, willing it to last as long as possible. I reached out and she poured herself into my arms. I was as hungry for the embrace as I had been for the kiss. We kissed this way for a long time and the longer it continued the more desperately I wanted it. I had no idea how much I was starving for this until it happened.

After several minutes, Ally pulled back slightly and touched her hand lightly to my face, looking deeply into my eyes at the same time. It was a remarkably tender gesture and whatever level of restraint I maintained was gone.

Ever so slowly, like people who believed they had limitless amounts of time, we made love. Each step progressed slowly from the previous one. Not because we were tentative or afraid – at this point, I set aside every thought other than those of Ally – but because we wanted to bask in that particular moment. I wanted to feel our bodies together at various phases of undress. I wanted to touch her over and over again and explore each stroke's differences and similarities. It was only toward the end, when the energy built inexorably between us, that our movements intensified and crested. I had been numb for so long that this level of sensation was nearly overwhelming.

We held each other on the couch for a long time afterward without saying anything. I wanted to tell Ally what this meant to me, but I didn't have those words. I simply pulled her more tightly against me and hoped that this would speak for me.

Eventually we made our way into my bed. I held her close and stroked her hair while her fingernails played across the small of my back. Occasionally we kissed some more, but we barely spoke. Conversation truly didn't seem necessary.

At some point, we fell asleep in each other's arms and were still together that way around 3:30 when Reese woke us up with his crying. I don't know what awoke him, but he seemed unusually rattled by it. I knew that kids began to have nightmares around this age and I assumed that's what was happening. I walked with him, sang him a song, and allowed him to rest his head on my shoulder while he calmed down. But when I put him back in his crib, he cried again before I even left the room. I knew there was only one way he was truly going to settle.

I carried him into the bedroom. Ally was propped up on her pillow.

"Is he okay?"

"I think something spooked him while he was sleeping."

"Poor guy. Is he up for good?"

"No, he'll get back to sleep. But only if I let him lie next to me. Is that too weird for you?"

She sat up in bed as I put Reese down on the mattress. "Do you want me to go home?"

"No, not at all. I mean, I would completely understand if you wanted to, but I'm certainly not asking you to leave."

"Let's just see if we can get him back to sleep then."

I put Reese between us and slowly, as he always did, he worked his body next to mine. Predictably, he was asleep within minutes. I reached over for Ally and saw that she was sleeping as well.

I tried to get back to sleep myself, but the minutes and then the hours stretched in front of me. At some point, I realized that I wasn't going to get another wink.

I used the time instead to try to make some sense of everything that had happened and everything that was happening.

FIFTEEN - *Subversive Thoughts*

"What would you do if I ever died?" Maureen had said to me several years ago, sitting on the couch. I guess most married couples have this conversation at some point in their relationship.

"I'd regret the fact that we didn't increase your life insurance."

She punched me on the arm and I kissed her on the top of the head. "After that."

"I'd probably spend most days wandering around looking for you."

"Would you mumble anything while you were doing this?"

"I'd just call your name over and over again. Eventually the police would come."

"You're not taking this seriously."

"Seriously? I don't have any idea what I would do if you died. I'm not entirely sure that I'd survive it. It would be like those stories you hear where one spouse goes and the other follows a few days later."

She looked up at me and held my gaze for several long moments.

"Really," I said.

"I don't want you to talk like that."

"We've been together since we were nineteen. I'm not sure I could even walk correctly if you were gone."

"But you'd eventually figure it out, wouldn't you?"

"I might need a cane."

"Don't walk around with a cane if I die. Maybe just a black headband or something." She kissed me surprisingly passionately at that moment and then sat back.

"You wouldn't feel the same way?" I said.

"Maybe for a week or so, but jeez, you gotta move on." She looked up at me and smiled. "Of course I would."

I held her tighter. "Because I'd want you to. I mean, I know the thing I'm supposed to say is that I'd want you to be happy and all of that, and I'm not saying that I'd want you to be miserable for the rest of your life. But to be honest, I'd like my loss to be a big gaping hole for you."

She squeezed my arm and didn't say anything for a minute or so.

"I could still enjoy chocolate, right?"

"As long as you thought about me while you ate it."

* * *

When Ally left late the next morning, I attempted to distract myself by playing on the floor with Reese. But I was kidding myself. Of course, I thought about what happened between us the night before. To say the least, these were not simple emotions. Almost simultaneously, I felt giddy and melancholy, liberated and guilty. Making love with Ally had been a joyous experience made all the more joyous by the fact that it was entirely unexpected. The only problem was that I was also completely convinced that it shouldn't have happened.

It wasn't just about feeling like I cheated on my late wife. I felt that I became smaller in my own eyes by allowing myself to do this. I'd never considered for a second that something like this might happen a mere five months after Maureen was so suddenly taken from me. I wasn't that kind of person and we didn't have that kind of marriage. I knew that for an absolute fact.

But at the same time, it would have been absurd to try to hide my feelings for Ally from myself. I liked being with her, I liked talking to her, I liked touching her. When Reese responded so well to her, it tickled me, and I loved the fact that I felt instantly better when she was around. I didn't ask her to come into my life. In fact, at the point at which she did, I was entirely incapable of inviting anyone in. And yet she still managed to reach me. That had to mean something.

And she had reached me in a profound way. I spent much of that Sunday imagining her there with Reese and me. When we went out in the car, I imagined myself talking to her in the passenger seat. When we stopped at the park, I saw her pushing Reese on the swings and making him giggle. As I made dinner that night, I wondered what she would think of the meal I'd made and what she was eating. And when I went to bed, I still felt her next to me. Ally moved me. *Where* she moved me was something I was more than a little confused about. But she unquestionably moved me.

For the last five months, the strong embrace of grief confined me. It wasn't a comfortable or comforting place by any stretch of the imagination, but at least it was a *specific* place. The hold loosened ever so slightly Saturday night. It certainly wasn't that I felt any less pain over losing Maureen, but I allowed myself to feel emotions that had been gone so long they might as well be new ones. I felt passion, desire, and even a brief bit of exultation. And because of this, I didn't particularly know my place any longer. Could I be the grieving widow if I wanted another woman the way I wanted Ally? Could I be the guy with the weight of the world on his shoulders if I had so recently felt so good? I knew it wasn't going to be easy to move forward with Ally, that I would feel doubt and recrimination every step of the way, that I was quite possibly doing it solely because I couldn't stand being miserable any longer. But I also felt a very real urge to move forward with her, at least a few steps. This was baffling and downright scary.

After putting Reese to bed, I turned to Tanya's journal. Last night was the first time I didn't write a word in it since I started, and the realization of that set off yet another wave of guilt. *I didn't write in the journal I created for my daughter because I was too busy sleeping with a woman who wasn't my wife.*

Something surprising happened last night. You know, at this point I probably should have figured out that life doesn't come with a script, but if someone told me a year ago that I would be writing in this journal because you disappeared from my life and that while doing this I faced the consequences of having a girlfriend, I would have told that person to seek professional help.

Yes, I said having a girlfriend. I'm not even sure that guys my age are allowed to use that term. The last time I had one, your mother might have been referred to as a "girl" in some circles. Ally's not a girl. She's 36 and she's smart and attractive and she makes me think subversive thoughts – like that I don't need to feel awful for the rest of my life. When we became friends at work, I just felt comfortable talking to her. When we went out on an ill-advised date about a month ago, I had a great time and then got scared to death and retreated. But then we spent the day together yesterday and that surprising thing happened. And I'm seriously thinking about continuing it.

I've tried to imagine what you would think of this if you knew. I've tried to imagine your face when you read this, assuming that you ever do. I'm worried that this would be the final straw for you, the ultimate confirmation that your dad was a pretender who never really cared for the people he said he loved. And I'm worried that I wouldn't know how to defend myself. What would I say? That I love your mother? That she occupies a huge place in my heart and always will? Of course I do and of course she will, but what can I say to you to convince you that these sentiments aren't diminished by my involvement with Ally?

And what can I say to myself?

That Tuesday, Reese and I went out for pizza with Tate, Zak, and Sara. While formal restaurants were out of the question for a while with my impatient son, I wanted him to get accustomed to the rhythms of eating in public places. I loved going to restaurants and I wanted to pass this along to him.

This was Tate's night during the week with the kids. Gail had insisted on it. They argued back and forth about whether Zak and Sara would sleep at Tate's during the week and finally settled on his bringing them back at bedtime. Tate was still too furious and too wounded to give me any clear sense of what exploded in his marriage, but what was obvious at this point was that Gail wanted things from him that he either couldn't or wouldn't provide. I still didn't know whether she tried to make him understand her needs along the way or if she just let her frustration build until she couldn't take it anymore.

I couldn't help but notice the kids differently, especially after taking care of them that afternoon a few weeks back. The breakup changed their lives dramatically and they would feel the effect of this for the foreseeable future. This made them realer to me, less accessories of Tate's and more individuals with delicate and tattered psyches. Zak's reaction was to try to act older than his age, though he remained fascinated with

Reese's baby food. When they all wanted different things on their pizza and Tate fumbled over how to negotiate this, Zak worked it out with the waitress. Later, when Sara grew frustrated over how long it took the food to come, he produced a coloring book and crayons and played with her. Meanwhile, Sara seemed to be going in the opposite direction, talking in baby talk and seeming unusually captivated by Reese's toys.

Tate was as befuddled and oblivious as ever. I never knew him to fluster easily, but he was getting progressively worse in this regard. He didn't even seem to have much of an appetite, which was entirely out of character, though at the same time I noticed that he'd put on a few pounds.

We always could talk easily. This was one of the tent poles of our friendship. No subject was off limits between us and I sometimes found myself telling him things that I didn't realize I felt strongly about until we started talking. I told him about the date I had a month ago with Ally, but I hadn't mentioned her since. But now it seemed necessary to do so and I really wanted to talk to someone about this.

"Ally spent the night on Saturday," I said after the pizza arrived.

"Ally?"

"The woman at work I went out with that one time."

He arched his eyebrows. "Jeez, really?"

"Yeah, really."

"And?"

I looked at him crossly. "You want details?"

"Yes, and please be as graphic as possible, especially in front of Sara. What did it *feel* like, you moron?"

I cut a piece of my pizza crust to give to Reese. "It felt like seventeen things at once."

"Name five."

I shut my eyes for a moment to search for a way to convey what I felt. "It was exciting and fulfilling and mind-blowing in a very real way."

He snickered. "If you have seventeen things like that, you're a lucky man."

"It also felt insanely confusing, bittersweet, and more than a little frightening."

"Not as good."

"No, not as good."

Tate's eyes narrowed. "You think it's too soon, right?"

"The thought has crossed my mind several thousand times."

"But you also think you want to keep doing this."

"More than I ever thought I would."

He shrugged. "Sounds like you gotta play it out."

"You don't think less of me because of this?"

He frowned. "First of all – huh? And second, what the hell difference does it make what I think?"

"I rely on you for honesty."

"I'm *giving* you honesty."

"Okay, so here's the other thing I wonder. Of course, I feel guilty over getting buzzed about a new relationship so soon. But what if I've blown my feelings for Ally entirely out of proportion out of some desperate need for companionship?"

"You need to stop thinking so much."

"Yeah, *that's* gonna happen."

"It has to happen. You can't resolve this by thinking. Just play it out. If I remember correctly – and forgive me if I haven't memorized every detail of your personal life these days – Ally is a very nice person. She's also, I assume, a consenting adult. In other words, she might be great for you and she can take care of herself. There are no rules about this stuff."

I waved a hand at him. "Ah, what the hell do you know about it?"

"Nothing. What do *you* know about it?"

"Exactly the same."

"So I recommend that you stop asking my opinion and you stop asking *your* opinion."

"It's not that easy."

"No kidding."

We settled into the pizza and then Sara asked Tate to take her to the bathroom. Zak and I talked about his soccer team while he repeatedly picked up the pizza crust that Reese repeatedly threw on the floor. Throwing things on the floor was a big thing for Reese at this point.

When Tate returned, I said to him, "Any new lunch dates?" He had told me that the woman he spent the afternoon with while I watched his kids had come and gone. As did a few others.

"Nothing on the calendar this week. I have a couple penciled in for next week, though."

"There's no chance I could do what you're doing."

"Why? What I'm doing is easy. What you're doing is way, way harder, my friend."

"I don't think I could trot out my story for a continuing procession of women."

"Trust me, I don't trot out much. Before it gets to the story stage, I usually move on to the next one in line."

"What's the point?"

"You didn't do a lot of dating when you were single, did you?"

"You know all about the people I dated."

He shook his head sadly. "I was convinced you were holding out on me. Let's just say there's a certain recreational value to playing around that you might have missed."

"Are you telling me to sow my wild oats?"

"The truth? I'm not telling you anything. Just giving you the view from my side of the fence."

At this point, Sara whined that Zak didn't allow her to play with Reese. It seemed like a very good time to ask for our check.

As we left the restaurant, Tate put his arm around my shoulder and drew me closer to him. He never did that before. I smiled over in his direction.

"You can call me later with the graphic details if you want," he said.

"Yeah, wait by the phone."

He laughed and pushed me away.

* * *

I called Ally that night after putting Reese to bed. We talked for more than a half hour. I brought her up to date on Tate and his situation and she told me about dinner with another member of our team. She said my name came up and it took everything in her power to avoid giving away details about our new relationship.

I never liked talking on the telephone for any length of time. I saw telephones as a medium for conveying essential information. Anything more than that was unnatural. But I really liked talking on the phone with Ally. The conversations weren't forced or artificial; I didn't struggle to come up with things to say. And when we talked, it really felt like she was in the room with me, something else I never experienced before. Still, it couldn't replace having her next to me, holding me. Toward the end of our conversation, I told her that I missed her. She told me that she missed me as well and said she could come over if I wanted her to. I wanted her to, but I wasn't entirely sure I was ready for it. That would necessitate introducing her to Lisa in the morning and that stopped me cold. I told Ally I was tired, which was certainly true, and that I was going to crash early. She seemed a little disappointed – I think the idea of an unplanned evening rendezvous was exciting to her – but she said she understood.

I felt miserable after I hung up. Like I'd missed out on something. Like I said the wrong thing. Like I was letting her down.

This was yet another set of emotions I'd put in deep storage. And I wasn't nearly so happy about bringing these out again. I hadn't worked on a relationship in a long time. But still, I knew I could.

SIXTEEN - *Visiting with Royalty*

Ally slipped into the side door of my life and made herself at home without moving any of the furniture. Whether we played with Reese (or attempted to stay just slightly ahead of him on his mission to pull everything onto the floor), read to each other from my new subscription to *Food and Wine* (or snickered at the hopelessly inept new restaurant reviewer for *Newsday*), brainstormed catalog ideas (or cajoled each other over preposterous concepts), or tossed epithets at the television screen during Yankee games (or celebrated a frustratingly rare victory), Ally quickly wove herself into the fabric of my life. She spent a number of weeknights at my house and most of every weekend. She and Lisa became fast friends, and Lisa even stayed for dinner on a couple of occasions. We even made plans for a vacation together in the late fall.

We decided not to announce our relationship at work, though it wasn't a state secret. Ben knew what was going on, as did Ally's assistant. I was also relatively certain that some of the people on the team knew we were together and maybe Ally's boss, though no one actually said anything to me. I wondered what my colleagues thought about this. Were they happy for me that someone as great as Ally had come into my life, or were they furrowing their brows? I set these questions aside, along with the numerous others that mounted in that place in my mind that I fenced off. I needed to take Tate's advice and let this play out. And I had to be less concerned about what everyone – including me – thought.

Our physical relationship was electrifying. Our lovemaking was an utterly holistic experience; I could feel it on any number of levels at once. I wanted to touch Ally constantly. I took inordinate pleasure in twining her fingers with mine or wrapping our legs around each other's while we lounged on the couch. I had convinced myself that my lustful urges mellowed over the years, replaced by what I considered the deeper satisfactions of comfort and affection. But Ally aroused me in an almost unearthly fashion. This wasn't just pure sexual desire. It was more like meta-intimacy.

And it was most surely intimate. While it would have been foolish – absurdly foolish, as it turned out – to say that I knew everything about Ally in our first month together, we were hungry to experience as much of each other as we possibly could. We always talked in bed after making love, sometimes for hours. About inconsequential things, about topical things, about things that happened during the day to one of us, to someone else we knew, or even to the Yankees. I loved these conversations, even the most trivial of them. Ally's voice sounded different to me late at night, almost incantatory.

We talked more about Maureen as we spent more time together. Ironically, I was a little self-conscious about doing this at first. Since it wasn't acceptable to me to understate how much I loved my wife, I tended to give the briefest possible truthful answers when Ally asked about her. Finally, she confronted me about it.

"Do you not want me to do that?" she said.

"Do what?"

"Ask you about Maureen."

I held her closer to me, though doing so meant that we could no longer see each other's eyes. "No, of course you can ask me about her."

"As long as you can respond in sentences of no more than four words."

"Do I do that?"

"Every single time."

I kissed the top of her head. "I'm afraid if I start that I'm not going to be able to stop."

"Why do you need to stop?"

"Because it's hard for me to imagine, after making love, that you want me to tell you how completely devoted I was to another woman."

Ally propped herself up on one arm. "But I do want to hear it."

"Why?"

"Because it's you. Because she kinda fills this house and I want to have a better sense of her. Because she's Reese's mother. And because I actually want to know what it's like to be that much in love."

"You've never been that much in love?"

"We're not talking about me now. And besides, even when you aren't saying more than four words about her I can tell that *most* people have never been that much in love."

I held her a little tighter. "She was everything."

"Do you think you could be a little more specific?"

"I don't think so. I mean for nineteen years, it was-n't just that my world revolved around her but that my world *became* my world with her. You know, I really only started living when we started dating. So we did just about every significant thing together."

She reached for my hand and squeezed it. "That must be incredible to have with a person."

"It was. Incredible."

She tilted her head up to mine and kissed me. "Never feel like you can't talk about her. I want to get to know her more. Maybe the two of us can become friends in some kind of spiritual sense."

I laughed. "That's just what I need, the two of you getting together at some cosmic coffee shop and snickering over my shortcomings."

"I won't snicker. Chortle every now and then, maybe, but never snicker."

"You're very kind."

She hugged me. "I mean it. I want Maureen to be an open topic between us. I know you think about her. There'd be something seriously wrong with you if you didn't. So let me think about her as well."

"As long as it doesn't freak you out."

"Everything about us freaks me out."

I sat up a little when she said that. "It does?"

She pulled me toward her. "I don't consider that to be a bad thing."

* * *

The next day, the check for Maureen's life insurance policy arrived. It took an inordinate amount of time because the company kept asking for more information and each time they did, I put off providing it. At one point, they even sent me a notice saying they were "closing the case" (which I don't think they could actually do, legally) because I was being unresponsive. When we took out the policies, I never bothered to think about the details involved in cashing one in. I never for a second thought I needed to think about this.

But now, more than six months after I found her lying dead in our bed, I stared at a check for a considerable amount of money. I refused to see this sum as the equivalent of the value of Maureen's life because there weren't enough digits in the world to represent that figure. What this number did mean, though, was that Reese (and Tanya if she returned) would have plenty of money for college and we could weather my unemployment if Eleanor Miller suddenly decided they no longer needed me.

I decided to spend one very tiny bit of this money on a present from Maureen to Reese. For days, I thought about what Maureen would choose if she'd had the opportunity. It had to be something he could enjoy as a child but hold dear to him later. I ultimately decided on a spectacular cherry rocking horse handmade by an artisan in Rhode Island because it reminded me of the painting that Maureen bought for Reese just weeks before she died. I imagined this horse becoming a family heirloom – one of the antiques she loved so much – passed down from generation to generation in the memory of Maureen Rubato who would have galloped off into the sunset with her son if fate had been kinder.

While we were in the craft store, I spotted a gorgeous handmade autoharp. I strummed a few chords and the sweetness of the sound sent me back to days in Washington Square Park, sitting against a tree with Maureen in my arms, listening to someone playing a Joni Mitchell song. It was April and warm enough to make us want to be outside, but cool enough to need the warmth of each other's bodies. Maureen said that I was at my softest while we held each other like this. And she told me now that she wanted me to have this autoharp – and to play something from *Ladies of the Canyon* in memory of her.

So I bought it too. Maybe I could learn to play some of my old songs on it. Songs sounded different when played on a new instrument and they would certainly sound different coming out of this beautiful piece of artistry. Maybe I'd even write some new ones. That was a fitting thing to do with this gift from my wife.

* * *

I'm sure your mother told you how we met at NYU, though I doubt her memory of our early days matches mine exactly. She was on the entertainment committee and I was just back from the club tour I did with the band. She wanted to hear us play and I told her about a gig we had coming up at a club in the city. She tried to clarify herself and I finally realized that she wanted us to audition for her. I snickered and told her the names of some of the clubs we'd just played. I then told her that I wouldn't audition for my own school. She wasn't pleased with this response and I assumed I would never see her again. I shrugged it off with the attitude I was full of at the time, but this really felt unfortunate because I wanted to play on campus and your mother was always really great looking.

You can imagine my surprise when she showed up at the club a few nights later. She came to me after the show and told me she thought we were "pretty good." Then she laughed. Much later, I found out that the laugh meant that she actually thought we were very good.

We had a drink at the bar and then ultimately pancakes at a seedy diner at 3:00 a.m. By my second cup of coffee, I was certain that I was in love. It wasn't just that your mother was gorgeous and that she became more gorgeous when she talked about things that mattered to her. It was that I was thrilled to be in her presence. It's impossible to describe this unless you've been through it yourself, but I knew that what was going on here wasn't just physical. There was something elevated about the whole experience, like I was visiting with royalty or had been granted an audience with John Lennon.

I swear I became nicer from that moment on. My friends probably thought that it was your mother "straightening me out." But the real reason was that I understood that by being a jerk with her the first time we met, I ran the very real risk of alienating her completely. Can you imagine what I would have lost?

I wanted to be with her every second after that. I swear I thought about marrying her when I walked her back to her dorm that early first morning. This was a huge shock to me, as finding a permanent relationship was somewhere around 87th on my to-do list. But while I might have been guilty of arrogance at this point in my life,

I definitely wasn't stupid. I went out with enough women to know that your mother was like absolutely none of them and that I could consider it a decent life if I dedicated mine to keeping her happy.

One of the Big Lies about relationships is that they require a lot of work to keep them alive. I don't think anything ever came more easily to me than loving your mother. Of course, we had rough patches. Of course, there were times when we didn't see eye to eye. Of course, there were days when she pissed me off pretty badly (and I'm sure many more when I pissed her off worse). But loving her and wrapping my world around her was always a breeze.

I guess I can officially say now that our love lasted forever. How's that for a horribly bittersweet notion?

SEVENTEEN - Capers

On a Saturday in mid-July, Ally and I took Reese to his first game at Yankee Stadium. Like so many other things I did with him at this point – talking to him about my day, describing various items around the house, explaining why I couldn't allow him to do certain things – it was more to get us accustomed to the behavior than because I thought he derived anything from it. I wanted him to feel natural and comfortable amongst the large crowds that gathered at Yankee Stadium and I wanted live baseball to be a meaningful part of his childhood. He still seemed surprisingly attentive when I had the television tuned to a game. And the plush ball I got him for Opening Day was still one of his favorite toys, both to throw and to teethe on.

The drive to the stadium was a hassle, as always. Construction slowed us on the L.I.E. and more construction did the same on the Cross Bronx. This meant that by the time we got to the Deegan, there were huge lines to get into the parking lots. As painful as this experience was, I knew it would be worse going home. For this reason alone, I didn't go to nearly as many Yankee games as I wanted to over the years.

"Does Reese get his first taste of a hot dog today?" Ally said as we took our seats in the loge along the first-base line.

"He just might. Of course, what he would love is the Cracker Jacks, but they're a major choking hazard."

Reese seemed fascinated with his surroundings. This was by far the largest crowd he'd ever been in and certainly the noisiest (and this was before the game). I got a little nervous on the drive because our crawling along made him impatient and he fussed for most of the last forty-five minutes. But now that we were here, his eyes were huge, and he seemed just stunned by the immensity of it, standing on my legs, looking out toward Monument Park and working his mouth into an O. Then just as suddenly, he flopped down onto my lap and began gnawing on my index finger.

The first baseball game my father and uncle took me to was a Mets game, since we were Long Islanders and the rest of my family were Mets fans. The Mets beat the Chicago Cubs 4-0. The details of the game I know only from the scorecard I kept in my room until I moved out of my parents' house and still have in a box somewhere in the basement. But my sense memories are very strong: the smell of the grass and french fries, the blustery voices of fans unaccustomed to winning, the vibration of the stands when the Mets scored a run or staved off a rally.

I also remember the way my father and uncle talked to one another during the game, seemingly arguing while actually sharing the same point of view. This is a form of communication particular to sports, maybe even particular to New York sports. Even if you rooted for the same team, you showed your true dedication and knowledge by saying everything combatively. It took me a little while to understand that my father and uncle weren't actually angry with each another, and then the rhythms of this peculiar method of discussion appealed to me. My father and I took it to an entirely new level later when I became a Yankee fan, and then we actually *did* argue, though we managed to constrain our most vocal differences to the playing field.

If Reese became a Mets fan when he grew up, would I take it personally? Rooting for the Yankees was an essential part of my makeup, like loving the Beatles or Gorgonzola cheese. Tanya's ambivalence about baseball (or Maureen's for that matter) didn't bother me because they were choosing *no* team, not *another* team. But if Reese became a Mets fan, especially after I shared my passion for the Yankees, would I see it as a betrayal? If he became a Red Sox fan, I could only interpret this as an outright act of rebellion, but there wasn't anything this clear about the Mets.

It wasn't worth worrying about. This was a special day at the stadium: "The Kid" was coming to the Bronx. Last night, they called Bobby "Kid" Kitterer up from the Scranton/Wilkes-Barre Yankees to make his first start in right field. He'd compiled monster statistics in half a year at AAA – a .340 batting average, 23 home runs and 57 RBI's – and Yankee management decided it was foolish to give him any more "grooming" time. And the team unquestionably needed a boost. They were only two games over .500 and six games behind the surprising Toronto Blue Jays in the American League East.

"I can't believe we lucked into seeing 'The Kid's' first major league game," Ally said.

"I know. I've been following him since he had that big year with Staten Island. I just knew he was going to do something."

"Let's hope he's for real."

"He's for real. He has all the tools: the swing, the arm, the legs. The only thing that might mess him up is if New York scares the hell out of him."

Ally and I didn't argue/talk when we spoke about baseball, but it was still nice to have someone with whom to share this. Earlier in our friendship, it tickled me to have a "buddy" with this common interest. But now it was more than that, something we built evenings around and called each other about during the day.

The Yankees took the field and the crowd cheered wildly.

"This would certainly scare the hell out me," Ally said.

Reese bit my shoulder. His teeth had been slow to emerge, but I felt the first little bud this morning and at this point he chewed on everything in the vicinity.

As the first Kansas City Royals player stepped into the batter's box, the Bleacher Bums in right field began their "roll call." Starting with the left fielder, they called the name of every Yankee in the game except the pitcher and catcher (who had other things going on at that moment) and continued to do so until that player turned in acknowledgment. It was a long-standing tradition, one of the many that elevated the Yankees' relationship with their fans. They saved Bobby

Kitterer for last and when he turned and waved, the crowd in the bleachers roared. Even this crowd, who had seen so many special players and witnessed so many dramatic sports moments, felt that this was a signal event. It probably wouldn't have seemed this way if the Yankees had a ten-game lead, but regardless of the reason, it made "The Kid's" (and of course, Reese's) first game a festive one.

The Yanks gave up three runs in the first. The same problem that plagued them all season. No one understood why, but their starting pitchers consistently began poorly before straightening out. As a result, the team regularly played from behind and all too often never caught up.

Kitterer's first three at-bats were unremarkable. He popped up to third on the very first pitch he saw, grounded to second his next time up, and struck out on three pitches his third. He saw five pitches total in his first three times at the plate and looked jumpy. He did, however, make a gorgeous running catch with two runners on to end the fifth, bringing the crowd to its feet.

In the bottom of the seventh, the Yanks were down 4-3. Reese decided that hot dogs weren't to his liking and that bouncing up and down on my legs was much more entertaining than anything happening on the field. He was so well behaved and I only needed to get up to walk with him a couple of times, but it was obvious there were many things he would prefer over sitting in a box seat for three hours. I tried to keep him occupied while watching the game at the same time.

A strikeout and a very close play at first left the Yankees with two outs and no one on when Kitterer came up again. He watched a ball in the dirt and then another up and in. The Royals pitcher then made a significant mistake, leaving a ball out over the plate. The Kid pounced on it, sending it six rows deep over the right field fence. The entire crowd jumped up when he hit the ball, and after it sailed out of the park, Ally kissed me hard before turning back to the field to scream her approval. Even Reese looked out and smiled as Kitterer rounded the bases, though it was probably because he just caught the glint off a mustard package.

The score remained tied as the game went into the bottom of the ninth. The Yanks blew a huge opportunity the previous inning, failing to score with the bases loaded and one out. But this inning, with one out and a man at first, Kitterer came to the plate again. He fouled off five 3-2 pitches in a row before driving the eleventh pitch of the at-bat into the right center gap. The ball went all the way to the wall and by the time the relay throw arrived at the plate, the Yankees had won the game 5-4.

It did in fact take more than an hour to get out of the parking lot, but the time went much more quickly than usual. Ally and I listened to the post-game show on the radio and relived Kitterer's last two at-bats repeatedly. There were other Yankees to applaud – a bullpen that provided four scoreless innings of relief, a couple of great plays in the infield, the timely hitting that got them back into the game – but a new Yankee legend had been unveiled. He could hit .183 and be back down in Scranton by August, but for now, he was larger than life.

"Reese, you're a lucky boy," Ally said, patting him on the knee. He clapped in response, showing nearly as much dexterity in doing so as "The Kid" had shown in the bottom of the ninth.

* * *

It was of course a trudge back to Port Jefferson. We even hit a construction delay on 347 only a few miles from the house. Reese, unquestionably fed up with his hours in the car, flat-out screamed for the last fifteen minutes of the ride in spite of our best and varied efforts to appease him.

I planned pasta *puttanesca* for dinner. But when we got home and settled Reese down, I discovered that we didn't have any capers.

Ally sat at the kitchen counter next to Reese's high chair, helping him eat some pureed peaches. "Can you make it without them?"

"You can have your food magazine subscriptions suspended for a question like that."

"Wouldn't it just be a different dish?"

"Yes, a blander, much-less-interesting dish. We need to go to the supermarket."

I moved to get Reese out of his high chair. I hated the idea of making him get in the car again. He would probably cry the entire trip.

"Why don't I just stay here with him?" Ally said. "He could probably use the break. Do you mind if we hang back?" She looked at me with Reese's spoon still poised in his direction. But he had lost interest in eating and had both hands in his bowl.

"No, that would be great, actually. You might want to get a washcloth before you pick him up, though."

The roundtrip to the supermarket was mercifully quick. I certainly understood Reese's frustration with being stuck in his car seat. At this point, the last thing I wanted to do was drive again. But you really needed capers to make the dish right and I looked forward to it all afternoon.

Ally and Reese were no longer in the kitchen. As I put the capers on the counter, I heard a loud thump followed by my son's full belly laugh. I found them in the hallway. Ally was crawling next to the baby and then she suddenly collapsed comically onto the floor. Again, Reese found this hilarious. They turned in my direction.

"We've been doing this for the last fifteen minutes," Ally said.

"Exactly this?"

"Pretty much. I think the kid has a taste for slap-stick."

She crawled forward again and Reese crawled next to her. Ally did her pratfall and Reese cracked up. This could go on indefinitely.

I went back to the kitchen, and while I chopped tomatoes and put the pasta water on to boil, Ally and Reese played on the floor together. She did the crawling thing with him for another ten minutes before the joke finally wore off. After that, they goofed around in the family room while I finished getting dinner ready. Ally almost seemed disappointed when I told her it was time to eat.

"I'm loose now," she said after putting Reese in his high chair and sitting down at the dining room table.

"Loose?"

"Yeah, like after a great workout."

"Were the two of you doing aerobics?"

"Kinda. The baby version. He's very physical, you know."

"Sounded to me like *you* were very physical and *he* was very spectator-like."

She smiled. "Yeah. That's probably true." She reached over and squeezed my hand. "The two of you provide me with a lot of exercise."

She tried the pasta and nodded. "Yum, great. Definitely needed the capers; I don't know what I was thinking." She looked over at Reese's high chair and the teething biscuit he was working on. "Hey, where's his?"

Ally went to the counter and spooned some plain pasta into one of Reese's plastic bowls, putting it down on his tray.

"He won't eat it," I said. "Unless you snuck in some maple syrup while I wasn't looking."

As I thought, Reese regarded the bowl indifferently while continuing to gnaw his biscuit. Ally reached for a noodle and held it up to him. Reese looked at her and then took it from her hand, stuffing it into his mouth. A moment later, he took another from the bowl.

"I could tell he wanted it," she said.

> The first dish I ever cooked that you really loved was spaghetti with anchovies and garlic. Not butter and parmesan. Not macaroni and cheese. I made both of those for you and you were fine with them, but you really got excited about this new dish. Anchovies. With lots of garlic. You ate most of my bowl. You were three, I think. It was as if you

were saying, even then, "You don't need to treat me like a kid, Dad."

You always had a sophisticated palate and I loved that because it meant that we ate as a family. I didn't need to make one meal for your mother and me, and something flavorless for you. I remember the first time Tina Molson had dinner at our house, though. I made chicken cordon bleu – chicken, ham, cheese, nothing a kid hasn't seen before – and she looked at her plate as if I put a reptile on it. It was a good thing we had some hot dogs in the refrigerator or Tina might have called the police.

After that, we were always careful to make "simple" food when your friends were over. Marinara sauce. Burgers. Barbecued chicken. I thought it was so great that you were in on the joke – "Darcy's coming over, gotta make something easy." The only time we didn't have to do this was when Melanie had dinner with us. She was always my favorite of your friends and yes, it had a little something to do with my overhearing her tell you that she thought I was cool, but it had a lot to do with the fact that she ate like a real person.

You and I connected over food at a deeper level than we did anything else. Saturday morning shopping trips were our thing together. Menu planning was a major topic of discussion on Friday nights (at least until you stopped hanging out with us on Friday nights). We made some good meals together. And then there were all those lengthy conversations we had about restaurants and celebrity chefs. We talked about cooking the way other parents might talk to their kids about sports or pop culture or fashion.

The thing is, I don't know why we didn't connect on other stuff as well. Now that you're gone, I see you in me all the time. The music thing, of course. Movies too; you were the first person to mention Amy Adams in our house and you were totally right about her. I even noticed recently that we like many of the same colors and I have no idea how I missed that all these years. Maybe, back when things were fine between us, we both thought our shared interest in food was enough. Maybe if we bonded over all of these other things you might have felt you didn't have enough to share with your mother (though considering the way you two were together, you would have bonded over the Weekly Pennysaver).

The other thing is that I never regretted it until now. I'm supremely conscious of missed opportunities these days. Given what's happened, it would probably have made me insanely clingy if you were still around. Guess you got out at the right time.

But I made a great puttanesca sauce tonight. It's too bad you weren't there to have some of it.

EIGHTEEN - *Avenue*

"I'm going to ask you an extremely personal question," Codie said on the phone a couple of nights later.

"Go."

"Do you think you might have gone for me?"

"What?"

"Do you think, if circumstances had been totally, completely different, that I might have been the kind of woman to interest you romantically?"

"There are at least a dozen reasons why I shouldn't answer that question," I said tentatively.

"Jeez, Gerry," Codie said broadly. "I'm not coming on to you. I'm just having a little crisis of confidence and I thought I'd talk to a guy who would give me an honest answer."

"You're having a crisis of confidence?" This in itself was surprising. Codie had always struck me as one of the most put together people I ever met. That she was having a crisis of confidence about her attractiveness seemed like folly to me.

"I've been on twenty-eight dates this year. I counted the other night, if you can believe it. Of those, fifteen have been first dates, eight were second dates, four were third dates, and a whopping one was a fourth date. I haven't gone out with a guy *five times* all year."

"You might want to get help on the counting-the-number-of-dates-you've-had thing. As far as the rest of it is concerned, you're in a little bit of a slump, that's all. That happens with dating, doesn't it? And this hasn't exactly been a normal year."

"I know it hasn't. But I was too depressed after doing this bit of analysis to pull out last year's organizer. It wouldn't be much different. Or the year before that, for that matter."

"And you think this has something to do with you?"

"Kinda has to, doesn't it?"

"Yeah, I guess it does. But it certainly isn't because you aren't smart enough, beautiful enough, or a clever enough conversationalist."

"Keep going with the compliments. I can use them right now."

"Codie, have you thought about the fact that you might be a little *hard* on your relationships?"

She was quiet for long enough to make it clear that she hadn't considered this. "What do you mean?"

"How much do you talk about your job when you're on a date?"

"The normal amount."

"The normal amount for *normal* people or the normal about for Type A crazies like yourself?"

"What's your point?"

"How different are your first dates from a lunch meeting with a new client?"

Codie hesitated again before answering. "I know the difference."

"I'm sure you do. And I'm just guessing here based on, you know, a certain amount of insider information."

Codie sighed. "I don't know; you might be right. I mean, there's something to be said for dealing with the beginning of a romantic relationship like a business transaction."

"And it's worked so well for you."

"I came to you for counsel, not sarcasm."

"Sorry."

"And some of this – at least recently – is your fault and Reese's fault."

"Explanation, please."

"It's your fault because I figure if I can talk this easily to my brother-in-law, then there must be other guys in the world I can get this comfortable with. And it's Reese's fault because ever since we've been hanging out together, he has me thinking about guys as potential fathers rather than just playmates."

"But that's good."

"Yeah, I suppose. But it's kicked me from hypercritical to some level of critical that science hadn't previously identified. Not that I don't love both of you dearly and even kind of appreciate what you've done to me."

"This'll work itself out," I said softly. "It actually sounds like it's in the process of working itself out already."

"You think there's a fifth date in my future somewhere down the line?"

"Without question. And Codie?"

"Yeah."

"If circumstances were utterly, totally, a million percent different, I would have gone for you."

"You would have?"

"Yes. If you weren't my sister-in-law and if you didn't look mind-bogglingly similar to Maureen, I would have found you scintillating."

"Really?"

"Really. I mean, I still find you scintillating but, you know, not *that* way."

"That's unbelievably sweet."

She sounded happy. I was thankful that I could make her feel that way. "When are you coming out again?"

"Sunday?"

"Can't this Sunday."

"Next Sunday?"

"How about sometime this week. Wednesday?"

"Nope, date – like it matters. Tuesday? No wait I have that schmuck from Peregrine Communications. Thursday?"

"You're on."

"Kiss the baby for me. And Gerry? Thanks. You're a rare commodity."

* * *

"Lisa is here," Ally said. "Are you ready to go?"

I turned in my chair at the computer to see her at the door. "Yeah, I was just checking my e-mail."

"Anything?

"No, nothing," I said with a shrug. "You look spectacular."

I wanted to take Ally somewhere fabulous. Though we were together most of every weekend and several days during the week, we went out relatively few times. Ally seemed satisfied with the bifurcated evenings that existed before and after Reese went to sleep, and it was certainly the easiest way to go. But I didn't want our relationship to become so completely domesticated that we didn't have nights where we dressed up, ate slowly, and didn't have one ear cocked toward the baby's room. This was important to me. So I got us reservations at Chimera, easily the most elegant restaurant in Suffolk County.

Ally wore a blue sleeveless dress that landed just above the knee. I never saw her dressed this formally before and it was breathtaking. From the waves in her hair to the contours of the dress, she *flowed* and I noticed all over again how gorgeous she was. It was at times like this that the hungry teenager really took over in me. I wanted to undress her nearly as much as I just wanted to stare at her for hours. I got up from my chair, held her close to me, and kissed her deeply.

"Thanks," she said.

"No, really, thank you."

I had been to Chimera only once, several years earlier, and forgot how beautifully appointed it was. Everything in the room was a form of illusion, from the sheer curtains that divided the reception area and the dining room, to the candles at the tables whose flames somehow changed color, to the menus that revealed different items depending on how you turned them to the light. It was like being in some grand magical parlor and yet it managed to do this without seeming like a silly theme restaurant.

We ordered a bottle of wine and held hands across the table. It felt good to be in this setting with this woman. Saturday nights had perhaps all too quickly evolved into playdates with Reese, and I liked that we weren't wearing jeans, putting on funny faces, or getting down on all fours. Though the natural progression of our time together was increasingly comforting to me, there needed to be an element of *dating* to our dating.

"By the way," Ally said while we looked at our menus, "while you were in the shower, Reese said 'avenue.'"

"He said 'avenue'?"

"It might have been 'Evinrude.' Or it could have been 'am I nude?' I suppose."

"Any reason why he would have said any of these things?"

"He wouldn't explain."

Reese was trying out syllables for a couple of weeks now and recently began stringing them together. These seemed to bear no relation to the words we said to him and certainly no relation to anything he might actually want to say. I don't think he really understood the point of verbal communication yet, but he definitely seemed to enjoy the sound of his own voice.

"I wonder if he's going to sing well," I said.

"He'll need some work on his phrasing. Did Maureen sing?"

"She was terrible. Fortunately, she was fully aware of her limitations. No, if he has that gene, it came from me."

"You sing?"

"You don't know that I sing?"

"Was it in a brochure I forgot to read?"

"You've never heard me sing?"

"Along with the iPod. That doesn't count. Is the piano yours?"

"Yeah, the piano's mine."

"That's great. Maybe you can *serenade* me sometime. Wanna know what else he did when you were in the shower?"

"Algebra?"

She smirked. "Don't mock. He winked at me."

"You mean that 'hey baby, how's about coming over to my crib' wink? He does that to all the girls. I tried to explain to him that it's rude."

"You've seen him do it?"

"I was being sarcastic."

"I got that. But he *really* did it."

"I think the technical term is 'twitch.'"

"No, he really did it. I winked at him and then he winked back."

"You winked at him?"

"Yeah, I do that sometimes."

"You were making advances at my son?"

"You're turning a wonderful story into something smarmy."

I smiled. "No, really, it's great. Except I don't think kids can do that kind of thing at his age."

"He did it, I'm telling you."

I looked down at my menu, chuckling. "Did you notice him cruising around in the family room today? I think he'll be an early walker."

"Wouldn't surprise me in the least. He's already an early winker."

I laughed and then concentrated on deciding what to order.

"Are you starting to get upset about the fact that you haven't heard from Tanya?" Ally said as our appetizers arrived a little later.

"I'm way past upset. In fact, I think I'm so far past upset that it's manifesting as resignation."

"Trust me, you're not resigned. If you were resigned, you wouldn't be going to the computer every night or writing volumes in her journal."

Ally was right, but I was still utterly confused about my feelings. "It's just so damned empty," I said. "I literally have no idea where she is. She could be traveling with the Riverriders – they're in North Carolina tonight, by the way, I wonder if she stopped in on my in-laws. Or she could be *anywhere*. I mean, literally anywhere. She could be behind one of these curtains."

"I can't imagine how frustrating this must be for you."

I shook my head. "You know, I've gotten better about not carrying it around with me all the time. And writing in the journal helps. I'm surprised how much. But I've been hanging on to that very last bit of actual communication I had with her. You know, the message she left at the hotel? What if I'm interpreting it entirely wrong? Maybe she didn't mean for me to jump ahead to the next two lines of the song. There was absolutely no way she knew that I even *knew* the song. Maybe she just quoted the lines she did because she thought they were a graceful way to say, 'Have a good life.'"

Ally reached across and squeezed my hand. "What would you do if that were the case?"

"I can't even think about what I would do if that were the case. I mean, I've been clinging to this thread. It's amazing how little a person needs in order to delude himself."

I took a sip of wine and then a bite of my food. I didn't like the way I felt. For one thing, I intended this evening to be quiet and romantic. I didn't want these emotions roiled up at this moment. And yet I couldn't help myself.

"And then there's this whole thing about Mick," I said. "I can't get it out of my head that he's completely taking advantage of Tanya."

"I know you think that he's this seriously *older* man, but you have to keep in mind that he's essentially a kid himself. He's probably still working out a bunch of his own stuff."

"He's *a lot* older than she is."

"He is and he isn't. A little more than three years. Given the discrepancies in emotional maturity, they're the same age." Ally smiled at me. There was nearly the same amount of space in ages between Tanya and Mick as there was between the two of us – though there was a world of difference.

I took another sip of wine and tried to dial it back a little. "Did you ever go out with older guys when you were her age?"

"I was a senior in high school when I dated Vince Hemphill. He was twenty and he raced cars, which seemed unbelievably sophisticated to me at the time. That was the first time I really had my heart broken." She sat back in her chair and shook her head. "Vince Hemphill, jeez. We went out for five months and then suddenly he just clicked off.

I eventually learned that what really clicked were him and Maria Caruso."

"Did you have trouble getting over it?"

"Really getting over it? I think you could say it took a little time. A few months, probably."

"So Vince Hemphill got to you?"

"Yeah, he did. I mean in retrospect, our relationship was ridiculously shallow. A lot of making out in his convertible and groping at the movies. But at the time, it seemed monumental. He was the first person I ever said 'I love you' to other than my parents."

Hearing this made me feel uncomfortable, which surprised me. "So why haven't you mentioned his name before?"

"We haven't really had this conversation before." Ally was right. While I was certain it was standard practice for people to share their romantic histories with one another very early in a relationship, we never got to this topic. Certainly, my romantic history had documentation all over the house. But while Ally and I had lengthy conversations about Maureen, and what she meant to me, we never talked about the previous men in her life. At least some of this was because I didn't ask. But it was primarily because she didn't tell. We spoke in vague terms about dating, romance, and sex, but she never got more specific than that. I in fact knew more about her affection for the Yankees' shortstop than I did of any boyfriend she ever had.

"Let's have it now," I said, convinced that this would pull me back from where I was dangling thinking about Tanya and Mick. "Tell me about the great loves in your life."

She smiled. "There weren't that many loves. And for the most part, they weren't that great."

"No preamble. Details, please."

She seemed at once to be reluctant and eager to do this. And over the course of the meal, little of which I recalled later, Ally told me about the men who were important to her. The guy she went to the senior prom with and with whom she had an intense summer affair before they went their separate ways. The TA during her sophomore year of college who she discovered romanced three students at the same time. The friend of a friend who was one of her three roommates in her senior year and whose casual friendship became something much more meaningful for a short period. The man she lived with in her early twenties. And the man she thought she was going to move in with a few years later until she found out he was a little more married than he'd previously indicated.

This triggered a reaction in me that I didn't expect. I was fascinated because it painted in Ally's background. And I genuinely wanted to know as much about her as I could. But at the same time, it made me a little skittish. As the list went on, I kept wondering when it was going to stop. Given her age, it wasn't that Ally had been serious with a huge number of men, but I was unaccustomed to being with a woman whose dating history extended past college. I envisioned Ally laughing with these men the way she laughed with me, talking about her desires the way she did with me, making love with them the way she did with me, and I found I didn't want these thoughts in my head. I remembered feeling some jealousy over Maureen's past boyfriends, but that was a lifetime ago. And those thoughts faded completely as we built our life together, a life I knew she had never come close to sharing with anyone else. But this was something entirely different.

"And then there was Philip," Ally said. "The guy who had me picking out china patterns – literally. We were together for three years. It was beautiful and intense and it sure felt like the real thing. When he asked me to marry him, it was the single most romantic experience of my entire life."

"Wow, you were engaged? What happened?"

Ally's eyes clouded over and she took a drink. I decided to do the same. "I thought I was pregnant and he completely freaked out. We talked about having a family, of course, but he wasn't thinking about having one *right away*. We had these huge arguments over it and I started to wonder if he ever wanted to have kids, and how I would feel about it if he didn't. And then, when it turned out that I *wasn't* pregnant, he freaked out even more. I mean, it was like he had been wearing a rubber mask the entire time we were together. I called it off and ran away. That's how I eventually wound up at Eleanor Miller, actually."

The procession of men who sat down at our table that night rattled me a little and I could swear this last one took a bite from my entree. I didn't say anything right away.

"Now you know," Ally said.

"Did you think you couldn't tell me about this?"

"Why do you say that?"

"Because you didn't tell me about it until now."

"We just never really got onto this subject."

"Ally."

She shrugged. "I'm a little sensitive about the Philip stuff."

I nodded and let it drop, though I didn't really understand what there was to be sensitive about. It seemed to me that Ally had every right to break things off with the man if they didn't see eye to eye about having children, especially because Ally's affinity for kids made it obvious that she would be a caring and dedicated mother.

When we got into the car after dinner, a dinner that had a tenor entirely different from the one I intended, Ally leaned over and kissed me gently on the temple. "It was good talking to you about this stuff tonight. Thanks for listening."

I smiled and kissed her. But I had to admit to myself that the experience was a little disquieting. I did-n't like hearing about Ally's other lovers and I didn't like having this new set of pictures in my head. I wasn't sure what this meant. Had I begun to feel possessive about her? Had the conversation of the last hour and a half altered my impression about her in some way? Or was this simply some dumb-ass male competitive thing that I preferred to consider myself too evolved to experience?

The one thing that was certain was that she found a way to divert me from my thoughts about Tanya and Mick.

We got back to the house and said goodnight to Lisa. Then we walked into Reese's room to check on him in his crib.

"He's such a gorgeous little boy," Ally said as we stood over his slumbering form.

He's looking more and more like his mother every day, I thought, but didn't say. I lay my hand lightly on his back, making sure not to rustle him. I turned toward Ally and saw that she was smiling down at him. "He is pretty cute, huh?"

"Yeah, he is." She kissed her finger and placed it on his forehead. "Sleep really tight, Reese-y."

Then she reached for my hand and drew me into the bedroom. She began undressing me as soon as we got there. We made love as hungrily and passionately as ever. In some ways, it felt as though we were doing it for the very first time. I wanted to make love to her since she walked into the library at the beginning of the night. Now I realized that through all of the conversation, even the parts that I found disturbing or uncomfortable, that desire had been simmering. I wanted all of her and I wanted it all at the same time.

And I had to admit to my conscious self – what little there was at that moment – that I was competing a little here. I wanted to show Ally that she never had a lover like me before, that Vince, Philip, and all of the others in between couldn't come close to my combination of experience and attention. It was a ridiculous reaction, of course, and hopefully one that Ally remained entirely unaware of. But it was definitely there.

We kissed for a long time afterward, much more than we normally did. I felt energized and not at all like sleeping. I thought we might stay up and talk into the morning, and while I knew that Reese would make me pay for this later, I didn't mind. But then Ally snuggled into me and told me she was suddenly very sleepy. Within a few minutes, she was out. I held her against me, stroking and kissing her hair.

As I did, I started to think about Tanya again and, believing that I was a long way from sleep, I got up to write her.

I know you thought I hated Mick from
the moment I met him. You wouldn't
be entirely wrong about that. But I

don't think you completely understood why I hated him. What I hated about Mick was that he was the antithesis of everything good about you. He was Darth Vader pretending to be some kind of postmodern James Dean.

The part that I missed – because, frankly, I wanted to miss it – was that he was the first guy who stole your heart. Regardless of who he was and how horrible, that still had to be really exciting for you. I wish I were able to step back for even a millisecond to see that from your point of view. It's such an enormous moment.

My first real girlfriend was Belinda Madsen. Sophomore year of high school. We sat in the back of the room in chemistry class making increasingly ludicrous drawings of the teacher in each other's notebooks. It took me months to realize that what we were doing was flirting and I didn't actually ask her out until the spring dance. We dated – which primarily consisted of hanging out on the football field after school – for three weeks, during time she absolutely captivated me. I nearly failed a test because she distracted me so much. When I offered this as an explanation to my father, he said, "Years from now, which do you think is going to be more important to you: this girl or your education?" As it turned

out, neither was particularly important, at least as far as chemistry was
concerned.

You've been with Mick a lot longer
than I was with Belinda. And I'm sure
right now you consider him a great
deal more than a distraction. Interestingly, by the time you read this, you'll
probably be trying to remember what
he looked like, grinning about your little fling with him, or cringing over what
a jerk he was. I'll therefore dispense
with all of the "fatherly advice" I could
offer about the transient nature of
early romances. Sadly, I also won't say
what I should have said to you when
you were around about guarding your
heart. You'll have to figure that out on
your own.

You seem further away from me again.
As I write this, I feel like I'm doing it
only for myself. It's the middle of the
night and my mind is filled with all of
the things I could have done or said
differently in those last few months we
were together and I wonder how much
what I did say and do has contributed
to driving you away to stay.

It's all a little daunting to me. I just
want to reach you, Queenie. I just want
another chance to do a better job.

NINETEEN - Ready Is Always an Issue

Ally and I were outed at the office that Tuesday. Whenever she stayed over, we took separate cars to work the next morning and the voluminous traffic on 112 or the Nesconset Highway usually separated us at some point along the way by. Somehow today we stayed side-by-side the entire trip, parked only a few spaces from each other, and wound up entering the building together. Less than an hour later, Frank Marcus came into my office, closing the door behind him. Frank was yet another person Maureen and I went out with on occasion.

"You and Ally Ritten?" he said provocatively.

I looked up at him from behind my desk with an expression that I hoped conveyed confusion. He simply stood there with a half-smirk/half-smile on his face.

"Me and Ally Ritten?" I finally said.

"Do you know about the rumor that's burning up the halls this morning?"

"What would that be?"

"That you and Ally are *a thing*."

I felt my stomach roil. I didn't want to have this conversation with Frank Marcus. I understood it was inevitable that I would have this conversation with someone. I just didn't want it to be someone who looked as bemused as Frank looked right now.

"Ally and I are dating, if that's what you mean by *a thing*."

Frank sat down in the chair opposite my desk. "Man, really? You and Ally?"

"Do you have a problem with her?"

"Ally? No, she's terrific. I just didn't expect you to get – "
he leaned forward in his seat " – back in the saddle so soon,
you know?"

"Could you make it sound just a little more tawdry,
Frank?"

He threw up his hands. "No, hey, I'm certainly not judg-
ing you. I mean I loved Maureen – who didn't? – but you're a
young guy and you've gotta get on with your life."

This was going worse than I imagined it would. Certainly,
I assumed that some of my colleagues would be surprised
and maybe even a little dismayed that I became involved with
a woman so soon after my wife's death. How could I blame
them? But I guess I really hoped that the people who chose
to address it with me directly would be more compassionate,
maybe even suggesting that they were happy that someone
had come along to make me feel a little less sad.

"You're saying this is hot news in the halls?"

"There are literally people standing near water-coolers
talking about it. When does that ever actually happen?"

I closed my eyes and willed Frank out of my office.
He was enjoying this much too much and I didn't understand why. Frank and his wife went out with Maureen and
me enough times to understand what she meant to me. He
couldn't possibly think that I had just tossed her memory
aside to be with Ally.

"It's cool, Gerry, really. I just thought you'd want to hear
from a friend before someone else barged in here."

A friend. Yes, a friend who I hadn't seen away from work
since the funeral. "Yeah, thanks Frank. It's good to be fore-
warned."

He stood up and patted my desk. "No problem, buddy.
And listen, I hope things go well with you and Ally. Like I
said, she's terrific."

Frank left and I called out for Ben.

"It's not on CNN yet," he said as he entered, "but I hav-
en't checked their website."

"Is this really the kind of thing that gets this building
motivated?"

"Seems to be."

"No wonder we're having a lousy year. Is everyone enjoying this as much as Frank is?"

"Hard to say. I probably don't hear any truly nasty stuff because I'm your assistant and everything. I also try to do the 'above it all' thing, so I get left out of the loop a lot."

"I'm proud of you."

"Thanks. I assume you want the door closed as much as possible today."

"Yes, please." Ben turned to leave. I stood up to follow him. "I'd better go check on Ally first."

I don't think I was ever more uncomfortable walking through the halls of Eleanor Miller than I was at this moment. I imagined every person I passed revising his or her opinion of me on the spot, visualizing me as the happy widower partying the night away with his new squeeze. Even when someone stopped me to ask about the specs on a product, I convinced myself that what this person really wanted to do was ask was whether or not Maureen had been lowered in the ground before I bedded another woman.

I turned into Ally's office and saw someone from the finance department I barely knew standing there with her. She smiled at me and turned to Ally to say, "I'll leave the two of you alone."

"We've been found out," I said.

"I know," she said, smiling and kissing me. "Elaine Dunham has the fastest pipeline in the business."

"How did Elaine Dunham find out?"

"I told her."

"You *told* her?"

"She saw us walking in together and said that it looked like there was something going on between us. I figured it was silly to lie to her at this point."

"You did?"

Ally tilted her head and moved to sit down behind her desk. "We've been together a while now, Gerry. Were you planning on keeping it a secret indefinitely?"

"I thought we agreed to decide together when to tell people and how."

She sat back in her chair and I leaned against one of her walls. "Why is this a problem?" she said.

"It's not a problem. But it is an issue."

"Gerry, I'm extremely happy with what we have between us. It's hard for me not to share this with the people I spend so much time with."

"And if you had told me that, we would have talked about how to let people know. Having Elaine Dunham turn it into a breaking news story probably wasn't the best way. There are people here who have known me since Tanya was in second grade."

"And you're worried about what they think of you."

"I'm *not* worried about what they think of me."

"Of course you are."

I put a hand out. "Yes, I am. Is that such a terrible thing?"

"Am I a fling?"

The question seemed to come from some other conversation entirely. "What?"

"Am I a *fling*? Did you just assume that this was a little dalliance and that it would be over soon and you'd never have to mention it to anyone?"

"I didn't assume anything."

Her face got hard. "Gee, thanks."

"I didn't mean it that way. I meant that I literally didn't *assume* this relationship. I never thought it would happen and once it did, it just took on a life of its own."

"So it could be a fling."

"It's not a fling. I don't have flings."

"You haven't had a new relationship since the first George Bush was President. How the hell would you know?"

I sat on the edge of a chair. "I know."

Ally looked down at her desk and shook her head. "I was actually having a lot of fun this morning."

"Ally, Frank Marcus leered at me when he asked me about it."

She reached out for my hand and I took it. "Sorry," she said.

I squeezed her hand and then released it. "Hey, they say there's no such thing as bad publicity." I kissed her softly on the top of her head and squeezed her shoulders for a second. She looked up at me and I bent down to kiss her again. I couldn't get Frank's expression out of my mind.

On the way back to my office, I stopped to see Marshall. There was a chance that word hadn't gotten around to him and he might actually appreciate hearing it from me first. Of course, he was on the phone and of course, he was agitated. I asked his assistant to let him know that I came to see him, but as I moved to leave, he called out to me and gestured me in. I sat across from him and waited until he ended his call.

"The good news is that your new comforter is selling through the roof," he said when he hung up the phone. "The bad news is that we've grossly underproduced it and will be out of stock for six weeks. Do you know how much I'd pay for something to go well *without qualifications* right now?"

"Hey, at least it's selling."

"No, it *was* selling. Now, it's *not* selling because we don't have any to sell."

I stood up. "This isn't a good time."

He gestured me back down. "If you wait until a *good* time to talk to me, we may never speak again. What's going on?"

I leaned forward a little. "Listen, I wasn't really ready to go public with this, but it happened anyway and I want you to hear it from me. It's about me and Ally Ritten."

Marshall laughed. "I've known you've been boinking Ally for weeks now."

"Boinking. *That's* the word I was looking for to describe our relationship. How'd you know about this?"

"You don't get where I am without having a first-rate intelligence system."

"Does this involve cameras and listening devices?"

"Yeah, because I spend all day and night thinking about your personal life. What's your point with this little bit of info?"

"It's an inter-office thing. I thought you might have some concerns."

"And if I did and I told you that I wanted you to end it for the good of the company, would you do so?"

His attitude threw me a little. "That's a little extreme, don't you think?"

"Then any thought about my *concerns* really isn't an issue, is it?"

"You know, Marshall, there was a time not that long ago when we could actually have a conversation."

This seemed to give him a moment's pause. But then he leaned forward in his chair and said, "Gerry, believe me when I tell you that I don't give a shit who you're screwing. My assistant can be giving you lap dances for all I care. Hey, if you're gonna go out with anyone, it might as well be someone from here. Might make you think about work a little more."

I stood up again. I felt angry and a tiny bit humiliated. "That's all I came here to say."

"Thanks for the update."

I turned and headed for the door. As I got there, Marshall called out to me. "You ready for this?"

I looked back at him. "Sometimes ready isn't an issue."

"Don't fool yourself. Ready is always an issue."

* * *

I remember the first time I played one of my songs for someone else. I'd played it to myself dozens of times and imagined it with a full production and the backing of world-class musicians. But having someone else in the room made me hear it again the way it actually sounded and I realized the song needed considerably more work.

Presenting our relationship to my colleagues had the similar effect of causing me to see it anew. And where I let pure emotion and a certain amount of relief carry me for a couple of months, all kinds of things that I'd sublimated came rising up again. It wasn't that I felt ashamed that others believed I'd moved on from Maureen's death so easily or that they thought this was a worthy topic for gossip, but that this forced me to confront my own ambiguities. I suppose it was just a matter of time before this happened. At some point, I had to realize that I couldn't run away from my own most intense feelings, and there was so much that was still unresolved.

This forced me to face two daunting questions: was I ready for the world to perceive me as part of Gerry-and-Ally as opposed to Gerry-and-Maureen? And was I ever going to be able to get to that point? For whatever reason, whether it was my being overly concerned about what other people thought or how going public made me "hear the song a different way," this event made me look at what I was doing with Ally and wonder if I'd let it go much further than I ever should have. People coming to the company now would know me as someone who dated someone else in the office rather than as someone who was married for nearly two decades to a remarkable woman who died much too soon.

And I didn't want Maureen's memory diminished like that. Not in the minds of others. And certainly not in my own mind.

But at the same time, this wasn't just about choosing not to move on anymore. Ally was here, she was real, and I had very strong feelings for her. I didn't float along the past two months because I decided to take a vacation from grieving. It happened because she got to me. She inspired me to believe in enjoying myself again. She excited me and seduced me. She befriended me and captivated me. She wasn't just a playmate for Reese and me. She was someone I cared about deeply. A more cautious man never would have let it get this far. But I was way past the point where I could do anything about that.

This was difficult stuff. No easy answers were available, nor were any forthcoming. For two months, I gave my head and heart a reprieve from the consternation and the complications. It was impossible to continue that way.

This is not to say that I didn't try. Not knowing the best way to deal with this with Ally, I went with the easiest available short-term solution: I did absolutely nothing. That night, when she asked me how I felt about what happened, I shrugged it off, telling her that surprise made me apprehensive earlier and that, as the day went on, I gained some perspective.

It also helped that Reese was especially diverting. He was now an expert at cruising and thought it was hilarious that he could make his way completely around the coffee table. He did this literally dozens of times, picking up a little bit of speed with each revolution and laughing loudly and pounding the table. Later, when he tired of this exercise, he grabbed a stuffed animal and chomped down on it. When this elicited a chortle from us, he did it again, glancing over to make sure he was still getting a reaction. He did this easily ten times before crawling over to me to pick him up. He obviously loved being the center of attention, but he also seemed to be a born entertainer. Maybe this meant he would write his kids songs for their birthdays some day. Hopefully, what it really meant was that he would always keep the happiness of others in mind.

It would be healthier if this didn't include enabling his father to run away from his issues. But for one night, I appreciated it.

* * *

The next night, Codie came over again for dinner. Though we talked on the phone nearly every other day, it had been a couple of weeks since we got together. Seeing Codie after yesterday's events made my quandary much realer. I hadn't felt before as though I was lying to her by not mentioning Ally, but now it seemed absurd and dishonest. And here in front of this woman especially, the last thing I wanted to do was be dishonest.

I macerated plum tomatoes in olive oil and garlic all day, grilled some halibut, and tossed it all together with tagliarini, fresh oregano, and crumbled ricotta salata. I brought our dishes to the table, where Codie fed Reese his second bowl of ditalini. He'd decided since that night with Ally that starchy carbs were as acceptable as sweet ones.

"Listen, I have something to tell you," I said with probably more gravity than I intended.

"Tell me you're moving to Duluth and I'll break your arm right now," she said sharply.

"Why would I move to Duluth?"

"It was the first place I thought of."

"You have an interesting mind. I'm not moving. There's a woman." She tilted her chin forward exactly the way that Maureen did. This was more than a little disconcerting under the circumstances. "I've started going out with someone."

She twirled a forkful of pasta, but didn't bring it to her mouth. "Going out with someone the way *I* go out with someone or the way *you* go out with someone."

"I don't know how *I* go out with someone. The last time I went out with someone you became my sister-in-law."

"My point exactly."

"It's hard to say. I mean, it should be hard to say, right? We've only been together for a couple of months."

Codie's expression shifted and I swear that her eyes misted over. "You've been going out with someone for a couple of months?"

"I know. That sounds like a long time to me too when I say it that way."

"Wow."

"Do you hate me?"

"For not telling me about this sooner? Yeah, I think I might. I thought we had an everything-on-the-table relationship happening between us."

"I meant do you hate me for *doing* it."

"Why would I hate you for doing it?"

"Because of Maureen."

"*She* might hate you for doing it. Me? I think it's good for you. What's her name?"

"Ally. Why do you think it's good for me?"

"What's the alternative?" She looked over at the baby. "Reese doesn't need a dad in a cocoon."

"Saying I'm conflicted about this is a serious understatement."

She patted me on the hand. "Which is why I love you, Gerry. But feel what you feel. Don't worry about whether I hate you or whether anyone else has an opinion about this. Does Reese like her?"

"He seems to."

"Not as much as me, though, right?"

"She doesn't have as much money to spend on his affections."

Codie smirked. "He would adore me even if I did-n't bring him things." She fed Reese another spoon of his pasta. "Remember," she said to him, "I'll always be your aunt and I'll always be around to give you anything you want." She turned back to me. "She has no reason to take you to Duluth, right?"

"None that I'm aware of."

"And you really like her?"

"I think I really do."

"Does she have a brother?"

"Sorry."

She squeezed my hand again. "This is good for you."

"Do you think so? I'm worried about losing touch with my feelings for Maureen."

She regarded me skeptically. "Is that *really* a possibility?"

"I don't know what is and isn't a possibility. I wouldn't have thought that *this* was a possibility. For that matter, I never thought it would be possible to be sitting here right now with you instead of my wife."

She laughed quietly in that way that people laugh when they think of something that shouldn't be funny. "I can't answer that for you, Gerry."

I smiled. "Can you try? It would be a huge help." She looked down at her plate and twirled. "The pasta's good."

THE WORLD found out about Ally and me the other night. We were a hot story in the office for a couple of days. I told your aunt about her tonight and she took it well, though she may have been doing that for my benefit. Codie's really an amazing person. I'm not sure why I didn't notice that sooner.

Ally's an amazing person too, Queenie. She's been a real lifeline for me. I think the two of you might even like each other once you cross some ridiculously high hurdles (not the least of which include your never meeting at all for a variety of reasons). Your brother has been a tremendous diversion and inspiration, as has this journal. But providing care for someone isn't actually moving forward and worrying about someone certainly isn't. What I have with Ally gives me a different kind of direction.

I guess most kids have trouble imagining their parents with another partner. I can just imagine what you'll think when you read this. Romance is usually accidental – a matter of events conspiring to throw two people together. Certainly, it was that way with your mother and me, and it was with just about every relationship I had in my life. One rarely gets the opportunity to plan this kind of thing and logic never governs the way these things start. To say the least, I wouldn't have designed the scenario under which Ally and I started dating. There isn't a single thing about it that makes sense or is even advisable – except for the connection we have to one another. That makes an unusual amount of sense and while I struggled with the notion of being with her (still struggle with it, actually) it is impossible to deny that there is something significant there.

It may turn out that none of this amounts to very much in the end. Things might simply not work out between us. Or the considerable guilt and confusion I feel over anyone taking your mother's position in my life – even if only physically – might undermine it. There's an excellent chance that my ability to see things clearly was seriously impaired on a bitterly cold January night and that when I recover, I'll realize that everything I did since then was one massive case of bad judgment.

But regardless of how this plays out, the fact will remain that I made room in my heart for another person. One might have thought that I didn't have any room left in there between the space dedicated to your mother, you, and your brother, along with the annex I built to accommodate missing you and your mother. But it turns out there was still a spot available. Maybe the heart is like an expandable file, filling to accommodate everything you need to carry with you.

Hopefully it's not like a hall of mirrors.

BOOK THREE - Runaway Train

TWENTY - Scar Tissue

Dad,

This is probably going to make you insanely happy, but even still, I feel like I have to tell you. Mick and I have split up. You know, you freaked him out pretty badly that night in Pittsburgh (I know the feeling) and for a while back then I thought we weren't going to make it. I was a huge mess over Mom and he kept looking over his shoulder thinking you were going to show up with a SWAT team, even though I told him that you wouldn't. We weren't in any condition to have a relationship and I just wanted to be by myself while at the same time I wanted him to sit next to me and try to make me feel better. But we held on and some of the other people in the van really helped us out.

Things were okay for a while after that. I still think about Mom all the time, but I could finally go to a show again instead of sitting in the van by myself. And once

I started doing this, things between Mick and me improved and we really started talking. One of the millions of things you never understood about Mick was that he was a really, really good listener and his observations were unbelievably wise. We'd stay up late at night after the shows and I just told him everything that was going on in my head about Mom and about you and even about the baby. And doing it helped. We started to have fun again. That was another thing you never understood about Mick – he could be a ton of fun.

Then I went through this really horrible phase. Have you had stuff like this? I don't know what set it off, but I became obsessed with thinking about Mom and about the nuclear explosion that went off in her head and about how none of us was around to help her when she really needed us. It was all I could talk about and I would have these crying fits and these despondent hours and I said the same things over and over again.

I guess I did much more of this than Mick could handle. A few days ago, he sat me down, gripped me by the shoulders, and told me that it was time to "snap out of it." I burst into tears and told him that I couldn't snap out of it. And he told me that if that was the

case then we couldn't be together anymore. Things had gotten too real for
him and he didn't sign on for that. I'm
paraphrasing, but I'm sure you get the
point.

He told me he planned to leave the
tour after the next show. I told him that
I would leave instead. The whole Riverrider thing meant much more to him
than it did to me and I didn't want to
bring everyone else down. I left three
days ago. I'm out here now on my own.

This is probably better. I need the
time to myself – I mean completely by
myself. I've sort of gone from one artificial setting to another and if I'm gonna
make sense of my life and everything
that's happened, I need to do it entirely
on my own. Maybe then I'll finally figure a lot of things out.

I know what you're thinking. You're
thinking that you can look up the latest stop on the River tour and comb
the area for me. I waited to write you
until I was nowhere near Atlanta for
exactly this reason. I know you, Dad. I
know you're going to take this personally. You always did. I'm sure you think
you can help me, but you can't. I've lost
two gigantically important people in
my life. I'm sure I haven't even begun
to come to terms with what it means
to lose Mick.

Sorry I didn't write for all this time. I
didn't know what to say. I'll drop you
a note every now and then to let you
know that I'm okay.

And I will be okay. Eventually.

Hearts,

T

During one of our frequent discussions about Mick when he first started dating Tanya, Maureen reminded me that their breakup was inevitable. She tried to get me to remember that at seventeen, people never stayed together for any length of time. She asked me what I would do when that happened. I'm sure she assumed that this would help me visualize how much I was overreacting to everything. What I said was, "I'll party all night. It'll be like we won the lottery." She shook her head and walked away from me.

But now that the inevitable finally came – and much later than Maureen imagined – I didn't want to party. In fact, a new sense of desperation and frustration struck me. Because in splitting from Mick, Tanya had also severed that thinnest of all possible lines that connected the two of us. While before I didn't know that she was still with the Riverriders, I knew now that she was not. This meant that I once again had absolutely no idea where she was, who she was with, and what she was doing. And even more compelling, I knew that she was *somewhere*, a few days from Atlanta in the throes of unmanageable grief over her mother and unknowable upset over the loss of her boyfriend. Was she curled up on the side of the road? Had she thrown herself into the arms of another? Was she even more vulnerable to deceit and exploitation than she was at other times since she was gone?

Tanya was right. I wanted to run out right this second to track her down. But because she believed that I couldn't help her, because she insisted that I *not* help her, doing this was several levels beyond futile.

I stood up from the desk and once I did, I couldn't get myself to stop moving. I tried to sit back and think, but I couldn't stay in one place. I tried cleaning, taking a shower, playing the piano – all proved useless. My daughter could at this very moment be heaving with sadness and I wasn't there to put an arm around her. Because she actually thought it was better to go through this alone than to go through it with me.

How did I cause her to feel this way? How did I ever send the message that I wouldn't be there for her, that I wouldn't set aside everything to help her get through this? I'd given so much away. I let so much distance build up between us. And now, when I really believed I could help her, when I had learned things that could benefit her, she ran away from me yet again.

I called Codie first because she knew Tanya. We talked for a while, but I did little more than vent. Codie was no more capable of suggesting a useful strategy than anyone else would have been at that point, and I really wasn't capable of having anyone mollify me anyway. After I hung up, I called Ally. She volunteered to come over, but I demurred. I was much too agitated and I not only didn't want her to see me in that state, but I didn't want to think about how I appeared to anyone else at that very moment. Like Tanya, I believed this was something I had to handle on my own.

I eventually returned to the library. I read the message on the computer again, trying to glean some different meaning from it. When she said she thought she'd be better eventually, did this also mean that she thought she'd be able to reach out to me again sometime? Was there something for me to hold onto when she said that she would write to apprise me of her progress? I was ready to grasp at anything.

My eyes fell on Tanya's journal, still open to the page I wrote the night before, some rambling trifle about the difference between work and a job. I had written it to a different Tanya: a Tanya I imagined who was farther along in the grieving process and who was open to fatherly advice – a Tanya who would be interested in reading what I had to say to her. And I wasn't ready to let this Tanya go. She simply had come to mean too much to me.

With the image of her back in my home – or at least reachable to the point where I could send this journal to her – I picked up the pen and wrote.

I wonder about the scar tissue that builds up between people. I was never first in your heart and I never really had a huge problem with that. You adored your mother and I could hardly fault you for feeling this way, since I adored her as well. And the two of you spent a tremendous amount of time together in your early years. The time I could offer you was a trifle in comparison. Sometimes I would get jealous at being on the outside looking in, but you took such joy in each other – especially those first few years after you started talking – that this couldn't help but warm me. You were, after all, the two most important people in my life.

But there were also times when you actively relegated me to second-class status. I remember several occasions when your mother was busy and I was free but you insisted that only she could help you get dressed, peel you an orange, play Old Maid with you, etc. Sometimes I felt a little pin-prick from these snubs, sometimes even a little more than that. It was never a huge deal, but I wonder if even pinpricks will leave a scar if inflicted often enough.

After a point, I know I settled on my place in your life. I wonder if the scar tissue prevented me from trying harder to form a different connection with you.

In the last couple of years before you left, this manifested itself in new ways. I always loved you and admired you. I defended your right to question authority and make sure that you got to air your (sometimes ill-informed) opinions. But I didn't make as much of an attempt to explain myself to you when we disagreed. And to be honest, I didn't take it as hard when you blew me off.

You were less predictable (which in itself was very predictable) and though I never made a conscious decision about this, I became less willing to tolerate your inconsistency. Even when it came to Mick, I would get angry because of who he was or what he was doing to you, but I could step back from it. It never really got all the way through to me and because of that I never made the extraordinary effort that I should have made to help you see where I was coming from. And maybe get a better sense of what this guy meant to you and why you felt so compelled to stick with him.

In one of our rare screaming matches, your mother called me on this and I tried to explain that things were different for her with you than they were for me. She could negotiate these difficulties with more grace because the two of you had built up a lifetime reserve of affection. I truly believe you could have set her hair on fire and five minutes later the two of you would have been in your room hugging and talking it through.

This is on my mind now because I realize that this journal isn't just a place to say things to you while you are out in the world, but also to say things to you that I wish I'd said while you were around. You should know that I have never consciously withheld my love from you. I might have avoided entanglements and I might have walked away rolling my eyes on occasion, but I can't recall a single situation where you needed me (or could use me) and I wasn't there for you. And I know that I would be there for you now if you wanted me.

You probably won't recall it this way – in fact, you might not recall it at all – but one of my favorite memories of us together came when your mother and your aunt went away for a long weekend. You were nine and we hung out at the mall, went to the movies, and made ridiculously elaborate dinners together.

All of that was fun, and I remember having a great time, but those things weren't what put this memory in my top five. What did was what happened that Saturday when you came back from an afternoon with Carrie Nicholson (someone I never liked, by the way, but whom I let you form your own opinion about). You were unusually quiet during the car ride back from her house. When I asked you why, you told me it was nothing. You went off to be alone in your room for about a half hour and when you came out, your eyes were red. I asked what was wrong, and this time your face crumpled. You told me how Carrie made you feel awful about some social error you made at a party. We sat at the couch and talked it through. I explained that when people went out of their way to make someone feel awful it usually exposed a flaw in their personalities, not their target's. You didn't buy this right away, but we kept talking and after a while, you cataloged all the terrible things that Carrie did to other people. Eventually, we found ourselves laughing hysterically over the way Carrie's voice cracked during her big solo in the class musical – after she pranced around the entire week telling everyone that she was the star of the show. In the end, you leaned over, kissed me on the cheek, and said, "Thanks, Dad."

I would have moved Kilimanjaro for you at that point. This was a fantasy moment for me, the kind of thing I envisioned between us within days after you were born. I always wanted to be a person you could rely on.

But like all of these other moments in our lives, it didn't last. Your mother came back and I assume the next time Carrie or Leslie or Carolyn did you wrong you went to her. And I told myself that it was a great thing that the two of you were so close and that I didn't mind being a bench player. Even though I sorta did.

I got the message about your breakup with Mick tonight. And even though I seriously didn't like the guy (for reasons I don't think you've even begun to understand), I realize that this was an incredibly sad event for you. I'm not going to lie and say that I know just what you're going through because these feelings are absolutely and utterly personal. It's not even particularly useful to experience them yourself because the next time it happens it's going to feel completely different. That's the upside and downside of relationships – each one is unique and comes with its own collection of highs and lows.

The first time a girl broke my heart, I had the most maudlin possible reaction. I actually went to the record store to buy sappy breakup songs so I could play them in my room and sing them to myself. It was a totally over-the-top reaction, driven as much by my need to feel like the relationship was important as it was by any real sense of loss. The next time a girl broke up with me, my depression lasted all of about four hours because Vicki Krenski called that night and asked me to go to the movies with her. Of course, the time after that, I went into the mother of all funks and nearly split a band because of it.

The best news I can give you here is that at some point the roller-coaster ride ends and you leave the amusement park altogether arm-in-arm with someone who really matters. That's the way it was when your mother and I met.

I'm sorry Mick broke your heart. I'm sorry that as I write this you're hurting. But I'm not sorry that things didn't work out between you and Mick.

I also learned tonight that you split with the Riverriders and that you're off on your own. What's most unnerving about both of these pieces of news is that they happened because you're struggling with the death of your mother. I wish I could help you through this. I wish you'd let me. It wouldn't

be anywhere near as simple as making fun of Carrie's singing voice, but I
really think in this particular case that
there is no possible way you can learn
as much on your own as we could learn
together.

I'm not going to shrug this off, Tanya.
I'm not going to shake my head and
walk away. Whatever scar tissue there
was has been lasered away by what
we've both been through since October. If you ever, EVER need me, I'll be
waiting.

I closed the journal and sat with my hand over it for several minutes. I could do nothing to will Tanya home. But
if there was even a moment in the past few months when I
thought I was okay if she didn't come home, I knew now that
would never be the case.

I called up a map of the South on the computer and
stared at it. She was there somewhere. Even as I realized how
absurd it was, I thought about simply picking a location and
beginning a search for her. I thought about hiring a private
investigator or a team of them.

I realized for the first time that, though they were a roving band of neo-hippies, the Riverriders at least represented
a community of some sort, and I had convinced myself that
this community offered her at least a modicum of safety and
support. But now even that was gone.

Tanya had disappeared again into the fabric of the landscape.

TWENTY-ONE - *Home-Baked Goodness*

One of the constants in my life for a long time now was my lunches with Tate. Since he'd come back to Long Island, I don't think we ever went more than three weeks without getting together some mid-week afternoon. The tone of these sessions was materially different from any time we spent as a foursome with our wives. It was more confessional and in most ways more candid. I always assumed that this happened because it was easier to talk this way when there were only two of us and because when we were together as couples it was more about entertainment and less about checking in on one another. But given what developed between Tate and Gail, I suppose it was entirely possible that he simply couldn't be as open and accessible when she was around. It saddened me to think that he could have spent most of his home hours this way.

When we had lunch that Friday, I planned to have a long conversation with him about Tanya. Since I received that last e-mail message from her, I couldn't stop thinking about where she was and what she was doing. Never in my life did I feel more helpless. Over the years, Tate made me look at things from a new perspective and I was certainly open to this now, since all of my own perspectives on the subject were bleak. But a couple of minutes after we sat down together, I realized he had his own agenda.

"I've found a new job," he said.

"Wow, I didn't even know you were looking."

"The situation arose. I'm gonna be president and CEO of Highpoint Foods. You know; the Mr. Tasty people."

"Really?" I reached out to shake his hand. "That's great. CEO, huh? It's about time."

"Yeah, I crawled my way to the top," he said with a smirk.

I was genuinely pleased for him. I knew he needed a boost at this point nearly as much as I did. "I had no idea they were located anywhere around here. For some reason I always assumed they were out in the rest of the world someplace."

"They are. Their corporate offices are in Seattle." This stopped me cold. "I don't suppose Seattle is the name of a new neighborhood near the Hamptons."

"Washington, Gerry."

"You're moving to Washington?"

"In a couple of weeks. As you can imagine, once I gave notice my current employer didn't see much reason for me to stick around."

"You're moving all the way across the country? What about Zak and Sara?"

"They're staying here with Gail."

This made me angry instantly. "And you'll send them postcards?"

Tate put up his hands. "We worked it out, Gerry. It was actually the first civil conversation Gail and I have had since I left the house. I'm gonna fly back here one weekend a month. And then they're gonna come out to stay with me every July."

He presented this in such a matter-of-fact way. "So you'll be like their rich uncle or something," I said stiffly.

"Give me a break, will ya, Gerry?"

"You're gonna be a freaking appendage in their lives. They'll have a mother and an appendage."

I could see that Tate was a little surprised by my response. He shouldn't have been. But now he leaned closer to me and his eyes flared. "I'm their father. You think they're gonna forget that?"

"I think you're going to be making guest appearances as their father. Seattle? Why didn't you just take a job in Singapore?"

He reddened. "You know, this holier-than-thou thing can get old really fast."

I sat back in my chair to take the edge off this confrontation. The other choice would have been to take a swing at him. "Tate, do you really see yourself as someone who lives three thousand miles away from his kids?"

"Dammit, Gerry," he said, slapping his palms on the table. "I didn't just do this without giving it any thought." He turned away from me and for a moment, I thought he was going to get up and leave. He turned back and leaned forward. "I *suck* at being a single parent. Some of us are more adaptable than others. I can't just jump into the breach. I love those kids; I really do. But all three of us have been completely out of control when we're together." He looked down at the table. "I think I'm actually hurting them by being around."

"That's not possible. And you would work it out."

"We might. Or I might just keep screwing up. I don't want to take the chance. I went after this job, Gerry." He chuckled sadly. "I'll do a much better job as their rich uncle."

"They're your *children*, Tate."

"I get it," he said, his eyes darting up to meet mine again. "And every family is different. I'm gonna have to play this out my way."

I didn't want to concede this point, but of course, I didn't get a vote. Still, it rankled. Though I was less certain about most things now than I once was, I knew absolutely that I would never make the decision that Tate had made. He was giving up without a fight and leaving behind two kids who needed him far more than he realized.

"Do they know yet?"

"We spoke to them last night. I told them to pretend I was on a whole lot of business trips."

"They bought that?"

"How the hell am I supposed to know? They did-n't start crying or latch onto my leg or something, if that's what you mean."

I shook my head and neither of us said anything for a short while. Then I clapped him on the arm. "This stinks for me, too. I'm gonna miss you."

He patted my hand, and then reached for the beer he ordered. "Wanna come out for the month of August?"

"Yeah, maybe." I tried to get the waiter's attention to order a drink for myself. "Does Highpoint make any *good* food?"

"Hot n' Flaky Biscuits. Home-baked goodness in just eight minutes."

"Great, send me a couple of dozen cases," I said sarcastically. "You know, if you were going to abandon us, the least you could do is go someplace where I could get some decent freebies."

Dad,

I've spent the last few days in a college town and I actually kinda like it. A lot of bookstores and coffee shops and posters for concerts by people even I've never heard of. Discussion groups about everything imaginable. Yesterday, I got a job at a music store, a real independent with CDs from local bands playing all the time and an owner who thinks he knows everything about every WORTHWHILE song that has ever been recorded. Last night this guy came in who must have been in his early forties. He talked to Syd (the owner) for about a half hour about all kinds of music. I was working the cash register so I couldn't hear everything they said, but they were all over the place. I thought that you would like Syd. And then I realized that you could have easily been that guy that Syd was talking to. I remember how clueless most of my friends' parents were about music, but it was always pretty cool that you knew so much.

This town is okay. I don't know if I'm going to stay here or what, but it would be kinda nice to be in one place for a while. There are some cheap places to crash and there's lots of stuff to do. And when I walk around here, I kind of feel like there are a lot of other people trying to figure things out the same way I am. It's not like Port Jeff where everyone in school is trying to show everyone else how together they are. Out here, it seems to be okay to be a mess, even a little preferable.

Good thing, because I'm definitely still a mess. It's like that stupid joke where a guy goes to a doctor and tells him that his head is hurting. The doctor steps on the guy's foot and says, "Now you won't think so much about your headache." In my case, the pain in my head is Mom and the pain in my foot is Mick. (Gee, maybe Mick thought he was doing me a favor by dumping me.) They're both throbbing pretty much all the time, but one hurts just a little bit more than the other depending on where I am in the day.

At the same time, I'm getting these tiny indications that I might be doing a little bit better. Yesterday, I thought of something funny Mom once said to me and I smiled about it for something like twenty minutes. That's gotta be some kind of progress, right?

Syd's letting me borrow his computer, so I can't really take a lot of time here. Tell Aunt Codie that I'll write her when I get a chance. And kiss the kid for me.

Hearts,
T

* * *

Here's what I learned so far about the thing that you and I are going through about your mother: it never feels better. What does feel better is the understanding that you can keep living your life even though you know it's never going to feel better, and that there is still more joy to be found. I suppose in some way, you understood some of this intrinsically before Mick bolted on you.

It's so easy to for tragedy to defeat you. It's seductive in the way that I heard freezing to death is. Being consumed by grief is in many ways much more comfortable than battling your way out of it – especially when you realize that no matter how hard you fight you can't reverse the situation you're grieving over. But it's so important to engage in the battle anyway. It's really the only way to stay alive.

Admitting defeat is almost never advisable. Tate told me today that he's moving to Seattle because he got a huge new job. But a big part of the reason why he went after the job in the first place was because he didn't believe he could handle his kids as a solo parent. Rather than taking on a challenge that could very well beat him, he decided to throw in the towel. I have no idea what his future relationship is going to be with his children, but if this is where he is with them right now, it's hard to believe that the relationship will be a good one. I hope that you never shrink from tough situations, no matter how hopeless they seem. I can't tell you how often I have to convince myself of the same thing.

It's at least a small comfort to me that you're a little bit settled in this unnamed (new remailer, I noticed) college town of yours. Thinking of you working in a record store where smart "old guys" like your father shop is decidedly better than imagining you hitchhiking on some highway in the middle of nowhere. And yes, the thought did come to mind that I should try to call every independent record shop in every college town in the South and ask for Syd. I might still do it, but I'm holding off for now. I know that you don't want me to swoop down to drag

you home. And I know that if you come
home on your own we're both going to
be much better off.

See, I refuse to admit defeat. Even
when it's killing me.

* * *

Early the next week, as Ally and I watched the Yankees take
another pounding, Codie called.

"I'm not interrupting anything, am I?" she said.

"Ally's cursing at the baseball game on the television
right now and I was beating a pillow when the phone rang."

"This is something that you think is romantic?"

"People tell me I'm cute when I'm angry."

"Put Ally on the phone. I want to tell her to get out while
there's still time."

"Love you too, Sis."

She chuckled. "Listen, if you're not too strung out on
that stupid sport of yours to pay attention, I could use some
advice."

I stood up and walked toward the library where I couldn't
hear the TV. "Shoot."

"I need you to tell me if you think I'm losing my mind."

"I only occasionally think that."

"I haven't told you what I might be losing my mind *about*
yet." She waited a beat before continuing. "I'm giving very
serious thought to in-vitro fertilization."

I flopped down into a chair in the library. "That's sensational news."

"You don't think it's insane?"

"You're not going to try to buy a Nobel Prize winner's
sperm or anything like that, are you?"

"No, jeez, of course not."

"Then I really think it's great."

"You do?"

"*Really* great. World class great. Do it tomorrow."

"Too many meetings. Maybe the day after. You don't think being a single parent is impossible?"

"You're asking *me* this?"

"You don't think it'll seriously complicate my professional life and have a huge impact on every date I ever have, assuming I ever have another one?"

"Yeah, I think it'll do both. I also assume you've made peace with that."

"I *have*, but what if the baby comes and I realize that I didn't *really* make peace with it."

"You'll deal with it."

She sighed. One huge difference between Codie and Maureen is that Maureen never sighed. "You don't think I'll just be the world's worst mother?"

"That was a shameless bid for a compliment."

"It wasn't, actually. What the hell do I know about being a mother?"

"You'll be a sensational mother. I can tell these things. You're going to be and extremely good one. I knew this about you since you were in your mid-twenties."

"You did?"

"I could tell just by watching you with Tanya. You displayed more than *aunt stuff*."

"Wow, I had no idea."

"You're a natural."

"Thanks. This is because of you, you know. I probably would have sat on the fence the rest of my life if I didn't see you with Reese. You just make it look so possible and so worthwhile."

This touched me. I hardly considered my handling of Reese to be inspirational and I spent so much time these days beating myself up over what I did wrong with Tanya that I hardly thought about the kind of parent I was to my son. But if I helped Codie make this decision, I was glad. "So how do you go about doing this?"

"I went to a seminar about it a few days ago. It's really not that complicated, but if you take it seriously there are resources all over the place."

"And you just call the sperm bank and place an order?"

"Yeah, it's exactly like that," she said sarcastically. "More to come. I have a lot of research left to do. I'm really glad you're with me on this."

"With you all the way. Reese needs a cousin."

"Maybe you'll be my Lamaze partner?"

"I'd be thrilled. Of course, I'll warn you now that I'm a tough taskmaster. Maureen nearly threw me out of the delivery room."

"I'll bear up."

"I'm really glad you're doing this."

"I'm really glad you're really glad."

We talked a while longer and I found myself feeling better about this than I had about anything in a week. This was such a good decision for Codie, such an optimistic decision. I was proud of her for making it and glad she was moving her life in this direction.

Like me and like Tanya, Codie had been felled by Maureen's death. But she wanted to keep living and she wanted to make more of her life. I really needed to see this at this very moment.

TWENTY-TWO - *Veered Away*

As shaky as I was about Tanya, Ally and Reese at least offered me balance. Ally listened to me and worried with me and commiserated or debated, depending on what was necessary. And at some point, she simply pulled me away, taking me into her world and offering relief.

Reese was just Reese. Thank God.

Ally and I now referred to Reese as the "cruise missile" because of his ability to dash with unusual speed while holding onto tables, chairs, or whatever kept him upright. He even stood unsupported a couple of times before realizing he wasn't grasping anything and plopping to the ground.

The cruising thing became a game for him, made more exciting if I chased him around the coffee table in the family room. He found this hilarious and a few times lost his balance because he excitedly threw his arms out away from his body while we raced. Not wanting him to feel bad, I tumbled after him, and the two of us laughed while we lay on our backs.

"I wonder if Laurel and Hardy started this way," Ally said while she watched us. We got up and did it again. When we flopped this time, Ally came over and flopped on top of me, which got a huge belly laugh from Reese. Of course, she did it again. And, for that matter, three more times before I suggested another manner of entertaining my son. Ally reached across my body and snatched Reese up, rolling him over and tickling him while he laughed uncontrollably.

That afternoon, we'd bought him a little color-coded xylophone. I brought it over to him, showing him how to make a sound by striking the keys with a mallet. He smiled when I played a note, but didn't do anything other than that.

I put one of the mallets in his hand and helped him use it. This led to a volley of wild banging accompanied by his off-key wailing.

"Bet you can't sing as well as this," Ally said to me.

"Maybe not, but I can sing more quietly."

Reese put down the mallet and I picked it up, seeing what I could make of this toy instrument. I started to pick out the notes to the Beatles' "Here, There and Everywhere," which required some imagination since the xylophone didn't actually have all of the notes. Reese found this mildly amusing, but Ally was more interested.

"That's pretty," she said.

"I never played it on a ten-dollar xylophone before."

"Will you play some songs for me sometime?"

I nodded. "Yeah. Maybe after we get this guy to bed."

"I think I would like that."

I stopped playing and Reese took the mallet from me and put it in his mouth. I picked him up and raised him over my head, twisting him back and forth. He giggled, but as I looked up at him, he drooled down on my face.

"Can't let my guard down for a second," I said as I wiped my cheek.

As was often the case on Friday nights, we decided that "Reese needed ice cream" and drove off to the local Ben & Jerry's. He didn't get more than a lick of our cones (though he would have eaten much more if given the opportunity), but he seemed happy and we were more than satisfied. Then it was back to the house for a few crawling races before it was time for the baby to go to bed. As had become our ritual, Ally sat in the rocking chair with him and read from a book. After this, Ally usually left the room while I sang him a couple of songs and put him in his crib. On this night, though, he snuggled into Ally's chest while she read and he was asleep before she finished. She looked up at me, bemused, and then leaned down to kiss him on the top of the head.

"I guess we wore him out tonight," she said with a dreamy smile. She lay him down in his crib and then walked over to me and put her arms around me. "That was nice."

There was no question that Ally was smitten with Reese and he with her. She was a willing audience for every trick or gesture he performed. And there were mornings during the week when she was late getting into the shower because she couldn't pull herself away from him. Recently Reese had trouble sleeping through the night again and Ally not only accepted bringing him into bed with us – the only way he would go back down – but she even seemed to welcome it. At the same time, Reese was more openly affectionate with her than anyone other than me. He loved playing with her face and gumming her chin, and he was tolerant and amused by just about anything she did with him, whether it was rubbing noses or her flipping him around on the couch.

His falling asleep on her warmed her in a way that I hadn't seen before. She was even more tender than she usually was the rest of the night. She just cuddled with me on the couch with some music playing softly in the background and she didn't even seem particularly interested in speaking. And when we finally went to bed, she made love to me with more softness and affection than ever before. She fell asleep shortly thereafter, and I swore I saw an entirely new level of contentment on her face. I kissed her on the cheek and lay my head next to hers. I was glad that she felt this way and glad that I could play the part in this that I did. In that one moment, everything made sense to me.

True to form, Reese woke up around 2:30 and spent the rest of the night with us. I knew that in some way it was a cheat to bring him to bed with me, putting off the string of sleepless nights required to get him to stay on his own. But at the same time, I wasn't entirely averse to having him here. He always settled down quickly and his body next to mine was reassuring in a way. I knew at some point this wouldn't be nearly as cute as it was now – not to mention that in the future he might want to go to bed *with* me as opposed to joining me in the middle of the night and that simply wouldn't be acceptable – but I had time to address that issue.

Some time later, I had the most incredibly vivid dream. In it, Reese sat on the floor of the family room when he caught my eye. He gathered himself up to a standing position and, with a huge grin on his face, toddled over in my direction. I called to him while he took halting steps that grew more confident as he got closer. But then as he neared, he veered away from me and threw himself into Ally's arms instead. As she gathered him up, he buried his face in her neck and said, "Mama."

The dream actually woke me up, as though I envisioned myself falling off a cliff instead. I sat up in bed and found both Reese and Ally fast asleep, his little arm resting on her back, both of them content in their slumber.

I tried to get to sleep again, but it was absolutely no use. I lay in bed for maybe forty-five minutes playing the dream over in my head. What did this mean? Did I believe that Reese was walking away from me because of his affection for Ally? Did I think that Reese thought Ally was his mother? Did I think that Ally thought *she* was *his* mother?

Though it was barely 5:30, I slipped out of bed. In so many ways, this dream provided me with the most disturbing thoughts I had since Maureen died. While I struggled with the fears of what a new romance would do to the memory of my love for my wife, I think I always understood at the most meaningful level that I would never forget that love and that it would never vacate my heart. But that Ally could replace Maureen in Reese's mind before I could ever teach him who Maureen was and what she meant to our world, – that another woman could seem much more real to him as a mother – this was an idea that I didn't even consider. It didn't matter whether Ally was trying to insinuate herself into Reese's life this way or not. My guess was that, as sensitive as she was, she was trying very hard to avoid precisely this. But the fact was, given the way in which they'd connected and the situation the three of us were in, Reese could very easily come to see Ally as his only real mother figure, relegating Maureen to some kind of myth, a fanciful figure like Santa Claus, or a guardian angel.

For the first time since Ally and I got together, I felt truly anxious over what I had done. This was way beyond concern over what my colleagues, my family – or even I – might think. And I had absolutely no idea what to do with these feelings. Was I supposed to tell her to back away from my kid? How ridiculous would that sound and how could we possibly move forward after a conversation like that? Was I supposed to tell her that I needed time to make sure that Reese had a palpable understanding of who his mother was before I brought another woman into his life? That would take years to accomplish and I might as well ask her to wait for me while I did a tour of duty with the Marines.

But this was scary. The very first promise I made to myself as I held Reese after Maureen died was that I would raise him in her memory. That not only would he know who she was, but that I would always parent him with her in mind. I owed her that. She was such a good mother and I learned so much about being a parent from her. To think that I broke this promise only months later and that I did it in the most provocative way – by bringing a woman in to replace her – was unconscionable.

And I once again had to wonder to myself who I was. Was I the kind of guy who obliterated the memory of the woman he loved at the first opportunity? Was I the kind of guy who made that woman a footnote in her son's life because he found himself in the thrall of someone else? If I was that guy, did I have to take all of the mirrors down in the house? And if I wasn't, then how did I get where I was right now?

I tried to convince myself that I was overreacting, that this was the result of too little sleep and an unusually clear dream. But the reality was that the scene in that dream could very easily happen sometime in the near future. Reese was very close to walking and he could as easily walk to Ally as he could to me. And he was babbling a lot lately. If I stretched my imagination, I could even convince myself that I heard him call me "Dada." How much of a leap would it be for him to say "Mama"? If the scene actually did happen, how would I react to it? Would it stun me speechless? Or would I smile and enjoy the little family moment like any other thoughtless soul?

To quiet the voices in my head, I turned on the television. The YES Network was broadcasting their "Yankeeography" of Thurman Munson, the great catcher on the Yankees' World Series teams of the '70s. Even this was a form of taunting for me. I adored Munson and he was my first real favorite baseball player. And when he died in a plane crash in 1979, I knew that no other ballplayer would ever mean as much to me. But only a few years later, Don Mattingly joined the club and I became a passionate fan of his. And then there were those great teams from '96 on. And while I still had a soft place in my heart for Thurman and could get choked up just seeing his image on TV, I let others co-opt his space.

I switched the channel. First to VH1, but they were playing a video by River, of course. Then to the Food Network, which at last offered safe harbor. There was nothing about the preparation of stuffed pattypan squash to torment me, though perhaps I was simply too defeated at this point to find it.

The cooking show soothed me and even proved a bit inspirational. Ally came out of the bedroom with Reese in her arms a while later to find me in the kitchen making French toast.

"When did you get up?" she said as I walked over to them. Reese reached out for me and I kissed him on the cheek and hugged him.

"A while ago."

"Everything okay?"

"I just couldn't sleep." Ally touched me on the arm. I'm sure she thought I couldn't sleep because of Tanya. I squeezed her hand. I got Reese his first bottle of the day and sat him in his high chair. "Sorry to make you get up with him. Do you want to go back to bed?"

"No, I'm fine." She looked over at Reese and then grabbed his foot. He smiled, but kept the bottle in his mouth. "We cuddled for a little while, but then he got really squirmy."

"Yeah, he can be like that in the morning." I chuckled, but I could feel myself getting anxious again. I hoped that seeing Ally and Reese together in real life would convince me that I was overreacting to the dream, but it did nothing of the sort. They just had a thing for each other.

I finished making breakfast while Ally made coffee. Even the fact that the coffee and the French toast were ready at the same time set me off a bit. Still, as was the case with several of these bouts of uncertainty, I let my concerns go unstated. What could I say? If Ally knew that something was bothering me, she didn't mention it, and even if she did notice something, she probably assumed it was one of my *usual* things.

After we ate and showered, I dressed Reese while Ally and I talked about our plans for the day. We intended to go to the park in the afternoon, but I had a number of errands to run first, including a stop with my accountant that could take a little while. Our practice on Saturday mornings was to attend to our personal business separately before getting back together after Reese's nap.

"Why don't I keep Reese here while you do the stuff you need to do?" she said.

"Don't you have things to do as well?"

"Nothing that can't wait. You don't want to have a conversation about financial planning while juggling a baby."

Given the thoughts I had all morning, I was loath to leave the two of them alone to bond some more. But at the same time, Ally made a huge amount of sense.

"Here, let me finish dressing him so you can get going," she said.

"No, I can finish dressing him. My appointment isn't until 10:00."

Without question, accomplishing what I needed to accomplish was considerably easier without toting Reese around. Still, I couldn't stop feeling uneasy about it. It seemed so silly; I'd left Reese with Ally before. But the dream initiated this creeping feeling of discomfort and an increasing sense that I needed to do something about what I was feeling, that this time around I couldn't simply put it off. I was distracted throughout the meeting with my accountant, forgot to get toothpaste at the supermarket, and had to turn around after I returned to the neighborhood because I didn't pick up my dry cleaning.

By the time I got back home, the lack of sleep had caught up to me and I was feeling edgy. This kicked up to an entirely new level when I heard Reese screaming as I entered the house. I rushed to his room where I found him lying on his changing table and Ally standing over him holding a tissue to his temple. The tissue was soaked in blood.

"What happened?" I said excitedly.

"I left him alone for a second to make a phone call and he fell. He must have hit his head on the edge of the coffee table."

I moved Ally aside and took the tissue from his head. Reese's face was crimson and he was screaming uncontrollably. I tried to inspect the gash, but blood pooled in it as quickly as I could wipe it away.

"This is bad," I said. "We need to go to the emergency room."

I swept him up and brought him to the car, strapping him in his seat while he wailed. I hugged and kissed the top of his head while I stroked his hand trying to calm him down, but I doubt he had any awareness of what I was doing. Reese seemed to have a high pain threshold and even when he did get hurt, he tended to stop crying quickly. That he was so hysterical meant that this was excruciating for him.

I held another tissue against his temple. Ally asked if I wanted her to keep it there while I drove and I asked her to drive instead. Reese barely stopped crying when we pulled up to Mather Hospital ten minutes later. I quickly unstrapped him and carried him into the ER. There were a half-dozen people in the waiting area, but a nurse came to triage Reese right away. She checked his vital signs and then, while I held him tightly against my chest, I gave our insurance information to a clerk at the registration desk. He told us that a bed would be available for Reese within a few minutes and asked us to sit down. We went to sit with Ally, and it was only then that I noticed she was crying and probably had been for some time.

"I'm so sorry, Reese-y," she said as she reached for his hand and held it. His head was on my shoulder and his body was still shaking with sobs, though he no longer wailed.

We got a bed fifteen minutes later and waited another half hour after that for a doctor to see him. By this time, the bleeding had slowed considerably and Reese even smiled a little. But the worst was hardly over. The doctor took one look at the cut and asked me if I wanted to consult with a plastic surgeon.

"You mean there's going to be a scar?" I said.

"He's a baby. It's always hard to tell with them. But I do think there's going to be a mark of some sort. Plastic surgery is something to consider if you're concerned about a scar."

I glanced over at Ally. Her lips were set grimly.

"If I don't want a plastic surgeon, what would we do?"

"He'll need stitches. I think three will close this up."

Neither option was particularly attractive. I'd hoped that this was something the doctor could have treated and then closed with a butterfly bandage, but obviously that wasn't the case. I decided against the plastic surgeon. It would only extend the process for Reese and there was a very good chance that any scar would be barely noticeable.

What happened next was one of the most harrowing experiences I've had as a parent. A nurse and two orderlies came to our bed with a "papoose," a board with something that looked an awful lot like a straightjacket attached to it.

"What are you doing with that?" I said.

"We need to put him in here before he can be stitched," the nurse said.

"I can't just hold him?"

"He'll move around too much."

Reese had calmed enough by this point to stand up while holding my fingers. When an orderly came to take him, he latched onto my arm and started crying again, climbing up my chest. At that point, turning him over to these people was just about the last thing in the world I wanted to do, but I also knew it was necessary. The orderly pulled him away from me and placed him down on the board while the others strapped him in.

Reese started screaming again as loudly as ever. But it got worse. An orderly held his head still while the doctor first anesthetized and then stitched him. Reese fought this all the way. He had no idea what was going on and couldn't possibly understand why he needed to endure this. While this happened, I knelt next to him, patting his arm, singing to him and trying to get him to make eye contact with me – and at the same time trying to maintain my own composure, which quickly slipped away. I knew these medical people were doing their best to make this as painless as possible for him and to get it over with as quickly as they could. That still didn't prevent me from wanting to punch them for putting him through it.

When it was over and a nurse released Reese from the papoose, I snatched him up as quickly as I could and held him close to me until he stopped crying. Ally, who I lost track of while the stitching was going on, patted him on the back. All I could think at this point was that I wanted her to leave him alone. That I wanted this time by myself with my baby to reassure him and let him know that this horrible experience was over. Ultimately, I moved away from Ally, telling her that I wanted to walk him a little to calm him down.

Reese fell asleep during the car ride home. I'm sure the crying and his ordeal had exhausted him. I brought him into the house and put him in his crib, wishing I could join him there for the next several hours. I felt absolutely washed out and beaten down. And I wasn't particularly enthusiastic about going out to see Ally. Between what had been going on in my head that morning and then the accident, I wasn't at all sure what to say to her.

"Is he sleeping okay?" she said when I returned to the kitchen.

"He's fine for now. It would be great if he slept a couple of hours, but I'm afraid he'll wake himself up when he turns his head."

"Poor guy. I can't believe how fast that all happened."

"You can't?"

"You know what I mean. It was just the blink of an eye."

"You mean he was standing up against the coffee table already when you left the room to get the telephone?"

Ally's face fell. "He scrambles around that thing. I was going to be gone for a second."

"I'm sure the accident took *less* than a second." Ally looked stunned and disappointed at the same time. I'm sure she was blaming herself for this already, but I'm also sure she didn't expect to hear what I was suggesting now. "Are you saying this was my fault?"

"He was your responsibility."

"The exact same thing could have happened if I was in the room with him. We don't walk around him with a safety net."

"But you *weren't* in the room with him. This didn't happen because he just slipped. There had to be some velocity for him to cut himself that badly. Maybe he was running around the table. Maybe he was running after *you* because you left the room."

She threw her hands up to her face and then steepled her fingers and pressed her thumbs against the bridge of her nose. "I can't believe you're saying this. I love that kid like he's my own."

It was the exact wrong thing for her to say at that moment. Almost anything else would have made me see how upset she was about what happened and understand that this was very painful for her as well. But the events of the day conspired against us. So instead of feeling for her, instead of allowing this to be a trial that we endured together, what I said was, "Well, if you're going to play at being a mother, you might want to practice on something less valuable first."

Ally's expression told me everything I needed to know: I had crossed a line from which I could not retreat. She wasn't angry; she was humiliated.

"I won't let you talk to me like that," she said.

"I didn't mean it the way it came out," I said quickly.

"Explain to me how it could have come out differently."

I gestured with my hands, but found I couldn't think of anything to say.

"Look, Gerry, I think you're great and I think Reese is a gift from heaven, but I'm not going to be a junior partner in this relationship and I'm certainly not going to allow you to slap me in the face."

Something else replaced the anger I was feeling. It wasn't contrition; though I was certainly sorry I had said something so cruel to her. It was the realization that I had subconsciously prepared for this moment from the very beginning of our relationship. Realization that at some point the misgivings and hesitation I sublimated would rise up. Realization that I would always find something else to convince me that we started too soon, that I wasn't ready to let go of Maureen, that I wasn't prepared – and might never be prepared – to let someone all the way in again.

I knew that Reese didn't get hurt because of Ally's negligence. I knew that I had no reason to be angry with her. But I also knew as clearly as I knew anything on this fuzzy day that my striking out at her was a symptom of something much more pernicious. I was in over my head and I was now violently kicking my way back to the surface.

"Go, then," I said.

I know that wasn't what she expected to hear and she seemed deeply saddened by it. But while I could-n't possibly imagine what was going on in her head, I have a feeling that a light clicked on for her at that point. And what she saw in that light was a man who would never give her what she wanted or deserved.

She bowed her head. When she looked up at me again, there was new resolve in her eyes.

"I'll come by for my stuff sometime when Lisa is here."

I nodded.

"And you need to let me know how he's recovering. E-mail me if you have to. But I get to share that much."

"I'll let you know when I see you on Monday." She closed her eyes and took a deep breath, as though she just then remembered that we would cross each other's paths on a daily basis.

"Bye, Gerry."

When she left, I went to the couch in the family room, sat back, and stared at the ceiling for an incongruous length of time. Reese wound up napping for hours, leaving me uncomfortably alone with my thoughts. During this time, I realized I was at least as unready to move forward without Ally as I had been to move forward with her. None of my available options were good ones. If I could somehow get Ally back, I'd only subject both of us to the consequences of my next bout of guilt and indecision. But if she was in fact gone from my life, I was greatly diminished. I relied on her for so many things. And regardless of my anxieties, she made my life immeasurably better.

When Reese finally woke up, he looked miserable, the dressing at his temple drawing further attention to his haggard eyes. He'd been through so much and he had no idea why any of it had happened. And he wasn't even aware of the major surgery I did on his life while he slept. He was listless and didn't seem particularly interested in playing, so we sat on the couch together and I put on the Yankee game, which they won. Throughout the last four innings and the entire postgame show, he sat on my lap with his head tilted against my chest.

We were once again alone together.

I saw your brother's blood for the first time today. It seemed like there were gallons of it coming out of him. Everything is exaggerated when someone you love is hurt, especially when you feel like you can't do enough to help.

It was a scary experience and it got scarier before it got better. Ultimately, the solution was three stitches, which will leave a little mark on the side of his head. You managed to make it through your entire childhood without going through something like this. He couldn't even get to his first birthday. Hopefully this isn't an omen. But it's clear that he's a daredevil and it's unlikely that this will be our last visit to the emergency room. I can only hope that future trips are less upsetting.

I got five stitches in my scalp when I was seven. It was the result of a stupid summertime accident involving a skateboard and a broken bottle. From what I remember, the stitches hurt much more than the cut did, even though I wasn't supposed to "feel a thing." That was the first in a series of lies people told me surrounding that accident, the biggest of which was that the other kids wouldn't chide me about the patch of hair the doctors shaved off before they sewed me. I suppose Reese is lucky that he won't have any memory of this event, not to mention that he won't have to endure Frankie Wild's endless teasing the way I did. Though of course we subconsciously store absolutely everything from our early years and these things work away on us even though we can't recall them. For Reese's sake, I hope today is just a complete blank down the line.

Right now, I know the incident is playing on his mind. He was very tentative moving around the rest of the day and he sat in my lap this afternoon for a couple of hours. I have to admit I took some comfort in that. It's one of those parental guilty pleasures to enjoy cuddling with your kids when they're sick. Reese is so incredibly active all the time, and now that he's mobile, he rarely agrees to snuggle with me when we're not in bed. He's so much like you in that way. The only time you ever let me simply sit with my arm around you was when you first woke up on weekends and when you didn't feel well.

The house seems extraordinarily still tonight. I miss you right now even more than usual. There are times when I almost convince myself that it's okay for us to run on separate tracks these days. Today isn't one of them, though. I remember when little Billy Weston broke his leg a couple of years ago and how great you were with him, playing videogames with him, reading him stories, and even baking cookies for him. This was during the nascent stages of your drive for emancipation and it was so completely reassuring to see: to know that regardless of how hard you were pushing against your mother and me you could still be giving and patient and compassionate with others. I knew right at that moment (though I certainly believed it before) that you were the kind of person who others could count on, a great foul-weather friend, someone who came through in the clutch.

I could have used a little of that tonight when Reese went to sleep and I felt the full impact of the day. Since it was Saturday night, you would have gone out with your friends, of course. But maybe you would have made me some macaroons or something first. That would have helped. Immeasurably.

TWENTY-THREE - Mom's Old Recipe

Reese slept until a little after nine the next morning. This was an absolute first for him and an indication of how much his body and soul had been through yesterday. I didn't get up until I heard him babbling in his crib, which I guess meant I felt rather beaten up myself.

When I walked into his room, he smiled at me, scrambled to the edge of his crib, and threw his arms up. I took him out and he put his arms around my neck. He started giving me these little hugs about a month ago, but it meant something different to me this morning. I changed his diaper and he giggled when I tickled his belly. I needed to change the dressing at his temple as well, but I decided to give that a little time. I didn't want to remind him of his injury right after he got up.

We went into the family room to play on the floor. I pulled out a few of his toys and, while I did this, he crawled over to the coffee table. I thought I saw him hesitate for a moment when he got there, but it's very possible I projected that on him. Then he reached up and stood, turning to me and pounding the table at the same time. This caused him to slip and he landed on his bottom. But he immediately got up again and started working his way around the table. His injury was so *yesterday*. I was somewhat reluctant to play our little game of chase, nervous about his slipping and falling again. But I simply couldn't help myself. The fact that he wanted to do it was just too appealing.

Codie came later that morning. It wasn't until I saw her walk up the driveway that I remembered we'd planned a brunch together. This was the day she was going to meet Ally.

"You look comfortable," she said when she reached the door. "I'm so glad you don't feel the need to dress up for me." I wore a Yankees 2000 World Series Championship t-shirt and a pair of shorts. I was un-showered and unshaven.

"I forgot you were coming," I said regretfully.

"I'll try not to be offended by that. Where's my nephew?" Reese crawled up behind me. When Codie saw the bandage on the side of his head, she knelt down and scooped him up. "What happened to him?"

"We had a *day* here yesterday."

"Is he okay?"

"Does he look okay?"

"He always looks okay," she said, nuzzling his neck and handing him the electronic toy phone she brought. She pressed a button and the phone played a song. Reese thought this was very entertaining. I was glad he let Codie pick him up so easily. Sometimes he didn't. It would have been especially tough if he'd reacted badly to her today, though, after I told her she slipped my mind.

"What's going on?" she said.

"He fell. We went to the emergency room. There were stitches and this restraining device that I thought they'd stopped using in medieval times."

"Where's Ally?"

"And then there's the thing that happened with Ally."

While I made coffee, I told Codie about our breakup.

"I really screwed up. I keep seeing the look on her face. I can't believe I made someone look like that."

"Why don't you call her?"

"I can't call her. First of all, I doubt she'll even take the call. But more than that, I don't know what to say."

"You sound pretty sorry about this. Start there."

"I *am* sorry about it."

"But you can't call her."

"I can't."

"Is this one of those secret fraternity things that women aren't allowed to understand?"

I chuckled sadly and sat next to Codie, kissing her hair. She wrapped an arm around me and I rested my head on her shoulder. "I can't because I can't promise her that it won't happen again."

"Things happen, Gerry. People say things out of anger sometimes and hurt people unintentionally."

"I didn't hurt her unintentionally."

Codie pulled back to look at me.

"I didn't do it to hurt her, but I *did* do it intentionally. I just didn't see it that way at the time. I did it to drive her away."

"Why?"

"Because I'm not ready for her. I don't know that I'll ever be ready for her. So I can't call her because if I do we might get back together. And I can't promise her that I won't freak out all over again – for exactly the same reason – three weeks from now. It's kinda hard to realize that after all this time I haven't gotten very far."

Codie didn't say anything, only held me a little tighter.

"I should start making something for us to eat," I said. "I'm sorry; I kind of dropped the ball here today."

"You know what? You go take a shower. I'll make us something."

"What?"

"Go take a shower. I'll whip something up."

I laughed. "You whip things up?"

"I'm working on it. Look, if I'm going to have a kid, I need to be able to cook, right? The kitchen's the center of the home and all that stuff."

I kissed her on the top of the head. "You, on the other hand, have gotten very, very far. You humble me."

"Go take a shower."

I nodded and walked off to my room. It felt especially good to have water streaming over me this morning. Though it was early August and the air conditioning was working hard to counteract the dead-of-summer heat, I turned the hot water high, allowing it to massage the back of my neck for several minutes. I might have stayed like this for hours if I weren't so curious about what Codie was whipping up.

I went back to the kitchen to see Codie flipping pancakes and Reese tearing one apart on the tray of his high chair.

"Why don't you have any blueberries?" she said.

"I don't?"

"Not unless you've hidden them in the laundry room or something."

"Sorry."

She turned two pancakes apiece for us onto plates and then nodded me toward the dining room table. The pancakes were surprisingly good and I told her so.

"Mom's old recipe."

"I didn't know your mom had an old pancake recipe."

"Yeah, this was a bit of a cheat. I've been making these since I was ten."

"How is it possible that I didn't know about this after all this time?"

"Didn't Maureen ever make breakfast for you?"

I searched my mind. "She made me oatmeal a couple of times."

"Right. Because you always did the cooking and she *loved* that. I mean it wasn't just because she did-n't really like doing it."

"I know."

"She always told me – no, I think it was more like she taunted me – that you spoiled her."

"We spoiled each other, trust me."

Codie offered a knowing glance. "So she ruined you for any other woman?"

I looked down at my plate. "Yeah, something like that."

We ate in silence for a couple of minutes. I dipped an edge of Reese's second pancake (the one he didn't tear to shreds) in my maple syrup and gave him a taste. He worked his lips around the sugar the way he had from the time he was much, much smaller, and then ate the rest of the pancake without any more syrup.

"You know," I said, "I never stopped trying to show off for Maureen. I mean, when we first started dating, I always wanted to prove to her that there was no other man in the world she could be happy with. The songs, the food, the dates, the back rubs, all of it. But even after I, you know, won her, I refused to let up. I wanted her to be a hundred percent certain at all times that she made the right decision."

"She got the message."

"I know she got the message. But I still needed to keep delivering it."

"It was a good idea." Codie took a sip of her coffee. "Why are you telling me this?"

"I don't know."

"Yeah," she said, "you do."

* * *

That afternoon, Tate's family had a going-away party for him. I'd planned to take Reese, but Codie volunteered to stay with him and it was really better for all of us. It didn't elude me that I felt none of the concerns about leaving my son with his aunt today that I felt about leaving him with my now-former girlfriend yesterday.

Though we grew up in each other's households, I hadn't seen most of the people at the party since Tate's wedding. His cousin Laura, who I had a major crush on as a teenager, sat at a table drinking gin and yelling at her kids. His brother Stan tried to convince me to invest in a strip mall. It seemed that everyone there knew about Maureen and Tanya. Many people asked after Reese. Tate's mother asked after Ally.

Zak and Sara hung around with their cousins. Zak played "Running Bases," outside with a group of kids. Sara chose to stay inside to watch a Pixar movie. It dawned on me that they would have fewer opportunities to get together with these relative-friends in the future, though for all I knew, Tate would foist the kids off on his family when he came across the country to visit.

We hadn't gotten much of a chance to speak since he'd told me about the job. While the rest of our lunch that day wasn't nearly as contentious as it began, it wasn't relaxed. The few conversations we'd had since then were a little awkward. Still, we had been close for decades and would see a lot less of each other in the future. I didn't want to miss the chance to say a proper goodbye.

The party was crowded and loud. Unlike mine, Tate had a huge family and they always showed up at events like this one. For the first hour I was there, I couldn't get a second alone with him, as person after person dominated him.

On my way to get something to drink, I ran into Zak, who came in from his game. "Did you steal a lot of bases?" I said.

"I came in second. Danielle is 12."

"I'm impressed."

"Where's the baby?"

"He's staying with his aunt. He got a little bang on the side of his head yesterday and we thought it would be better if he stayed home. Want something?"

I got Zak a Coke and we stood drinking for a moment. "I'll get to see him again, right?" he said.

"Of course you will. Don't worry. I know it seems like he's going really far away, but everything is going to turn out fine."

"Yeah, I know. I was talking about Reese."

"Oh," I said, laughing. "Definitely. Anytime you want, really. Even if your dad isn't around. Your mom and I are friends, too."

"You are?"

"You knew that, didn't you?"

"I guess. Sometimes I get confused."

"I can understand that."

A couple of kids came by to tell Zak that they were going to be shooting baskets on the driveway. Zak told them he'd be out in a minute and then turned back to me.

"I guess I am a little worried about my dad," he said when the kids left.

"Try not to be. I know that sounds stupid, but try.

You guys will figure this new thing out." "Yeah. I can hang out with you and Reese sometimes?"

"No question about it. I'll give your mom a call."

He nodded and drank his Coke. Another couple of kids came by to tell him they were putting a game together.

"Wanna play with us?" he said.

"I'm an *excellent* basketball player."

"Good, I'll make sure you get on my team."

Just then, Tate walked in our direction and ruffled Zak's hair.

"Gerry's coming out to play basketball with us," Zak said.

"He is?" He turned to me. "Still got that little fade-away jump shot?"

"Who knows? I haven't touched a basketball in five years."

"I thought you said you were good," Zak said.

"I *am* good. You never lose skills like mine. I'll meet you outside in a few minutes. Don't let the other team pick me."

Zak gave me a thumbs-up and walked away. Tate got another beer.

"You ready?" I said when he returned.

"Movers came and took most of the stuff yesterday. We're staying with my parents until I leave tomorrow."

"When do you start?"

"I have meetings with a bunch of people Thursday and Friday, but my first day in the office is next Monday. I wanted a few days to get everything in order."

"Are you excited?"

"Pretty much." He looked around the room and raised his beer bottle to one of his cousins. "I don't know, now I'm starting to think about the kids. We had a good day yesterday. Figures, huh?"

"So go out there and blow people away for a little while. Then come back home. We'll all be waiting for you."

"Thanks. Where are Ally and the baby?"

"Reese is staying with Codie. We had a little emergency room incident yesterday. Ally is currently in the process of putting as much distance between the two of us as humanly possible."

"You split?"

"I said some things I shouldn't have."

"It was bound to happen, you know."

"I suppose."

"Swings and misses."

"Something like that."

Tate waved to another relative passing by, which prompted her to stop and make small talk. She left a few minutes later.

"Listen," he said, "I know what it looks like with me taking this job on the West Coast. Believe me when I tell you that I'm pretty sure I know what I'm doing."

"Just don't disappear out there, okay?"

He smiled. "I'll try not to." He looked around again. "All these people. The last time I left home a third of them weren't part of the family yet and another third weren't born." He patted me on the shoulder. "Hey, you've got a basketball game."

"Yes, I do."

"Think they'll let me play, too?"

"Not if your reputation preceded you. And *I'm* not guarding you."

"Oh, come on. Let me whip your ass one more time as a going-away present. If you insist, I'll even let you block one of my shots before I blow you out of the water."

Dad,

This isn't working either. Syd's great, the store's great, I even like the people I'm crashing with. But I'm not great. Syd played this old Eric Andersen album and when the song "Be True to You" came on, I was just barely able to finish helping a customer before I had to run to the back room. I thought about Mom and I just started crying uncontrollably. I mean I couldn't stop myself for something like ten minutes.

The weird thing is that it wasn't even Mom who played that song for me. It was you. The first time you played it was after I got a C in English because Mr. Edelstein didn't like what I said about *"The Yearling."* Do you remember that?

I think there might be something wrong with me. Not everyone who has a loved one die can possibly go through what I'm going through. I don't seem to be able to make it for more than a couple of hours without breaking down. It made Mick run away from me and I think I totally shook Syd up after this last episode. I just can't imagine that you're letting this happen to you – and I'm not saying that because I don't think it hurts you as much but because I just think you're stronger. You have to be. Do you think I might really be broken in some way?

One of the people I met here hooked me up with someone to talk to and I'm going to see her tomorrow. I don't know what she could possibly say to make me feel even a little bit better, but I hope she does. I need to feel better. I really need it.

Hearts,
T

In the face of everything else that had happened this weekend, this message was especially hard to receive. I was beside myself. I needed to hold Tanya. I needed to tell her that she was more okay than she realized. I needed to let her know that I would do everything in my power to ease her through this process, to share experiences with her and help her learn to move forward. But while she had been more forthcoming in this message than in any before, she still didn't give me any way to get back to her.

It was Sunday night and there was no one I could talk to about tracing her message back through the remailer she used. Maybe someone from the IT department at Eleanor Miller would be able to help tomorrow.

Back in October, Maureen's father hired a private investigator to track Tanya down. We called him off after a month when it was obvious he didn't have enough information to do his job. Feeling the need to do something now, though, I called his cell phone. I told him what little I knew about the record store and agreed to wire him a retainer in the morning. If he found the store, I would be on the next plane. I was no longer worried about Tanya's response upon seeing me. I needed to bring her back.

As little as it was, I felt like I was doing something. But it wasn't nearly enough to calm me down. I opened the journal and tried to write, but I couldn't put down a single word. It no longer served the function it had been serving for me. Not when my need to communicate with the *real* Tanya was this great.

I went into Reese's room to watch him sleep in blissful ignorance. He didn't know his mother was gone forever. He didn't know his sister anguished somewhere all alone. He didn't know that I'd bounced the woman he adored from his life. I envied him.

I went into my room and sat in the middle of my bed. I tried asking Maureen for advice, but she wasn't talking. I don't know how long I sat there, but at some point, I entered something like a meditative state.

Only to learn that there were no answers forthcoming.

TWENTY-FOUR - *Contact Information*

Ally didn't come to the office that Monday. Her assistant called Ben to tell him she wouldn't be at the team meeting; she got sick on something over the weekend and needed another day to recover. This was a relief for me. I didn't know what I was going to do when I faced her again.

I was much too distracted to work. I talked to a colleague in IT about tracing the remailer and he connected me to a friend who connected me to another friend. In the end, I learned a chapbook's worth of jargon, but nothing of Tanya's whereabouts. These remailer services were especially effective at masking the origins of the messages they handled. That, of course, was the point. I wired the investigator his money and spoke to him twice on the phone. He told me that his preliminary sweep of independent record stores in the South had netted no owners with the names Syd or Sidney. I didn't think until then that Tanya had probably changed the owner's name to deflect any efforts I might make to find her. The investigator could search forever and never learn anything based on what I'd given him. Still, I asked him to keep looking.

By mid-afternoon, after attending a meeting but not participating in it in the slightest, I realized that I needed to get away. I couldn't pretend that my life was in any way routine when Ally was down the hall hating me (as presumably she would be tomorrow), and Tanya was suffering somewhere else. I had to get out of the house and out of my job for at least a few days in order to gain a little perspective.

I went to see Marshall and, remarkably, he wasn't on the telephone.

"Listen, I'm going to take the rest of the week off as vacation time."

"You can't. There's too much happening here."

"There isn't too much happening here. The catalogs are in great shape, there isn't another board meeting for a couple of weeks, and because it's August half the staff is on vacation already anyway."

"This is the time when real executives step back to take stock of the company and plan for the future."

"I'm not in the best shape to do that right now."

"The company is in desperate need of creative solutions to its mounting problems."

"I've got a few mounting problems of my own and I'm going to explode if I don't get away."

Marshall picked up his pen and started doodling. He did so for a good minute before speaking again and I briefly thought he believed that our conversation was over.

"At some point, the regular recitation of your issues gets boring, Gerry."

I was instantly furious. "Sorry I can't be more entertaining for you. Ben will have the details of where I'm staying the next few days."

Marshall dropped the pen. "Maybe it's time for me to be as cavalier with you as you are with your professional responsibilities."

I moved around to Marshall's side of the desk and glowered at him. I think he thought I might hit him, because he shrank back a little. "How can you possibly be such an unmitigated horse's ass with someone who has contributed as much as I have all these years? I have taken hundreds of hours away from my family – hours it turns out I can never make up – for the good of this place. I did that because I love this company and I believe in this company. I have bled for this company and will bleed for it again. But right now I'm just a little bit out of my mind and if my taking some time off to try to deal with that is a problem for you, then fire me."

Marshall held my stare for several beats and for that time, I thought he was in fact going to fire me. It wouldn't have surprised me, given the way he acted with me over the past several months. Then he broke eye contact and said, "Go."

He returned to the papers on his desk and I wondered if there was more I should say. I decided there wasn't and began to leave his office.

"Gerry," he said, stopping me. "Leave your contact information with *my* assistant, not yours."

Dad,

I spent the whole day baring my soul, so I should probably do it with you, too. I spent a bunch of time talking to this grief counselor and she got me to think about a lot of things (A LOT of things), and then after I finished with her, I did another three hours with the woman who hooked us up, which I'm sure was a real thrill ride for her.

Here's the thing: I always felt like I was competing with you for Mom's affections. You may have figured this out a long time ago. If you did, Mom never said anything and you and I certainly never talked about it. But I felt it very strongly and I was very conscious of it even when I was really young. This probably sounds stupid to you. I mean, I know that Mom and I had a great relationship — better than the ones any of my friends had with their mothers — but she was just SO crazy about you. It wasn't like she dropped me on the floor or anything when you walked into the room, but I definitely had to share her when you were around. No one else's parents were married the way the two of you were married. You even fought differently than most couples.

Anyway, as long as I can remember, I always tried to get Mom to like me more. You know, asking her to help me out with stuff, taking a special interest in everything she did, taking a REALLY special interest in the stuff that you didn't like that much, that sort of thing. I know that sounds really childish but – oh, yeah – I was a child.

When Mick showed up, I was sure I had you. I could have all these dreamy mother/daughter conversations about men and what it was like to be in love. And the fact that you instantly despised him played right into my hands. I could have those "Dad doesn't get it" conversations, too. But then you two announced that Mom was pregnant. And as soon as I heard it, I realized that I was the one who had lost. Mom actually liked you so much more that she was going to replace me with another baby. After that, it was just a matter of letting things run their natural course. Mick painted this romantic picture of life on the road, away from the rules and the people who made the rules. It sounded like a little fantasy to me when he first started talking about it. But after your announcement, I started to think about it more and more. Then one night, a couple of days before we left, Mick started talking about it again, and I just said, "Let's do it." I didn't want to live in a house with you and Mom anymore. And if I heard one more word about the new baby, I was going to go crazy.

I blew it, Dad. I mean a piece of me always assumed that I'd come back to Port Jeff at some point after establishing myself and that Mom and I would pick up where we left off. I had no idea that I would be gone for the rest of her life. No matter how mad I was or how betrayed I felt, I never would have left if I thought that I would never see her again.

And I blew it with you, too. I mean almost right from the beginning. I don't know where this competition thing came from. For all I know, you felt the same way and were glad to see me bow out. But I couldn't help watch you and Mom together and feel a little jealous, even with everything she gave me. Maybe BECAUSE of everything she gave me. And it made me miss out on what you and I could have had together. Yeah, we did some fun stuff. And there were times, you know? But something always got in the way. I think the something was me.

Enough psychobabble. I feel moderately calmer after talking all this stuff
out with these people today. I even feel
a little better now that I've written you
this message.

Don't hate me too much, okay?

Hearts,

T

I had just finished packing for our trip when I checked
the computer. I had no idea that Tanya felt this way. Certainly, there were times (especially when she was little) when
she did something obviously intended to draw her mother's
attention away from me. That was something every kid did. I
didn't realize how much deeper it went.

And it explained so much. If Tanya had been more obvious, would Maureen and I have been able to intervene? *Had
she been obvious and I just missed all the signs?* I couldn't
understand why Tanya felt the need to compete with me.
Didn't she understand that people had room in their hearts
for more than one person? Did she understand it and still
find that it wasn't enough? Was it possible that Maureen and
I loved each other *too much* for her?

I read the end of the message again. *I feel moderately
calmer after talking all this stuff out with these people today.*
That was good. At least she didn't sound as desperate as she
did in her last message, though I knew all too well that one
never knew when the bad moments were coming. *Don't hate
me too much, okay?* That was easy. I never even came close to
hating her, even when she angered me or dismissed me the
most. This new admission couldn't make that happen.

If anything, it did precisely the opposite. Tanya had
never seemed this vulnerable and open to me.

This increased my need to see her exponentially. I called
the investigator and told him to redouble his efforts, regardless of the cost.

* * *

Finding a nice place to stay on the beach is always difficult. Finding one impulsively in the middle of August is nearly impossible. I could get a "last minute cancellation" with an acre of private waterfront in the Hamptons for $10,000 and there were any number of motels available "within driving distance of the beach." None of this was what I wanted. Eventually, I found a resort on a lake in northern Connecticut with one last room.

Reese and I made the three-hour drive the next morning. Once we settled into our room, we went for a walk down to the lake. Walks had taken on a different meaning for Reese in the last week. He didn't want me to carry him nearly as much and he flat-out rejected his stroller. What he really wanted to do was hold one of my fingers and toddle along the path. This was an extremely slow process since at any moment he might sit down to examine something or, inexplicably, just sit. While the exercise could be tedious at home, we had come here to do precisely this kind of thing.

It had been a while since Reese and I had a significant stretch of solo time together. Now, given everything that had happened recently, I found that I could take comfort in just about anything he did. If he wanted to crawl around in the grass for forty-five minutes, I watched him do it, interrupting his activity only to prevent him from putting an ant in his mouth. If he wanted to sit on my chest while we were in a chaise lounge and pat my cheeks for an inordinate length of time, we did that. I talked the teenaged son of a vacationing family into taking us out in a rowboat, knowing that I needed to hold Reese carefully during the entire trip given his propensity for exploring. And we spent a lot of time sitting at the edge of the lake, Reese completely naked and seemingly enjoying the gentle lapping of the water at his legs and bottom.

At night, we ate at the resort's restaurant. The food wasn't particularly inspired, but there were many kids there and I knew that Reese could do nothing that other kids hadn't done at least three times already that evening. And he was surprisingly well mannered, patiently waiting for our food to arrive while gnawing on bread with the three teeth that had broken through. As a reward, he got his choice of desserts, chopped up peaches in heavy syrup being his favorite. Then we returned to our room to watch the Yankees in what could very well be their last big series of the season.

The Blue Jays were in town with their eight-game lead and the Yankees really needed to sweep in order to get back into the race. Ultimately, they lost all three games instead and it became obvious that they would not play in October this year. The one bright spot was the reemergence of "Kid" Kitterer. After a very fast start, he went through a terrible stretch of games where he couldn't hit at all and even made mistakes in the field. There was talk of sending him back to Scranton just to get the pressure off him. But in this series, he tried his best to carry the team on his back, hitting four homers, knocking in ten runs, batting .625 and making two remarkable defensive plays. And though it perturbed me that the Blue Jays had all but eliminated the Yankees, I knew his efforts weren't in vain. He gave all of us a glimpse of the future.

I thought a tremendous amount about Ally and about how things turned out between us. I nearly called her several times, if for no other reason than to try to make sense of our last day together. I thought about telling her about my dream and about how the events unfolded for me from there, hoping this would give her some context. But I always came around to the same reason not to do it.

I really missed her. It wasn't just that I'd come to depend on her. It wasn't just that she made me feel better about nearly everything. It wasn't just that she excited me, entertained me, and kept me motivated. It was that she reached me. At the most impossible time, she became another central part of my life.

But calling her was out of the question. I wouldn't put her at the mercy of the endless flitting of my emotions. If I ever brought another woman into my life, I owed that woman the peace of mind of knowing that I could deal with our relationship on its own terms. Anything else was terribly unfair.

I had no idea what it would be like for us to work together. I wondered if Ally had gone to the office on Tuesday. Was it terribly upsetting for her to get ready that morning and drive to the building? I wondered what she thought when she learned I would be gone for the week. I even wondered if this was the final sign that it was time for me to leave Eleanor Miller. None of this would be easy.

On Thursday morning, Reese and I walked down to the lake when something caught his attention. He let go of my finger and took several clumsy steps in that direction before he stopped and, perhaps realizing what he'd just done, looked back at me. He had an enormous grin on his face and he sat down and patted the ground wildly with his open palms. I went to pick him up to hug him, but I realized that he would be happier if I simply boosted him back to his feet. He sauntered off toward the woods while I trailed behind him. When he fell down, I picked him up again and pointed him in the direction of the lake.

For most of that day, Reese wanted to do little more than walk as much as possible. Even when we were in our room – not a large space – he insisted on exploring everything he could. This would require an entirely new level of babyproofing when we got home.

His growth curve was extraordinary to me. In the last nine months, he'd gone from someone who could do little more than scream when he was hungry to someone who could traverse a path, splash by a lake, eat copious amounts of peaches, and make his audience laugh in a wide variety of ways. By his first birthday, he'd add countless other things to his resume. It was dizzying. And the fact that it happened to millions of children all over the world on an ongoing basis didn't make it any less unique or fascinating to me. For the thousandth time, I realized how thankful I was for this experience.

On Friday night, I got a call from the investigator. He'd made absolutely no progress in his search for Syd. I decided to put a halt to the investigation. He wouldn't find Tanya for me because she was clever enough to make it nearly impossible to do. She would come home when she could, when she wanted to, or not at all. As frustrating as it was to me, I didn't have any say in this.

The owners of the resort let me borrow their computer a couple of times during the week so I could check my e-mail. I did it once again on Saturday to find a message that Tanya had written days before, but which arrived only a few hours ago. All it said was:

"Life's mysteries seem so faded."

P.S. Syd made me a nice going-away dinner.

The lyrics were from Soul Asylum's "Runaway Train," a song Tanya knew was one of my favorites, a beautiful and sad tune about a teenage runaway that I'd somehow never associated with Tanya until this very moment. What was the message here? Was she the runaway train? Had things gotten worse again? What was I to make of this? And what could I do?

Of course, one part of the message was entirely clear. If Syd had made her a nice going-away dinner, that meant she had moved on yet again.

TWENTY-FIVE - *Just a Prior Engagement*

We went home the next morning. Concerned that my newly ultramobile son would have even greater difficulty with a long car ride, we made several stops along the way to allow Reese to stretch the legs that now served a new purpose for him. Even a rest-stop parking lot was a field of dreams in his current state of mind.

As we drove, I considered the reality I headed toward. Certainly, I didn't expect my problems to go away during this little excursion, but I wasn't any better prepared to face them now than I had been when I left. Tanya was on the road again and had been for a few days. Ally would almost surely be in the office tomorrow and we would need to come to terms with our new relationship.

It had been ten months since Tanya walked out on us. Nine since Reese was born. Seven since Maureen was taken. Through all of it, I persevered, or at least made a modest attempt at persevering. But as I worked my way through the days, I discovered only more uncertainty. In fact, at this point the only thing I could be sure of was that I couldn't be sure of much. There was something appealing about running away from this, about driving until I couldn't drive anymore and just putting down stakes. But I couldn't do this now anymore than I could when I rejected Maine and Halifax. Therefore, I continued east on the Long Island Expressway.

We pulled into the driveway and Reese started screaming. Had he just now realized how much he missed his home? Or was he protesting our return, wondering why we weren't going back to that place with the water and the interesting bugs? I took him out of his car seat and held him for a moment, but he wiggled out of my embrace so he could walk around on the lawn. I started unpacking the car and, keeping a close eye on him, brought my first armload to the porch. It was then that I saw the enveloped taped to the door. I recognized Ally's handwriting immediately. I scooped Reese up and brought him inside with me so I could read the letter without concern about him walking into the street.

Gerry,

When I learned you had gone away for the week, I have to tell you I was glad. I'm not sure what I'll do when I see you again. I've given some serious thought to leaving Eleanor Miller. I have some feelers out. I don't think I'll ever be able to simply smile at you as we pass in the hall and I can't work someplace where just taking a walk can cause me heartache.

I was so deeply, deeply wounded by our last conversation. I don't think anything has ever hurt me as much as what you said when we got back from the hospital. And what hurt the most was that there was some truth to it. I **was** playing at being a mother with Reese, though I didn't realize that this was what I was doing.

But if I'm going to be honest with both you and myself, I have to acknowledge that some of what I found so appealing about you when we first became friends was that you had a little kid and were taking care of him by yourself.

You see the rest of the story with Philip is that what ultimately broke us up wasn't that little pregnancy scare, but what followed. I learned that I would never be able to take a baby to full term. Philip wanted a family and when he learned that I was "damaged goods," he disappeared as quickly as possible.

So yeah, the idea of hooking up with a guy and his little kid and being needed by both of them seemed pretty romantic. And that was even before I met Reese. Afterward, I just flipped for him. The way he smiles with his whole body. The way his eyes shine. He wasn't just an attractive idea anymore; he was a living, breathing, magical thing and I was crazy about him.

Of course, I fantasized about being his mother. I started imagining the three of us doing things together. I started imagining doing things with Reese by myself. I felt like the luckiest person on the planet, someone who had gone from the heartbreak of childlessness to being a significant presence in the life of a kid like this. I knew I had volumes to learn about being a parent, but I was hungry to learn all of it.

And to learn all of it from you. It was amazing watching you and Reese together. You were just so natural with him and you cared for him so completely and you found it so absolutely satisfying. In our months together, you taught me things about parenting I never even considered before. But that was only a piece of it. What we shared as lovers was at least as important to me. I already admired you as a colleague and even more as a friend. But when we began seeing each other, I started feeling things I never felt before. It was passion and excitement for sure. But it was something much more complete than that. When I was with you, the entire world seemed more alive to me.

I was totally in love with you. I never told you that because I didn't want to complicate your life any more than it already was. I knew that you had so much you needed to work out. But I said it to myself all the time. I went to sleep every night telling myself that I loved you.

And when everything fell apart the way it did, I wanted to hate you with the same intensity. If you could hurt me this much, then I had to hate you. But I couldn't do it. Because when you love someone the way I love you, it doesn't disappear in an instant. I don't know that it ever disappears.

I thought that you should know these things. It'll probably make seeing each other on Monday even more awkward, but I had to tell you anyway. I hope you had a good time on your trip with Reese. And I hope you thought about you and me a little. And I hope you felt at least some of what I felt when we were together.

Love,
Ally

I was stunned. Not by the revelations in the letter, though some of them were shocking. But by Ally's willingness to lay herself out the way she did. After what I'd said to her, after what I'd done, she was still willing to reveal these things to me. She was remarkable.

And I needed her. In that moment, I realized that my ambivalence was never about her. I was as certain about my feelings for Ally as I had ever been about anything. All of my consternation had been over *having* those feelings, but none of it was about the feelings themselves. She emerged in front of me and made me better. She not only started to heal me, but she made me believe I could be strong again. And though I knew that Maureen would loom large in my life forever and that I would never let go of what we had together, I also knew that allowing her to come between Ally and me was a tragic mistake. I'd lost Maureen because fate intervened – something I'd never fully get over. But if I lost Ally, it would be my own doing – and that would forever diminish me.

Reese toddled past me and I picked him up and headed for the bedroom. There, I could close the door and have the hugely important phone conversation I needed to have while he roamed free.

"I love you too," I said as soon as she answered.

"You do?" she said in a voice I couldn't completely read.

"I love you. I knew I loved you. I was just *afraid* to love you. And I'm so, so sorry I let that hurt you."

"Are you sure you mean this?"

"I am *totally* sure I mean it. Do I still have a bunch of stuff to work out because of it? Yeah, probably. But there's no question in my mind. None whatsoever."

She was quiet on the other end for a long moment. I couldn't picture what she was doing. "Did you have a nice trip," she said at last.

"The trip was good." The baby stumbled past me, fell on the carpet, and picked himself back up. "Oh, Reese walks now."

"He does? I wish I was there to see that."

"Me too. Come see it now."

"I can't. I told my sister I'd take care of my niece. I'm just getting ready to leave."

"Tonight?"

"It might be late."

"Whenever. I really need to see you." I hesitated for a second "Ally?"

"Yeah?"

"This is a ridiculous thing for me to say, but please don't have second thoughts on me."

She chuckled a little. "No second thoughts. Just a prior engagement."

"I love you."

"I am *so* glad. I love you too. Give Reese a hug for me."

"It won't be the same. I think he really misses your hugs."

She sniffled. "You think so?"

"I know it. You weren't playing. This is very, very real and you are great at it. I can't wait to see you."

"I'll get there as soon as I can."

I put the phone down, grabbed Reese, and bounced him on the bed, tickling him. He laughed uproariously, even though he had no idea how much better his life had just become. We played like this for a while and then I sat up. We had errands to run – no food in the house, down to our last three diapers, that sort of thing – and while I was loath to get back in the car and suffer the consequences of strapping him into his seat again, I knew we had to do it.

While we finished shopping, the sun cut through a thick layer of clouds. I thought all day that it was going to rain, but now it looked like the weather was going to be okay. I took Reese to the playground – the one where he first got to know Ally – and we stayed there for nearly an hour, Reese squealing loudly or rapt with fascination. We had come here dozens of times with Ally and I knew we would return as a trio countless times in the future. That made me extremely happy. I pushed him on the swings and allowed myself – maybe for the first real time – to think about sharing the days to come with the new woman I loved. I'd cursed my luck more times than I could calculate over the past seven months, but it turned out that fortune hadn't turned its back on me. It had given me a new partner, someone to share the life I had now and welcome what lay ahead.

And someone who would always understand that there was another person walking beside us, inhabiting my most personal spaces. Maureen was eternal within me. She was a part of my eyes, my hands, my mind, and my soul. She helped me form the words I spoke. She helped me see the world I saw. I would never let her go, and I understood now that I never needed to. Love is always custom built. And every time it happens, it brings its own unique qualities. Maureen and Ally could co-exist and each remain vibrant in my heart.

* * *

Reese fell asleep on the ride back to the house. It was very late for him to nap, but I didn't try to wake him. He barely moved as I settled him into his crib.

I went back to the car to get some of the grocery bags. When I brought them into the kitchen, I found Tanya sitting there. For a moment, I thought my eyes were playing tricks on me. But no, she really was here. She was thinner than I remembered and her hair was unkempt. But she seemed healthy. And her eyes were bright.

I didn't move. I wasn't sure that I could. And I wasn't certain what she would do if I approached her. I didn't want to do anything to make her disappear again. So, even though I'm sure I looked ridiculous to her, I stood three steps into the kitchen holding my grocery bags.

"Turns out that the runaway train stops here," she said.

"One way?" I said tentatively.

She broke eye contact for a minute. "I think so." "Then that makes this a very good day."

Tanya looked around the kitchen. Her eyes stopped often and I followed her gaze, trying to get a sense of what she saw.

"Mom's really gone," she said.

"I'm so sorry, Queenie."

She smiled slightly. "I thought I told you I hated that nickname."

I closed my eyes for a second. *Don't do anything to make her go away.* "I'll never use it again."

"I didn't say I wanted *that*."

I was still holding the grocery bags. I put them down but then found I didn't know what to do with my hands. I wanted desperately to hold her, but I was still so fearful of her reaction. Only once before had I ever been this nervous in my own home.

"I have something for you," I said, turning to go to the library. I returned with the journal and handed it to her. It was the closest we'd come to one another so far. "I wrote this for you while you were away."

"This is that blank book from a couple of Christmases ago."

"Yeah."

She ran her hand over the leather cover. "I guess Mom was right." I didn't even realize she was aware of that exchange, though of course I knew she was in the room.

Tanya opened the book and looked at the title page. She glanced up at me. "I'm gonna go to my room for a while, okay?"

I nodded. When she passed me, I reached my hand out to her and she squeezed it for a moment and looked deeply into my eyes. Then she squeezed my hand one more time and walked away.

She was gone for more than an hour. It was so hard for me to believe that my daughter, who I'd lost in a variety of ways over the years and nearly completely ten months ago, was only a few dozen feet away from me. Her room was the same as it had been the last time she saw it. I hadn't touched it, had barely gone into it, since she left.

I put away the groceries and sat in the family room, staring at that antique wall hanging Maureen loved so much and wondered what she would think of everything that had happened today.

Reese woke up from his nap. As I went to get him, I glanced at Tanya's closed door, trying to guess which entry she was reading at that moment. What was she thinking? Did she understand why I wrote these pages? Did she know what it meant to me to do so?

Reese and I returned to the family room, and he walked around a little with no obvious destination before settling down on the floor to play with his blocks. I didn't sit with him, but unlike with Tanya, it wasn't because I was afraid to. I knew how Reese would react to me, how he always did. I just wanted to watch him for a while.

About twenty minutes later, Tanya came into the room. She glanced at Reese, but his attention was elsewhere and I don't think he noticed her. Then she looked over at me and our eyes met. Whether it was something about the way they touched or something she read in the journal or just the sheer power of being in this house again, I don't know. But she took several quick steps in my direction and then threw herself into my arms. She buried her head in my chest and we cried together for an immeasurable length of time.

"I missed you, Dad."

"I'm right here, Queenie."

We held each other for a long time without saying another word. At one point, I checked in on Reese, who had moved on to yet another toy but seemed perfectly satisfied to play by himself. It was almost as though he knew how much I needed to spend a little time with my daughter.

Eventually Tanya leaned back against the couch with my arm still around her shoulders. She tilted her head back and looked off into somewhere. Then she turned back to me.

"Ally?" she said.

I offered her a half-smile. "We have a lot to talk about."

"I guess we do." She smiled and then leaned her head into the crook of my neck. Once again, we did-n't say anything for several minutes. The feel of this girl in my arms was not all that different from the way it felt when she was four or eight or eleven. But at the same time, it was overwhelmingly new. And like everything else that mattered, it was imprinted upon me forever.

A few minutes later, Tanya leaned up, kissed me on the cheek, and got off the couch.

"Gotta get to know my baby brother," she said, kneeling down to see what he was playing with.

* * *

Maureen always told me I was too much of an optimist. She said I left myself open to too much heartache by believing the best was in the offing. I would be safer, she said, if I was at least marginally prepared for the worst.

In the last ten months, I'd done my share of preparing for – and experiencing – the worst. I'd had long-held notions challenged and sometimes proven wrong. I'd had the very foundation I built my life upon crumble underneath me. I'd experienced more dark moods, disillusionment, and defeat in three hundred days than I had in nearly forty years.

But as my daughter held a toy phone to her ear and made my son laugh with the exaggerated voice she used; and as Ally entertained her niece in some way or other as a prelude to returning to my life to stay; and as the hangings on the wall and the songs in the piano bench and the children on the floor confirmed for me that nothing I ever cherished would disappear from my soul, it was hard not to feel optimistic.

Under the circumstances, I think Maureen would have approved.

About the Author

Lou Aronica is the coauthor of the *New York Times* bestsellers *The Element* and *Finding Your Element* (both with Sir Ken Robinson) and the national bestseller *The Culture Code* (with Clotaire Rapaille) and the author of the *USA Today* bestselling novel *The Forever Year* and the national bestselling novels *Blue, When You Went Away, The Journey Home* and *Leaves*, among others. He lives in Southern Connecticut with his wife and four children. A long-term book industry veteran, he is the President and Publisher of the independent publishing house The Story Plant and a past president of Novelists Inc.

You can reach Lou at laronica@fictionstudio.com.